HYSTERICAL ORGASM~MEDICAL MURDER

BY KA SHOTT

I0648446

It is interesting. It is

(...shared by all...)

Time Passing.

It creates
divergent ways such that
Time becomes

merely steerage and we

but fares: for It remains
(—in one's often-forgotten—
) itself.

That, so very common, application
to everything and nothing else
more so than the crux of what It is

—is Passing.

Chapter One

In the small town of Ashland, Oregon, Mrs. Warrant thought:
Oh my GOD!
"Yes, Mrs. Warrant, very good. An excellent expulsion of fluid.
Strong paroxism."
My nerves are quivering. Mrs. Warrant thought.
"Mrs. Warrant."
How can THAT feel so good? Mrs. Warrant thought.

"Mrs. Warrant?"
"Yes, yes, I'm sorry."
"That's alright. I just wanted to make sure you were recovering
properly. These treatments can be quite strenuous. I'll leave you now
to get dressed."
"Very good. Thank you Mm. Genevieve."
"You're quite welcome. Let's hope this time the treatment will hold
you through
until. . .next week?"
"Next week!"
"Yes Mrs. Warrant—next WEEK."
"But. . .I get so. . .you know. . .suffering."
"I know that living with hysteria can be difficult but you MUST find a
way to cope. As I said, it's a strenuous treatment. It should only be
undertaken—at MOST. . ."

and you've been a thrice-a-weeker for years Mm Genevieve Pardieu,
the midwife, thought.

". . . twice weekly."
"Well," Mrs. Warrant replied, getting up from the treatment table and,
grasping her dress to her chest, "I'll just have to talk to Dr. Hill about
this."
***

Amidst City, streets beaded to near dripping with nature's effluent drizzle-rain

He's almost there. Good, the grunts. A few more thrusts and I get paid. AHHH there it is.

"Good boy. Good boy."

He never looks at me when he's done. Go figure. Five years ain't worth nothin' Not even a tip. Son-of-a-bitch!

"See you next week." she said.
"Yeah, yeah."
He shifted his cock back into his trousers.

Better get cleaned up The woman scurried inside.
The man walked the industrialleddesolation of the city. He knew each crook of its cranny...

SWAAAPPK

"Quick pull him over here."

SCCCHHHH SCCCHHHHH SSSSSCHHHH

"He's a heavy blighter I tell ya!"
"You think I don't know that. Who the hell you think is pulling the other end!"
"Oh shit! He's coming to. . ."
SWAPK
". . . that should do."

GALUB
"Don't waste it! That stuff's gold ya' know!"
"Oh shut up! You wanna' do it?"
"Nah," he said, looking at the ether bottle, "I don't like the smell of it."
"But Ieeel. . .

SHHNNIIIIIIIFFFFFFFFFFFFF

". . . doooooo. . ."
"Not so much not so much! Last time you cut the wrong way and it cost us."
"Always criticizing. All you do is smack. I have to do all the hacking."
"Yeah but my pipe-hand packs a deadly thwap."
"Oh yeah? Then why ya' need me?"
"You know darn well."
"Yes I do. Just don't YOU go forget it." *Grown man faints at blood. Daftie.*
"Awright, let's get it over with."
      He smiled: "You better look away nowowow."

DRIPPLEDRIPLLEDRIPPLE
   DRIPPLE

     DRIPPLE

       DRIPLLE

          DRRIp   DRIp
DR ip

     D
       rip p p
         d r i p . . .p   . . .p

"Are you done yet?"
"Jus' about..."
      CHINK...CRUNCHRISH

"Well what's taking so long?"
"This'uns a strong one."
       CHINK...CRUNCHCRUNCHRISH

"Yeah? That means they bleed more?"

"I bet you'd bleed a fair bit."
"That's not funny!"
"It wasn't meant to be."

I don't know about him. He likes this job. I don't. Mamma would turn in her grave if she knew what I was doin'. But times is hard. There ain't no work. No way to eat or place to sleep and he...what's takin' him so long!
"You ready yet?"

"Not. . .quite. . ."

God. I do not like this man—but we have a room...and I'm hungry. I wonder if we'll be able to buy a baked ham to share...with potato...and
"Stop your daydreamin.' It's your turn."

Big Bob grabbed the man's head. Everything in him tightened with precise muscular rhythm. . .
CRACK
...the tension eased then—

like a thunder's lightening cracking the sky's eye—
into a black-too-stained-with-blood-to-be-noticed bag
a bowlingballskull.

"What about the rest?"
"The Doc said he don't need the body. Just the head."
"So we're just gonna leave the body?"
"No. . . you DAFTIE! The school always wants bodies."
"True. How'd you find out about HeadDoc?"
"Friend of mine told me."
"Friend? I never seen you had no friends."
He snarled—sneered—"There's lots you don't see. . .friend."
"How the hell we supposed to get this body—with NO HEAD—to the school all the way cross town without anyone noticin'?"
"I have a plan."
***

The rain was gently falling on the warming fields of Iowa. Estimates (bets made by farmers [and their banks]) promised; promises made: some kept...others cast as chaff.

"Tristan, what are you going to tell your folks?"
"I don't know, Jake. I guess that I want to be a doctor."
"My folks laughed when I told them I wanted to be a veterinarian."
"That's all? Laughed?"
"Yeah. Then I told my dad I could help keep his livestock alive and he started 'figurin.' When he was done doing that he was alright with the idea."
"How about your mom?"
"She said that as long as I took care of the farm I could do whatever fool-blamed thing I wanted in my spare time."
"Fair enough. But. . . it's different with doctors."
"True. True."
"My mom and pop are expecting me to take over our farm too. So how do I break it to them that their only son won't be around?"
"Yeah, not much call for docs in small towns like yours or mine. Hey, who's the barber at your end?"
"Stan Smith."
"Ours is Danny Smith! Think they're related?"
"Could be. Could be."
"Yeah, Danny'll shave ya', cut ya', pull yer teeth, and stitch ya up all sittin' in the same chair."
"Same with Stan.   I'll have to go to a city. . . where there's a practice."
"Getting a bit ahead of yourself aren't you?"
"How do you mean?"
"I mean you have to graduate the Ag. Program first, get into a medical school—which I'd be bloked to tell you where one of them is. I'm just glad they started the vet program here this year. Talk about divinity."
"Don't bring THAT up."
"What up?"
"Divinity."
"Oh I see. Parents wanted you to be a preachin' farmer then. I've seen a few of them over the years sitting in the pews. Seriously though, the Agriculture program? That's a long way off from preaching."

9

"It sure is but even worse is that when I started Divinity here…I hated it."

"Why?"

"If I told you I'm afraid it would ruin religion for you."

"Ah come on! We're best friends. You can tell me."

"That's right. We are best friends and that's exactly why I WON'T. Anyway, I figured if I went Ag then at least my dad would be happy."

"And medical school? When did that happen?"

"The day you lost your finger."

***

Everywhere were prayers:
"Let us pray."

Lord, please keep my sister, Mom, Pa...

Father can you fix my mother

God help my family

Lord, I don't know how I'm gonna make it this winter now my husband's dead

Please help Momma and Pappa

God, keep my livestock safe

*God, let me find a girl with pretty hair to marry.
Dear Lord, ease my suffering from this dreadful disease.
God. Keep the business strong.*

Lord. . . forgive me. . .I'm such a sinner. But I can't seem to help myself. . .she's so beautifull

God save me from my daddy

Father, I pray, and you know I wouldn't ask if it weren't important, I never have: God, Tristan wants to be a doctor! I know you know this already, but please God don't let him do this thing. Please let the school say no. In Jesus' name I pray.

The "Heavenly Father, we thank you for all you do..." echoed the stained glassrooms and colored the world's sunlight.
***

On a midday Iowan farm:
"Go tell yer pa it's time for lunch."
Why do I always have to go?   "Yes Ma."

Ouch! Darn thistles.

Oh look. There's a stink bugohohAND a praying mantis.
            I remember Miss Thompson telling us about those.

"Emily!"
"Yes Ma?"
"Stop daydreamin' and get Pa."

I bet. . .   if I just go   slow   enough. . .
"Emily Marie Andersen!"
Darn it, Momma, it got away.

Great.
     He's
          all
                    the
                         way
                              down the pasture.

I should'a put my boots on.   *It's just too darned hot*
                    for boots.

  I bet the field's soft now anyhow—the cows have munched it good.

                    OUCH!
          'cept that thistle patch. Have to watch better.

Oh and the Monarch butterflies are out. Fall's comin'
There's My Bess. Her little guy is so darned cute! I hope Momma
doesn't have him butchered because if she does
I SWEAR   I WON'T   eat.

Whew, it sure is hot. There's Poppa.
There. . .

12

gees' that's still a long way off.
Just a little more. This fence—it gets me every. . .
OUCH!!   Darn it!   *I'm bleedin*

"POPPA!. . .

STEP STEP STEP

. . . POPPA!. . .

STEP STEP STEP

PAAAAA—PAAAA!"
"What's all this hollerin' about?"
"Time for lunch."
"Child you know better than to scream like THAT around all these cattle."

Emily Marie looked around.

All the rusted white steer paid no-never-mind
to anything not-green.

"Yes Poppa, I know. Animals don't like loud noises. It scares them."
"That's right. . ." *Plus it darn-well hurts my ears* ". . . I guess we better head on up. Any idea what's for lunch?"
"Cow tongue."
"My favorite!"
Yuck
"With gravy and potatoes?"
Double yuckyuck "Sandwiches—I think."
"Darn."

"OUCH!"
"Emily Marie, why don't you have your boots on?"
"It's too hot Poppa."
"You always say that then I pick thistleslivers out of your feet."

"OUCH   OUCH!   Darn thistles!"
"Watch your tongue! If your mother heard you we'd both be in a world of trouble."

"I know. I'm sorry."

Patting his shoulder, he squatted on his haunches,
"You want a ride?"
"MY favorite."
"I know. I know."
Little Sunshine
***

When Roy opened the black bag, revealing a human head, Dr. Stanley Hahn did not quite know how to handle the situation.

"Come in, come in!" he said, attempting to shove the very large man (known as Big Bob) through his backdoor. His efforts proving unsuccessful, he cried out in exasperation, "You can't just stand there you idiot!"

"Listen Mac!" Big Bob began to menace before Roy intercepted with, "Easy big guy," putting his hand against Big Bob's chest.

"Well he sure don't have no manners," Big Bob eased.

"I know. . .I know. . . but. . ."

    Roy's eyes narrowed to snake-slits,

". . .he pays. . ."

    watching a mouse nibbling its last tidbit

". . . dontcha?"

what I do for science "Yes, yes, but you must be discreet! You CAN'T just come here, unexpectedly, with human body parts."

  Roy looked at Big Bob.

  Something in their quiet exchange alarmed Dr. Hahn: a change of tactic was in order. He pointed to the kitchen table, "Please put it therethere. . ." but it was all so overwhelming that Dr. Hahn began subconsciously verbalizing, "Oh dear. . . what will the neighbors say…think Stanley, think."

  Big Bob looked at Roy but pointed his finger at the doctor, "He always talk to hisself?"

  Roy shrugged, "Beats me. This is the first time I laid eyes on 'im." Then turned to Dr. Hahn, "Okay Doc, time to pay up," he said.

"Okayokayokay. . . but you musn't come like this again. . .or. . ."

  Roy looked the way only he could:/
  like a scalpel-edge-waiting,

"Orrrrr WhaTT?"

"Ororor. . .I. . . won't pay!"

  Big Bob's eyes got big: he said, "Hey Doc, I don't think that'd be a good idea."

"I mean it!" the doctor continued, "If you come again like this I swear I won't pay. . . I'll turn you over."

Roy's pupils were already slashing, "I'd be real careful how you finish your words Doc."

Dr. Stanley Hahn was new to procuring flesh for research. A colleague had told him of two men who always seemed to have healthy young specimens, "But," the researcher cautioned, "You mustn't ask too many questions. Even though they don't charge much, when they come you must pay."

"I apologize Mr. uh. . .?"
"I'm Roy and that there's Big Bob."
"I'm sorry Roy and Big…Bob. It's just this is a little upsetting."
"You're tellin' me," Big Bob nodded, "I can't stand blood."
Roy hit Big Bob's shoulder, "Shut up!", then turned to Dr. Stanley Hahn:
"Now Doc, it's been nice chattin' with ya but we got other places to be so could you kindly give us our money and we'll be on our way."
The doctor went to a writing desk.
Roy hit Big Bob again.
"What'd I do?"
Roy tilt-nodded his head towards the doctor's desk.
Returning to the two men, Dr. Hahn said, "Here you go," and tried to hand the money to Big Bob (because—of the two men —he instinctively liked him best) but Roy grabbed the cash.
"No sir. Big Bob can't count."
Pity Dr. Hahn thought.

"If you don't mind me asking," Dr. Hahn said to Roy as he counted, "what happened to the body?"
"I do," was all Roy replied.

In an alley outside Dr. Hahn's house:
"Get the body," Roy commanded.
"I like the Doc at the school best."
"Just because he gives you a Lolly."
"What's wrong with that?"
"Nuthin'. . .just like a little girlie-daftie!"
"You BETTER take that back."
I've killed for less—even though he was my pa
I think he's thinking about killing me…

16

"I'm just foolin'" Roy said, jabbing Big Bob's arm.

"Whhhheeeeeuuuuwwww. Me too."

Roy eyed Big Bob:
I better watch him...maybe it's time...
***

Chapter Two

The morning sun cresting the Rogue Valley's silhouette meant a hot day for the forging blacksmith.

"Hi Doc Hill," Johnny the Blacksmith piped, wiping his hands on his leather apron, "Fancy ready fer me?"
"She's all settled in your back stall. I have to leave."
"Nothin' serious I 'ope."
"Not really. Broken bone."
"Yikes! Don't say that to me. I can't a'ford one a' those."
"Neither could she."
"She?"
"Yes. Mrs. Watkins."
"Widder Watkins?"
"Yes."
"Poor thing. Left to tendin' that farm all alone. Her man did'na leave her right."
"Sometimes it can't be helped."
"Ah know, ah know. That's why I can't a'ford no broken bones."
"You're not planning on dying any time soon I hope," smiled Dr. Frank Hill.
"Hope not Doc. Hope not."
"Well. . . better be off then."
"I'll take good care o' Fancy's feet."
"Remember, I need thick shoes. Too many housecalls."

After Doctor Hill rode away Johnny led Fancy out.
"Thickest I got right here," Johnny, the blacksmith beamed, "made 'em special jus' fa' you—Fancy.
        Ah, Fancygirl.
        How's my beautiful Fancy-girl,
        now thas' a good-ol'-gal, up ya go,
        NAH!! No leanin'"
SNIP SNIP SNIP SNIP   SNIP SNIP SNIP SNIP   CLUNK
PINCH/PULL,
        PINCH/PULL,
                PINCH/PULL

RASPRASPRASP   SCRAPE   SCRAPE

"You got the nicest feet I ever seen Fancy-girl.
    Now you just be easy now."
        PUMM___PAPAPA PUMM___PA PA PUMM SIZSSS SIZSSSS

        PUM___ PAPAPUM___ PA PA SIZS   SIZZLE

"That's a good fit."
                    SSSSsssssSHHHHHHHHHHHHHHHH

TAPTAPTAP   TAPTAPTAP   TAPTAPTAP   TAPTAPTAP
    TAPTAPTAP   TAPTAPTAP TAPTAPTAP   RASP   RASP
    RASP   RASP   RASP   RASP   RASP   RASP

*One down—three to go. Man, she's a fine animal. What I wouldn't
give to have a filly like her in my barn. But then what would I do with
'er? Not much use for someone like me…still, my God, she's a
mighty-beautiful piece of work.*

SNIP SNIP SNIP. . .
***

"Easy old gal," Dr. Hill cooed, "It's nothing to worry yourself about. Just some brush…"

I hate rattlesnakes. Funny. Animals sense so much more than we do

"That's it. Look, Ginger, there's Widder—I mean Mrs. Watkins' gate."

How can she stand to live up here all alone? It's so far from anyone, twenty miles at least to town, five to the nearest neighbor. I'm glad the Thompsons told me to come tend to her.

"Ah, Mrs. Watkins. Good day to you. I hear you need some medical attention."
"You heard wrong."
"Is that so?"
"The Thompsons I'd guess."
"Well," Dr. Hill smiled (rather matronly-like) "I'm not at liberty. . ."
"Save it Doc! I don't have the time or money for your 'services' so if you'd kindly leave I'll get back to. . ."
"Mrs. Watkins," Dr. Hill's voice assumed a bed-sided paternal tone, "how about if I don't charge you? Can I have a look then?"

"Don't charge me for looking at it. . .but for fixin' it!"
It's always about the money. People must think I have no heart at all
"I won't charge you for anything…except my supplies."
"I knew it!"
"Mrs. Watkins. I've come all this way. I'm willing to give you my services for free but I can't go into debt to care for you. I have a family to support as well."
"Yes. . .you do have a family."

She looks so broken. Bones being the least unmended.

"Please. . ." Dr. Hill asked, nicely.
If she'll let me look at it I know she'll let me fix it.

"Well, how about you come down   I'll give you a cup of coffee. We can talk a little, but then I MUST get back to work."

At the table:

"You know, watching how you're having to do everything with your right hand. . ."
"I'm right-handed."
"Yes, but being able to use two hands makes work easier. . . and if I can cast that arm, you'll be able to use it a lot more than you are now."
"I don't have any sugar. Cream?"
"Thank you."
It's hot! Wheeewwwwsip   wheeewwwwwsip whewsip
                    CLINK

"Okay Doc," Mrs. Watkins said, cautiously lifting her longsleeved shirt to the elbow.
Oh my GOD! How can this woman not pass out from pain?

Umgh, Dr. Hill swallowed, "This is serious."
"Let me guess. It'll cost me."
THAT'S NOT IT! DAMN these people and their country ways!

"No, Mrs. Watkins. It's just that. . . well, how long ago did you break it?"
"Ten days…maybe a couple weeks."
"And," he continued, removing from his bag a few key tools, "have you been. . ."

"OUCH!"
". . .cleaning these wounds. . ."
"OW! That REALLY hurts!"

". . .at least a couple of times a day. . ."
"I mean it Doc! You do that again I can't be responsible. . ."
". . .especially after handling your. . ."
          he set her arm down onto the table
". . .livestock?"
          She looked down at her purpleblackgreenyellow arm with rustyholes scabbed over once-white bone.
"I've done the best I could. . ."

22

He put his tools back in his bag.

". . .is it—bad?" she asked.

She really is a beautiful woman. Tough, obviously. Strong. What a fine wife she'd have made… life rather, death.

"Listen, Mrs. Watkins. . ."

"Hannah Lee, please."

"Hannah Lee. You have what's called a compounded-fracture and, I'm afraid, infection has set in."

"So I'm going to die."

"No, at least I hope not, but I must attend to you."

"My Burt died of infection."

"Yes, but his was different. His was an infection of the lung."

"It still killed him."

"I know but you're not him! And I believe we can fix this, but you must come with me to town and stay until it's properly healed."

"I CAN'T do that! Who'll tend my livestock?"

"We'll figure something out. You must come with me now."

"Figure something out! I've got milking to do, feeding, gathering. How is that all supposed to be done if I go off into town?"

"Please. . .Hannah…Lee…let's think this through. If you don't come—and you die. . ."

"You just said I wouldn't die!"

"I said I hoped you wouldn't IF I attend to your arm."

"So that's it. I either go with you or die."

"I'm afraid so."

"And my farm?"

"What good is a farm when the only one who cares for it is in the ground? Besides, I'll figure something out."

Her lips. They're quivering. My God, her mouth is plump. I'd love to kiss…whoawhoawhoa. . .married! Married! Yes. Married.

"Okay, Dr. Hill."

"Frank, please."

"uh. . .if it's okay—can I call you Dr. Hill?"

It's been three years since he died

"Absolutely. I'm sorry."
"No no nothing to apologize for. I just. . ."

"I'll get your wagon ready, who do you want hitched?"
"Sliver and Steel."
"Good, I'll tie Ginger on back."
"I'll get a bag ready," Hannah Lee said, as she left the kitchen for her bedroom.
"You won't be gone too long," Dr. Hill hollered.

I hope. And what in the HELL am I going to do to take care of her farm? Maybe. . .the Sherman kid? He'd probably do it for cheap but Mrs. Wat...Hannah...can't pay him AND me. If I pay him my wife will KILL me. When Marge finds out I'm not even charging her— she'll kill me. I'm a deadman either way. But I can't leave this poor woman to such a grisly fate. I know I can save her. Her farm, on the other hand, I'm not too sure of.

"Here we are," Dr. Hill tried to chime.
"Thank you Dr. Hill."
"I haven't done anything."
"You've cared."
That's the stuff right there. That's what makes it all worthwhile.

"You're welcome, Mrs. Watkins."
"Hannah Lee."
"Is it okay if I call you Mrs. Watkins?"
        She smiled—and it was beautiful.
***

Warrant's lumbermill had been the first industry to experience (to "know") the native (the naïve) Ashland hills.

Mike Warrant had worked at Warrant's lumbermill for ten years (even though he was only eighteen) for Mr. Warrant (the founder/owner of Warrant's lumbermill) was his father.

The father/son shared the same proper name. In fact, they shared the same given name (making one "senior" and one "junior") but there was, between the two of them, a striking physical dissimilarity. This "lack of physical inheritance" had some of the people of Ashland speculating.

Though impropriety was never proven, the constant whisperings brought poor Mrs. Warrant to wits-end. Of course the whisperers viewed Mrs. Warrant's state of agitation as the firmest affirmation that their assertions (of her having an affair that produced a bastard child) were correct.

However, Mrs. Warrant felt quite redeemed when the good doctor, Dr. Hill, properly diagnosed her behavior's "medical" condition because then no one could fault her. It was not improper to be ill, especially with such a vile disease as hysteria (and, as Dr. Hill observed—a quite severe case of it).

***

Curt Bell was the town's apothecary. He was a decent man (if one judges what is decent by the general consensus of one's townspeople): everyone loved him. He was liberal with his opium and never denied a person of it regardless if they could (or—which was more often the case—could not) pay for it.

Like Mike Warrant, Curt Bell was young. However, he'd already inherited his father's business because his father had met with an untimely end.

However, before his father had died from "consumption" (meaning: for reasons not otherwise understood by Dr. Hill) he'd essentially raised Curt—and apprenticed Curt—by himself.

Curt's mother's condition (a "poor constitution" requiring frequent medication with opium) made it necessary for poor Mr. Bell to raise his (infant/toddler/youth) son as well as run the shop and tend to the household (apothecaries, unfortunately, never made a great deal of money therefore rendering Mr. Bell unable to hire domestic help).

Much to the discomfort of Mrs. Bell, her husband's premature death meant widowhood at the tender age of thirty with no appreciable assets other than a son whose station in life, naturally, assumed a nearperfect image of his father's (work, work, and more work: all for the care and maintenance of Mrs. Bell).

However, he did have one passion—her name was Wendy Waeh.
***

Wendy Waeh was the burgeoning daughter of the town's newest mayor, Arthur Waeh.

Arthur Waeh had been a wealthy Bostonian (so rumor had it and rumor was the manner in which most "relevant" information was transferred throughout the townspeople of Ashland). However, upon his wife's death (during childbirth) Mr. Waeh quit life in the East and traveled west bringing his new daughter with him.

Ashland had not been their initial destination. It had been rumored by some that the Waehs had lived in at least 3 other towns [or 7, depending upon on the source]; those same some were curious about what seemed to them as wanderlust.

The fact remained that however many residences they'd had before (where they'd been) none dared ask Mayor Waeh about them. For Mayor Waeh had an intimidating air about him. A sort of aura that some found, rather, unsettling.

Some said this unapproachable aura was the result of his vast wealth. Others saw the way he watched his daughter's every move (like a voracious beast with its prey).

Such was the case for Curt Bell.

***

Oregon's Rogue Valley was the fold between two hilly legs—most juicy in the summertime. Golden: metal and fruit. An ambrosia for humanists, manna for spiritualists—its geographical slit was majestically offset by the tail end of a mountain range phalanx.

It was an Eden, some swore. Some swore, like Eden, it was the destruction of Man. This was not, however, the case with those early industrialists (particularly millowners) such as Mr. Warrant who seemed, above all, capitalist. And Mr. Warrant never took more interest in a venture than when it concerned his son…and Isaac Inns' daughter (for if the two were matched, their union would greatly profit both families): you see, the Warrants were gluttonously wealthy but land-less whereas Isaac Inns, though cash-poor, was obscenely land-rich.

Isaac Inns had inherited his land from his father who'd claimed the land his…under the authority invested him by the United States government (even though it'd rightly been property of the Rogue Indians).

Isaac's father had been one of the first white men to come to that particular territory and his staked claim remained unchallenged (by the Rogues—who'd been already been drove extinct). You see Isaac's dad was given the right to claim, "as far as an eye could see." This "freedom" proved quite profitable for the Inns' family as Isaac's dad had had the forthwith to climb atop Pilot Rock before staking the official claim.

However, being extremely patriotic (and in the spirit of the republic for which he stood) he voluntarily chose to take only the right side of the valley—to the shores of the shimmering Rogue River. The rest (meaning the left) he left for other settlers to claim thereby (perhaps inadvertently) creating an effective land shortage in the fertile (to-be-prospering) Rogue Valley.

Mr. Warrant was one of those who, naturally, lived on the left side of the valley; for all his manufacturing wealth could not convince (though not for lack of trying to—several dozen times) Isaac Inns to part with even a single acre of land.

Then Julie (Isaac's "mysteriously appearing" daughter) came along.

The rumor went:

Isaac Inns had never been seen in the company of a female ever. Some wondered if he wasn't a bit "touched" and those same "some" would shake their heads, speculating, what would become of all that land when Isaac died without ever marrying and/or having a child.

Well, the trails between San Francisco and Portland had become well-traveled…by all sorts of travelers—including actors. The rumor continued thusly:

Julie's mother was one of these. Her troupe had been riding the coach from San Francisco when they stopped at the Greenspring's Inn (it was a regular stopover for the stage) where there were a few miners, a few farmers, and a few loggers so the troupe decided to put on a small show (more likely in trade for food…or other things in exchange for money).

Isaac Inns had been checking his herd of cattle that had been ranging in the mountains. Always hopeful (that less of his livestock had been killed by mountain lions, cougars, bears, wolves and poachers than had been the case for the last season) however, Isaac found his typical luck: that his losses were, in fact, graver.

Needless to say, his mood was sour and the whiskey was doing little to sweeten it.

It was nearly spring's end. Summer's heat had hard-packed much of the shallow clay. Only the deeper pockets acted like tar so the stage line's driver allowed the opening of:
caskets of the actors,
        throats of voices,
                and the hope of something beyond
        the dreary death that common men—like Isaac
        Inns—found themselves living in.

That particular night, everyone was absolutely enthralled by one little actress (though she could hardly carry a tune) for her skin as white as rendered bacon fat…her name was Lily…
        …or so the rumor went.

The truth was:

One day Isaac Inns (the man most believed to be the loneliest, sorriest human being living in the Rogue Valley) instantly had a thirteen-year-old daughter. Of course he offered an explanation:

"An actress and I were in love: productive love. I offered to marry her. She refused. She asked that I keep our child, raise her in a good home, with good morals because she couldn't…being an actress. Well right after she bore Julie she left. I've never seen her again."

When people asked why they'd never seen Julie before (not once during her infancy, childhood, or the beginnings of womanhood) he simply said:

"T'wasn't no need. She was healthy as a polecat and never needed Doc Hill."

The fact was, Isaac Inns lived about as far away from town as one could—clear up on the side of the mountain range. He only ever came to town a handful of times each year (for supplies) just like his father had…before him.

Of course the good folk of Ashland condemned Mr. Inns for attempting to raise a daughter all on his own so whenever he did come to town some of the town's women felt it their duty to chatter his ears off with feminine advice.

Effectively, Miss Julie Inns became the topic of many-a-parlor room's conversation. People (meaning the women) just couldn't figure out how they'd never (ever) seen the little (but beautiful) girl during her first 13 years of life.

"Surely," they'd speculate, "he didn't leave her up there all alone when he came to town."

But their ponderings would forever be just that…for Isaac Inns never (ever) volunteered more. By the time anyone had actually met Miss Julie Inns she was (all at once) "coming out" and betrothed to Mr. Warrant's only son and heir.

***

"What's that?" George asked his wife, Elaine, as he came into his shade-cool farm's house for respite from an Iowan sultry day.
"A letter from Tris."
"Yeah...what's it say?"

Mr. Tristan E. Andersen
In Care of Dr. Emile Horn, Iowa

We are pleased to inform you that you have been accepted to the Pacific University Medical School of Portland, Oregon. Attached is your program of study. Please sign and return it to act as your acceptance. We look forward to meeting you in August.

Sincerely,
Dr. Mereth Hague, M.D., Ph.D.
Director, Pacific University Medical School

The woman stood up from her rocker. While walking into the kitchen to fetch her husband's lunch, she handed him the letter.

It took him a while to read. He was not like Elaine. She'd taken a fancy to reading (even though she'd only finished grade six). George (having finished tenth grade) could not stomach reading. To him it felt like idleness. Whenever he found Elaine reading he'd...*hgaaarrrumphfff* (clearing his throat) as if he'd swallowed something bad.

He tossed the letter onto the dining table, "What's this mean?"
"You read it."
"Yeah, but what's it MEAN? You know darned-well I'm not in for readin' so tell me what it's saying...please."

George had been married to Elaine long enough to know that even an unreasonably-put request had a chance of compliance if he tagged a "please" alongside it.
"It means Tristan has been accepted to a medical school in Oregon."
"Medical school! What in God's name! He...he's supposed to come help me...you know, TAKE OVER the FARM!"
"Here's your dinner. Don't let it get cold."

"I'm not hungry…DAMN!"

"Now! George Eugene, I'll not have you swearing."

"Yeah Poppa," the thirteen-year-old-Emily Marie piped, having just come through the front screen door, letting it slam behind her.

"Don't slam the door," he grumbled.

Emily Marie, looking at the plate, whined, "Oh Momma…this AGAIN!"

"Stop your bellyaching, child. Be thankful for what the Lord has given this family. Lord knows, we should ALL be grateful. God doesn't make mistakes."

The man and his daughter ate in silence while the woman kneaded her own concerns into the warm, yeast-risen dough.

***

Miss Julie Inns was beautiful. She had languid, dreamy aquamarine eyes (dollish: like glass instead of flesh) and creamy, buttery skin. She also had what some might call "an outgoing nature." Which was, of course, another topic of conversation (particularly for the town's women who vehemently condemned those prone to speaking their minds—especially if they were young women). "It's unnatural," some of the ladies would say (of course, never to Miss Julie Inns' face).

The men, however, seemed to like her. When they talked (in parlors separate from those of their women) they confessed it was a breath of fresh air that a woman could say what she thought (though even they would qualify, "within reason, of course").

However, what had brought Miss Julie Inns to the forefront of all parlor conversations was an interaction she'd had with Mrs. Warrant at Bell's Apothecary.

Julie (who was simply passing time by looking around the apothecary while Isaac did business at the granary) was looking at the various shades of blue glass (neatly stacked upon a shelf for display) when Mrs. Warrant came in for her prescription (of, naturally: opium).

Mrs. Warrant was shocked to find Miss Julie Inns out in public while unattended by a proper escort. When she voiced her concerns to her son's intended, Miss Julie Inns proceeded (in front of Curt Bell) to tell Mrs. Warrant that she was perfectly capable of keeping her honor intact while her father attended to his business. "Well," Mrs. Warrant stormed out the door (she was so beside herself that she actually forgot to pick up her medication. Though she went back for it a little later—all the while cursing the girl's lack of propriety in forcing her to make an extra trip).

Mike Warrant, on the other hand, was (to all outer appearances) the model of propriety. He'd lived a privileged enough life to hate wearing his hands to calluses handling wood. He only slightly less loathed business (though he displayed an excellent aptitude for it—as he was prone to paying attention to very slight details) and he absolutely abhorred horses (or anything that he equated to bodily excrement).

Julie Inns, however, loved all animals and her greatest joy was the riding of horses. She loved their smell, their hair, and how their strong muscles fluttered when they ran—like prairie grass on windy days.

Mike liked hair. Not his own: women's hair. His greatest joy came when women chose not to wear hats. Unfortunately for Mike, hats were the rage. But it wasn't just cranial hair (hair so often hidden beneath a hat) that spiked Mike's interest…it was everything "under" everything. He had a curious mind.

Julie's hair was exceptionally long (it hung well past the small of her back) blonde silk-like-soft but strong…and preferred going hatless.

For all their differences, these two agreed on one thing (well, 'agreed' perhaps may not be the correct phraseology, rather understood)—they were to be married. Their families had decided their fate. So there was only one logical thing to do: try to make the best of it.
***

Making the best of It—

        She closed her eyes
Father, no please no

"That's my girl…"
Please stop…PLEASE GOD…

"…Oh yes, that's Daddy's little girl…"
Please dear God in Heaven make him stop

"…just a little more…oh GOD! You're so sweet, so tight, so fresh!
UUUUHHHHH."
Thank you God

"Now what do you say."
"Thank you Daddy."
"Now clean up, you whore."
***

"Hello Mr. Bell."

"Please call me Curt."

Wendy looked side-to-side.

"I'd like to, but you know that wouldn't be proper. My father would kill me if he ever found out."

She smiled in a way Curt had never seen a girl (or woman) smile. There was something about her lips, her eyes that drove shivers of pleasure through his stomach.

"I suppose you're here for your order?"

"Yes."

"Is there anything else…I can help you with?" Curt asked.

He handed over the parcel along with the girl's change.

"No…I suppose not," she replied.

It seemed, to Curt, that when she looked at that brown paper wrapping a certain mournfulness came over her and it seared his heart with wonderment: why did Wendy purchased so much almond oil? He never dared ask…except this day, something seemed…

different…

and so he…

"Wendy?"

"Miss…oh," she looked around again, "Go ahead, you can call me Wendy. When no one's around…it's just between us okay?"

"Okay."

"You were going to ask me something?"

"Yes. I've never even heard of almond oil. I was wondering what you use it for. Because you order a lot of it."

"I'm supposed to say "cooking" or "baking." Would you like me to show you?"

"Show me what?"

"Do you have an office?"

"Yes, back there," he nodded with his head.

She grabbed his hand and ran: he followed like a puppy.

Behind the door he learned about almond oil and he learned— what he'd already known for as long as he'd known such things—that he was madly, passionately and deeply in love with Wendy Waeh.

***

Chapter Three

Big Bob hadn't always gone in for selling bodies to science.

His daddy'd come from England (with a small inheritance from an aunt he'd never met). Naturally, he set off for the colonies to farm. Settling on Virginia, Big Bob's father decided on slaves (which had proven—up to that point—a rather lucrative form of farming). Building a reputable slave stock required significant monetary investment (which Big Bob's daddy was all too happy to fork over in lieu of what astronomical returns such investments promised…at that time). However, timing was not in Big Bob's father's favor. For it wasn't more than a year after he'd sunk every Red cent he'd inherited into the trade of flesh that the government took its position on slavery (which eventually culminated in the Civil War) thereby effectively bankrupting Big Bob's dad (and such like him).

So his dad went to debtor's prison. On the day his pa got sentenced his mom took Big Bob to the sea (he was ten, then, and small). He'd never seen such vastness. He was ten when his mother drowned. 10 when he

vowed   (one day) he'd kill his pa… *for murder'n my ma*

Ten years he waited for the day. Free, his daddy (like a Salmon) returned to the only bit of land still left him…(even bankrupts kept something in lieu of—). Big Bob (then 20) split his father's head wide with an axe (but with only 1whack, for he was no woman nor lizard).   After the deed, Big Bob went back to the sea where he silently wondered if his mother was waiting down in the deep, pouring cups of tea.

It was that fateful day that Roy (who'd just arrived from England) watched him. Roy knew a thing or two (or three thousand) about making marks…and quickly assumed the appropriate manner: friend.

***

"You will never believe what happened today at Dr. Hill's office," Mrs. Warrant's frustration grew during the afternoon tea she was sharing with her husband.

"I don't want to hear about it."

"Well you need to hear…"

"You know I don't have a stomach for such things."

"But the insolence! Surely, you want to know…"

"Woman, NO! I told you. I don't EVER want to hear what happens at Dr. Hill's office."

Mr. Warrant adjusted his newspaper, in order to better shelter his eyes from his wife's. He mumbled, "It's all just too disgusting."

"Mr. Warrant! Put that paper down right this moment!"

Begrudgingly,
      he slowly lowered it
            (but only where he could, ever-so-slightly,
            perceive his wife's nosebridge above the
            corrugated paper's edge).

"You are my husband. You MUST do something about Dr. Hill's assistant, Genevieve Pardieu."

Mr. Warrant's spine folded (like newsprint). The only difference: the paper was allowed to rest itself on the table's soft linen. Contrastingly, Mr. Warrant's spine felt quite unable to bear what was being requested of it.

"Okay, okay, Vera. Since you WON'T let it go…what's the earth-shattering trouble at Dr. Hill's office?"

"Well, it all started when she said that I was only allowed to come twice a week…"

***

"Pastor Morgan I must speak to you."

"What is it Mr. Andersen?"

"Tristan."

"He's alright, I pray."

"Well, not exactly…"

"Oh dear, it's always hard for a parent to bury a son…especially one so young."

"No, no, Pastor. Nothing like that."

"Praise God!"

"Yes, yes, yes. But he's still going to be a doctor."

"A doctor! Lord, that *is* awful! I thought he was going to be a preacher…or farmer."

"Me too. Then we got this letter saying he'd been accepted to some medical school in Oregon."

"Oregon? That's even worse! Is it for certain?"

"Seems he left for San Francisco right after we set out on our way home from his college graduation."

"So he's already gone?"

"Yes sir."

"Why on earth didn't you tell me sooner!"

"I was trying to but…"

"I don't mean today. I mean, when you found out. Maybe I could have helped."

"Well, truth is Pastor, we didn't get the letter from Oregon until after we'd gotten home from Des Moines. You know how long it takes to get home from Des Moines."

"I do, yes. My family is from there."

"I know. Going to see them any time soon?"

"No, but thanks for asking anyway, back to Tristan. You say he's already gone?"

"Yep. We got home yesterday. So he must have been gone a good solid week by now."

"Dear oh dear. And Tristan didn't mention anything to you or Elaine, or perhaps Emily Marie, while you all were at his graduation?"

"Not a peep."

"Then I suppose all that can be done is to pray for him."

"Well that was what I was goin' to ask you to do in the first place."
***

40

It was at Tristan's graduation:
"Listen, Emmy, don't you DARE tell mom or dad where I took you tonight."
"I won't, Tris, " his little sister beamed, "But wasn't it absolutely GRAND!"
"Yeah, yeah…but you promise—not a word! They'll kill me if they found out I took you to see…"
"Those girls! Weren't they just SO beautiful? All shimmery like dragonfly wings…"
"Will you listen to me!"
"I HEARD you. I won't tell alright. I just can't believe how WONDERFUL it was. It must be perfect to be an actress."
"Emily Marie Andersen! What on earth are you talking about! You KNOW what kind of people actors are."
"Yeah, wonderful…like Jake."

Oh dear Lord…I should have known better than to take a thirteen-year-old to …burlesque…but really, what is so wrong with it? I can't understand why so many people condemn…

"Tris? Tris? Anybody home?"
"Yes."
"Honest. I won't say anything to anyone. Hey, your friend Jake. He's awful cute. Tell me about him."
"Another time, my sweet-but-devil-of-a-pain-in-the-neck sister. Mom and Dad will already be wondering where we are and I seriously doubt I can convince them we were at a my school's function if we get back much later."
***

"So," Mr. Mike Warrant Jr. said, twisting his head
    thisway
                    &
    that
in hopes of getting a better view of Miss Julie Inns' bunned hair.
"So," she replied, staring out the window {onto the lumberyard where men scurried like dirty mice}.

"So...you help your father then?"
    Mike shifted his bodyweight, yet again.
"Yes...you too I understand."
"Yes."

I wish she'd turn her head so I could see better. Maybe since we're to be married I might take some liberty
                    SWAPP!

God that stung!
"What on earth do you think you're doing!" Julie yelled, standing up so quickly that her foot caught her dresses' lace edge causing her to trip, which created just enough disruption for Mrs. Warrant to justify rushing into the front parlor from the kitchen (where she'd been pressing her ear to the door) exclaiming,
"What IS going on in here?"

"Nothing Mom."
"Most certainly something, Mrs. Warrant! I don't know what kind of woman you think I am or what "freedoms" your family feels it can take with me under the current arrangement but I assure you that you are GRAVELY mistaken if you think for ONE moment I'll let THAT BOY..."
"Boy? I'm a man!" Mike shouted (noticeably attempting to lower his voice as he stood).
"...touch me in such an INAPPROPRIATE way!"
    With that Julie stormed out the front door, got onto her wagon and drove herself home, all the while talking (ever-so-calmly) to her new best friend Rusty.
    Rusty, an Australian Shepard, was nearly two years old. Isaac had gotten him from his neighbor when (much to his neighbor's chagrin) the dog proved inept at sheep herding. He preferred to stay

at the farmer's side (begging a scratch). The farmer (a Traditionalist who believed that things living on farms had to earn their livings) decided to ask Isaac if he'd want the beast. Isaac (quite untraditional in that aspect always took what others cast off) was more than glad to take the pretty black/rust/white dog (that constantly tried to wag a tail that never was). The farmer visibly exhibited such relief that Isaac felt the way he did about cast-off beasts (because he secretly had hated the thought of putting a bullet into that friendly dog's head) that he offered, wholeheartedly, Isaac any favor in return. Isaac, unable to think of anything but the good-natured beast panting at his feet, simply said, "Thanks. I'm happy to take him." The farmer smiled (because he knew Isaac meant it), saying a brief goodbye to the dog he'd worked so hard to feign hatred for.

Of course, Isaac secretly had a special job for the dog (a job, it seemed, that had been specifically created for the beast to do): he was to be Julie's companion. When the two first met it was as if they'd known each other their whole lives.

She saw past his adult eyes to those powdery puppy blues and his eyes never remembered anything more than that they saw their mistress. So the two, from that meeting moment, proved inseparable …except…

***

In the night frightful sounds dance misting light so that even the mundane might drive a man insane. Much of one's mind can be held together by the glue of conscience. Yet, for those with skeletons…the night can be treacherously long—.

Dr. Mereth Hague found himself centered within just a night, when at his private door a tapping came…a loud, unmistakable rapping as if from a ghost unwillingly dismissed.

It was nearly 2 a.m.—the darkest hour of the darkest day of the winter.

"Hello sir," smiled Big Bob.

Dr. Mereth Hague's forced smiled betrayed:
"Hello boys. Glad to see you…come in…come in."

Dr. Mereth Hague looked side-to-side at the outside night.

His neighborhood was dark.

Closing the door [after the three had continued in], "What can I do for you?"
Roy sneered, "Well, it's more what we can do for you now isn't it?"

Dr. Hague looked at Big Bob—Big Bob, not Roy, because Big Bob seemed softer than Roy. So Big Bob spoke.

"What Roy here's tryin' to say is we got a nice one for ya."
"Here? At my home?"

Roy looked at Bob.
"You gonna' speak for me again?"

His eyes gleamed razor-like.
"No Roy."

"Good."

Roy fixed his eyes on Dr. Hague but paused, for effect, before he spoke.

"Doc you want bodies. We got you one. So go get your money and we'll bring it right in."
Dr. Hague stammered, "You've never come to my home before…"
"Is that a problem Doc?"

Roy's eyes turned rat-red.

"No, uh. No. I, well, let me see. I don't suppose you might bring it up to the school for me?"

"Now what do you think Doc? That we're a delivery service?

Dr. Hague stammered, "No. No. Certainly not. I...uh..."

"The money, Doc. The money."

Big Bob looked at Dr. Hague's rug. He didn't like coming to the Doc's house. He was afraid of something bad...that Roy would do something bad. Big Bob liked the Doc, but Roy was his partner...and they both had to eat.

Dr. Hague went to his bureau taking from it a leather money purse, pulling from its folds the correct sum for a body. Roy's eyes measured the remaining thickness...just as Big Bob's measured Roy's eye:focus.

He's thinkin' no good...I can see it...he wants to hurt him but I won't let him! If he makes a move...I'll make mine.

"Here you go boys," Dr. Hague said handing the money to Big Bob.

Roy snatched it out of his partner's hands.

"He can't count," he glared at the doctor.

As Roy counted every note he never took his eyes off Dr. Hague.

Dr. Hague looked at Big Bob.

"Sorry, I don't have a lolly for you...they're all at the school lab. Maybe next time?" The doctor smiled.

Big Bob smiled too.

"That's okay, Doc. It's not your fault."

Then Big Bob glared at Roy, who immediately shoved the money into his coat pocket. "Let's go get that body," Roy said.

The doctor held the door []

"In the kitchen please," he said. *I can clean the blood off easier there.*

"You're the boss," Big Bob smiled, almost cheerily, like a boy delivering an old woman across a street thus accomplishing a good deed.

It took a moment before Dr. Hague noticed that the head was missing.

"Where's the head?"

45

"Oh, it was no good," Roy blurted.

"Why not?"

Roy sneered, "Well, some head's take a bashin' better than others."

Doctor Hague looked at Big Bob, who refused to look anywhere but betwixt the doctor's knees and the doctor's floor.

When he said (to relieve his own awkwardness) that he liked Dr. Hague's rug better than the other doc's, "You know, your friend over the way," (which Dr. Hague knew to be Dr. Hahn) Roy's eyes hardly flinted. Big Bob knew he'd, once again, made a mess of things.

But for some reason, once outside, Roy grabbed Big Bob round his shoulder and was kind to him, "You hungry?"

"No."

"What's wrong with you?"

"I don't like how you were lookin' at Dr. Hague."

"Don't you worry about Dr. Hague."

"What'cha mean?"

"I mean Dr. Hague's alright."

That night, while Big Bob slept, Roy snuck out. He had things to accomplish.

***

Tristan Andersen looked out the window of the train carrying him south from Portland.

"How fitting," he thought, "A brand-new life riding the newly-launched Oregon & California Railroad." Tristan thanked God for the locomotive. Stagecoach travel (as he learned while traveling from San Francisco, California to the medical school in Portland, Oregon) had been far less comfortable.

Looking, alone, Tristan finally allowed himself a moment to acknowledge

his own becoming—a doctor.

His destination: the town of Ashland.

His goal: meet a Dr. Richard Hill, the town's sole medical practitioner, in hopes of retaining a partnership in his lucrative practice.

From his briefcase he pulled his freshly-inked medical license and a letter. The letter was from Dr. Hill.

It wasn't illegal—him having sole possession of Dr. Hill's request—but, perhaps, unethical.

Graduating medical students (from the handful of medical schools in the United States in 1887) relied [for their employment] almost solely on their medical schools. The medical school officials/teachers would receive job postings from: hospitals, asylums, medical schools, and private practices in need of new doctors. In return, the school informed its students.

Dr. Hill's request for a partner (in a growing small-town practice) had just so happened to find its way to the desk of the Oregon medical school's newest director (a man who, upon taking a particular liking to Tristan, felt only a mild wince of culpability for withholding the job posting from the other students).

A man whose name was Dr. Mereth Hague.

***

It's odd how, in one moment, all seems fine yet, in the next,
all seems foul…as if lives were metallic pinballs
      plunging=surging<>always: kinetic energy.

Energy that must move,
      even if the traveling journeys
            one into the throes of despair.

      Once Big Bob and Roy had left, Dr. Hague turned down all
his lights. He drew his curtains and lit a small candle in order to
inspect the body he'd just received.
      It smelled of cheap perfume (as had all the other bodies he'd
gotten from Big Bob and Roy):
Whores

      But there was something disturbing about this man's corpse.
Something Dr. Hague couldn't quite put his finger on at first:
He's well fed. That's different

      he rested the Dead's hand in his own
Fingernails trimmed…

      he held them close to the candle's flame
…and…buffed?

      Dr. Hague frantically searched the pockets of the man hoping
to find some kind of identification. There was nothing

(if there had been, Dr. Mereth Hague suspected that the boys would
have stolen it. None of the bodies they'd brought thus far had had a
thing on them except clothes…and blood).
*But if…wait…the clothes, these are not a gentleman's clothes. Why
would a gentleman wear such clothes?*

      The perfume answered back.

      Dr. Hague pulled off the man's shoe. He held the light to his
toenails. The nails shimmered with the same embossed sheen as his
fingers' nails had.

This man is a gentleman! My God! What have they done? What have I done? There'll be an investigation! What can I do...what can I do! I'm doomed! I'll go to prison!

"My God," he cried out.
        It—

was not much

            later when Dr. Hague used all of his strength:

he heaved the body
        into a river made notorious for such receptions.

That river of a city some called the Devil's.

        Some said it was White but there was nothing pure or
unstained about that place.

            Nothing remained untainted by the city's need to feed
        upon sin—and the river (filled with
                        such~and other~contamination)
                flowed.
            Fed by the greatness of lakes the size of oceans and the
        meat packers and the murderers and all the slimy things that
        did not walk erect upon the earth.
***

The lights at Dr. Stanley Hahn's house were out. Roy knew they would be. He shimmied the lock. It easily opened: "Just like a woman's legs," Roy thought.

Once inside, he went to the desk he'd seen the young doctor take his money purse from.

He could hear the rise and fall of two sets of breaths

I wonder who's in his bed

Roy slid Dr.Hahn's purse inside his jacket's inner pocket. He wasn't finished.

Behind the back leg of a lounging chair, Roy placed a single goldcapped^tooth.

Stealthing himself outside and across town to Dr. Hague's home (finding the doctor not at home) Roy performed the same ritual: a gold tooth carefully placed.

I wonder where he is. Maybe…no…he couldn't know

***

In their room, Big Bob woke to find himself alone.
"Roy?"

No answer came. He got up. He looked around the room. He went down the hall to the bathroom. Roy was nowhere to be found. This did not strike him odd. It had happened before. Big Bob remembered
He likes the whores after killing
so he went back to bed, falling quickly—again—into sleep.

Perhaps pulling a head from its stalk required sacrifice, for killing always seemed to exact Big Bob's strength—clear to the root#tendrils of his being.
***

Roy pulled the scalp from the skull, cleaned the blood from the flap in a puddle of water then pierced the flesh. Using twine, he fastened it around his head so the flap hung just across his forehead and covered his dark hair with red: the dead man's head had been red.

He pulled a hat over the skin's red-haired fringe, raising his jacket collar close to his neck. He heaved the body into a slump against the wall of a tall building's alley. Then he waited.

Outside the precinct:

It was nearly 4 a.m. (the time when the girls were finishing up their 'visits' to the officers who paid them in agreements of freedom). It was nearing 4:30a.m. when *she* came out: young…thin …*hungry*

He whispered for her to come to him—in the dark. He gave her more money than she'd ever seen. All she had to do was to carry the bag he handed her back into the station at 5:00 o'clock.
"Not before. You hear me?" Roy said.
"Yeah…what's the difference?"
"I'll kill you. That's the difference."

Her eyes widened.

"Yes sir," she said, "5 o'clock on-the-spot you can count on me."
He smiled.
"That's a good girl. That's a good, pretty little girl."
She winced when he brushed back, with one finger of one hand, a tuft of her hair that had fallen loose. Then she did exactly as she'd been commanded.
***

Dr. Stanley Hahn woke to what seemed a day like any other. He paid the whore extra for having spent the night through: he hated sleeping alone. When she'd gone he began his cleaning regimen.

It was 5a.m.

He had already washed his genitals with soapy water and was soaking them in a beaker of rubbing alcohol (for as long as he could stand the stinging repentance) when, suddenly, there came an unexpected knocking. His door conveyed a cadence of urgency. *I thought that's why whores got paid...so they'd leave*

To his surprise, it was Dr. Hague.
"What are you doing here?"
"We must speak."
"For God's sake man, what's the matter?"
"Those men...those ones who...you know... 'deliver'?"

Dr.Hahn moaned. "Yes. They came last night. I don't know where you get hold of people like..."

"There's been a murder."

Dr.Hahn laughed. "I suppose you can call it that. Some might call it a service to proper society. Me, personally..."
"Listen, Stanley, I'm not here to debate some philosophical stance. I'm telling you they murdered a man, a proper man...a gentleman!"

"Are you sure? How do you know?"
"Yes I'm sure. I'm leaving town right now. I suggest you do the same."
"But..." Dr.Hahn stammered.

Dr. Hague rushed to the door but Dr.Hahn ran past him, blocking his way: "Listen, we must stay calm! We must THINK for a moment!"
"You think. I'm leaving."
"What about the body?"
"I've taken care of it. I suggest you do the same with what you received."

Dr. Hague tried to push past Dr. Hahn (quite unsuccessfully as Dr. Hahn was strong in his body's lesser years).

The clock tower struck 6:00 o'clock.

"For God's sake man, let me go! I was good enough to warn you now be good enough to let me escape."
"Wait, please. If we run off it will look like we're guilty."
"Then you stay and prove your innocence. I'm for running and staying alive."
"Where will you go?"
"I heard there is a new medical school out west in desperate need of teaching physicians."
"Do you have any money?"
"I have enough for the train. Now I must go."
"What's the name of the school?"
"Pacific something…in Oregon, I think. Why?"
"Well, maybe we should both go."
"Then get your things. Time is of the essence I fear. I fear, deeply."

"Yes…yes…I can see that."
Dr.Hahn went to his desk only to discover that his purse was gone.
"They must have come in the night and stolen my money."
"Don't you have any more?"
"Yes…here."
As he pulled the lounge chair towards the floor's center he saw something.
"What is it?" Dr. Hague asked.
"I…I think it's a tooth."
"Hurry my dear man, hurry!"
Dr.Hahn pulled the back upholstery from the chair's frame to reveal a small leather purse…then reached for the gold glimmering— on the floor, just behind the chair's back leg.

Distractedly, he said, "I'll just get my things."
"There's no time," Dr. Hague cried.
"Listen, you go," Stanley waved him off, rolling the molar round in the palm of his hand, "Catch the train. I'll catch the next one. Oregon you say?"

"Yes, yes. I wish you well, my dear Dr.Hahn. And I hope we see each other again."

With that, the middle-aged doctor fled.

In the quiet that followed his departure Dr.Hahn began to think...*I wonder*...then quickly put on his coat, heading for Dr. Hague's house.
***

"I tell ya' sir," the young whore bellowed, "I don't know who 'twas!"
"Well, what did he look like?"
"He had a hat. And red hair. I think."

The police officer held up a patch of scalp.
"Like this color red?"
"Yeah, yeah that was it, I think. But it was dark."

"How much did he give you?"
She batted her eyelashes.
"Now, officer, I'm not the kind of girl to kiss and tell."
***

For Dr. Hahn, it had been easy to get inside Dr. Hague's house: the door had been left standing wide open. He didn't like that. It was unusual. Still, he had something to do.

He double-checked to make sure there were no signs of death (having disposed of his own scientific contribution in the same aforementioned river as his friend

{a regular Styx that split the city}

on his way to coming).

Then he went into the living room. There he found a wingback chair. Behind its one back leg, resting upon the rug, Dr.Hahn found what he'd suspected he would: a single gold tooth. Grabbing it, he ran.

It was 6:30 a.m. and getting light enough for people to see, so he took a circuitous way home.

He packed only his medical satchel and a small bag of clothes leaving his suitcases and wardrobe as they were.

His coffee pooled quietly cooling: his toiletries waited, vainly, upon the sink.

***

The police sergeant said to another officer: "Note says a man's been murdered by a guy going by 'Big' Bob."

The police sergeant held the note up for the other officer to see.

"Says the body's in the alley across the street. Says two Docs are somehow mixed up in all this and if we need evidence we can find it at their premises. Says where this "Big Bob" and these two doctors are staying. What d'ya think?"

"Probably should check it out."

They found the body easy enough. Naturally, they went to the doctors' residences first. Might as well deal with people less likely to do bodily injury than someone whose name itself sounded threatening.

The two doctors were nowhere to be found. So the police shook down their houses only to produce absolutely nothing except that both had mysteriously (and hastily) left town but on further investigation (at the university) found both had legitimate family excuses.

That left Big Bob holding the bag. He'd just come back from the toilet when police officers busted into his room shouting, "You're under arrest for murder."

It took four guys to get Big Bob down to the ground. Two more used their billys just to make his weight near-dead.

***

On the train, Roy looked out the window. He was dressed decently enough. He'd stolen what he'd judged to be Dr. Hague's nicest suit (Dr. Hague's size fit him close).

Yes, it should all be falling into place quite nicely by now. The police will have gone to the docs' places...maybe they've even found the teeth. Of course that might be giving them too much credit: maybe another couple of hours and they'll find them.
The newspapers will get hold of that story—they love
reporting that stuff—and that will divert attention.
They probably already have Big Bob in custody and, naturally, he'll tell them about me, which means they'll be on the lookout for a 'Roy' who never existed.

"Tickets. Tickets everyone. Tickets. Sir, may I have your ticket?"
"You most certainly may." Roy smiled. "By the way, how long until we reach San Francisco?"
"Oh, quite a while, Sir, quite a while. Enjoy your ride."
"I will," Roy looked back out the window.
***

Chapter Four

Dr. Mereth Hague stood at the window of his new office. It was springtime in Portland, Oregon. The daffodils were opening. He thought of roses—and his past:

It was good of the department to show me such kindness in their recommendation for the directorship position. I was scared they wouldn't believe me about my 'sick mother' in Portland and having to come away. I wonder...I never heard anything about it in the newspapers...

When he'd returned to his desk there was a knock at the door.
"Tristan Andersen to see you."
"Very good, send him in."
The young man entered.

"How are you today Mr. Andersen. Or should I say, Dr. Andersen?"
The man smiled at the young doctor.

"Sir, you wanted to see me?"
"Yes. There is a matter I want to discuss with you."
Dr. Hague stood then returned to gazing out his window.

Tristan remained reverently quiet. To Tristan, it seemed a long time had passed. He'd grown to expect such silences from Dr. Hague. He was often silently thoughtful. Tristan did wonder, however, if the silences weren't the result of the aging process upon his faculties; he never dared verbalize such a suspicion. Eventually, Dr. Hague did speak:

"Tristan, you and I have had many long discussions throughout your time here."
"Yes Sir, 'It is not unethical to use human cadavers to learn human anatomy for if we are to save human life then we must first understand human life.'"

Dr. Hague laughed.
"Yes, my boy, you have quite an adept skill for memorization. Particularly when it comes to quotes. But what I want to speak with

you about is your future. You know, ideals are often purchased at a price. Sometimes one must eat *and* have peace of mind."

       Tristan sighed (thinking):

Here he goes again. Sometimes I think he chose the wrong profession. He would have made a great philosopher

       but remained silent and listening.

"A position for a partner in a private practice has come to my attention. I believe you should pursue it rigorously."

"Where?"

"Ashland. It's a small town in Southern Oregon almost on the California border. Its settled at the base of the Cascade Mountain range. A growing town. The wagon trails went through it. So now does the train. It would be the perfect opportunity for a young man such as yourself. What do you think?"

***

"So you're telling us," the police sergeant re-stated, "that you, Big Bob, killed this man. Alone?"

"Yes."

"And you were all alone?"

Big Bob was silent for a moment (trying hard to think).

The sergeant pursued.

"And you were all alone? Simple question. What's the thinking for?"

Bob looked the bald sergeant in the eye. Without flinching he said, "I was all alone."

"So why'd you do it?"

"I was hungry."

"You make me sick…take him away!"

The sergeant motioned to an officer who took Big Bob away.

A little later the sergeant came to Big Bob's set of bars.

"So you say you were alone?"

"Yes, sir."

"So why'd you cut the guy's face off?"

"Huh?"

The sergeant smiled.

"I knew it."

"What?"

"Ah, nothin'"

He'd seen it before. His city had seen more murders than any city deserved to. Most times it was what he called 'bottomfeeders' who preyed upon each other. These were the cases that never got solved because, if truth be told (though no one spoke truth), cops and citizens alike figured they were taking care of themselves.

The guy with the red hair was no exception. A bum. A dead bum. But if there was one thing the sergeant could smell a mile away, it was a set up; if there was anything he hated worse than the scum of his city—it was scum trying to frame some other scum for what they'd done.

Looking at Big Bob, he just knew that that poor, dumb bastard was going to hang wrongly. He'd spent a career seeing it.

"Not this time," he thought. "Not this time."
***

On the train, Tristan thought of his last meeting with Dr. Hague. In his mind he could still hear him saying:

> "I can't tell you what an opportunity working with Dr. Hill might prove for you. In addition to being partner of a growing practice, I hear Dr. Hill is an ethical man...and quite skilled. It's a great chance for you to explore a broader spectrum of medical practice. You'll get to do a bit of everything. Oh sure, you'll probably work with the insane but, God willing, you won't have to do so exclusively."

That many of Tristan's classmates had no alternative to working in the asylums was true. For a physician, it seemed to Tristan (at least from Dr. Hague's portrayal) there was no worse a fate. But he had no choice but to rely on Dr. Hague's truth, for—in fact—Tristan had never been to an asylum (that fieldwork had not been required for his medical certificate).

Tristan closed his eyes. He felt the train's rocking. He listened to the metallic hum of the engine akin to a human heart beating. Slowly, he drifted into light dreams of his family.

His mother, Elaine, hung clothes on the line. His father, George, was feeding hogs and his sister, Emily Marie, was humming. Her voicenotes drifted on the humid air of beginning summer and atop the firefly nights. He could almost feel himself ascending with crescendoeing cicada calls...

—the train jolted.

Eyes opened.

The conductor announced the town of Drain.

Tristan pulled, from his attaché case, his license to practice medicine in the State of Oregon. The calligraphy read:

Dr. Tristan Andersen.

Replacing his license, he searched for the singular letter his little sister had sent him during his long years in Oregon.

Dear Tris,

I hope you are well. I am fine. I am so glad you're doing this whole DOCTOR-thing. See, you were always the "good" one. I was always the "bad" one but since you told Mom and Dad you were going to be a doctor, Pastor Morgan has been at the house nearly everyday praying for your soul. You'd think somebody died!

But I think they're just silly. After all, there must be SOME good in being a doctor. After all, you're going to be one and you're my most favorite brother in the whole world, which is why I'm going to tell you a secret. But only if you swear not to tell. I'm going to be an actress!

Anyway, oh, I forgot to tell you that Mrs. Wale came to the house the other day and told Mom that if you were her son she'd wish you dead rather that face the disgrace of knowing her son had entered into such a vile profession as to steal bodies from graves. Whatever did she mean? Anyway, you should have seen Mom. You'd have thought she was a cat "in season" because she darnnear scratched Mrs. Wale's arms to bits as she shoved her out the door.

I laughed and laughed. Of course, Mom punished me for it. But I couldn't help it. You should have seen Mrs. Wale's expression—priceless!

So…how is Jake?

> *Affectionately Yours,*
> *Emily Marie*

The truth was that, although Tristan was frustrated by his parents' condemnation of his chosen vocation, it hurt him to know they were suffering.

His family had farmed their farm in Birmingham, Iowa (of Van Buren county) just as hard as any of the other families (including the Wale's). They, too, proudly kept their generational kin inked in the family Bible. And they had worked hard, saving every bit of money they could, to send their son to Iowa's Agricultural College all because they'd expected him to take over the family's farm.

When Tristan wrote about exciting things he was learning in philosophy, his parents thought that maybe their son might become a clergyman (or lawyer), which didn't bother them too much—as the original plan of farming the farm would still have been in play.

Then when he wrote them that he'd discovered his "true" vocation: a medical doctor, his mother and father not only felt their hopes of their farming legacy crumbling but (being strict Methodists) were utterly distraught over the salvation of their only son's eternal soul: doctors were as bad as dancers: for both dealt in flesh.

After Tristan's vocational declaration had become public knowledge (which, in a small town like Birmingham, meant the day after the preacher knew of it) everyone began giving George and Elaine their condolences.

Pastor Morgan frequently paid George and Elaine Andersen visits. One day, while the three sat around the kitchen table sipping coffee (having duly dispensed with the social trivialities needed to broach the controversial subject) Pastor Morgan asked if Tristan's sister, Emily Marie, was presently at home. To which Elaine replied that she was not (she had gone to the neighbor's farm to watch their cow calf). So Pastor Morgan began:

"I've a nephew, a lawyer, who told me he'd been called in on a case of dead bodies being desecrated by medical students. He says they're digging them out of cemeteries almost as soon as they're put in the ground...and worse I hear."

Pastor Morgan then set his cup down and began rubbing together his creamy white hands (for effect, or so it seemed to Elaine, who had been watching his hands—hands nearly as smooth as the china cup Elaine had been given by her own mother as a wedding gift). She thought:
Hands not roughened with work are poor qualities in a man

"In fact," Pastor Morgan continued, "In the big cities there have been cases of people being murdered and used for experiments!"

Unlike when he delivered his sermons, he refrained from striking his fist against Elaine's table. He paused...looking contemplative...exchanging glances between the man and his wife.

When an expeditious amount of time had passed, he continued, (sighing, heavily, as if he felt the great burden of pure spiritual duty resting upon his fragile shoulders)

"There is such evil being done in the name of medicine."

He tilted his chin towards his chest (displaying utter reverence) darting his eyes between George and Elaine (for quite some time) before he continued, "I fear for Tristan's eternal soul."

Elaine stood. Leaned over her husband's shoulder, taking from him his cup and saucer. Pastor Morgan was mid-sip when Elaine reached for his, "I'll take that, if you please."

Shocked, he handed her his half-filled cup. While carrying the service to the sink she mumbled (under her breath, of course) "And which side of THAT ethical issue was your nephew on? The victims? I doubt it!"

"That's enough, Elaine," George scolded.

Awkwardly, Pastor Morgan excused himself claiming much work to be done at the church.

After the preacher had left, George went out to the barn. It was his sanctuary where he could, amidst the smell of warm hay and mewing cats of varying ages, put life in perspective.

Emily Marie had not yet come home from the neighbor's farm so Elaine was left alone to think her own thoughts. She pulled, from her private writing desk, the last letter she'd received from Tristan (the letter she showed no one—after all, it had been addressed only to her) to read it (for what must have been the hundredth time):

Dear Mother,

I hope all is well on the farm and that Emily Marie is growing strong. I pray everyone is healthy. Thank you for coming to my graduation. Please don't worry about my travels out West. I expect my journey will be arduous but I've saved money so I will be just fine on my journey to Portland, Oregon via San Francisco, California.

I wonder how much the stagecoach will be from San Francisco to Portland? I'll find out soon. Besides, if I am short on funds I can always work for the extra money, as I am leaving Iowa in plenty of time. I'm not due to start medical courses in Portland until the fall.

I am sorry I didn't tell you sooner. It's just that I knew you wouldn't approve...that you'd be disappointed. I couldn't have born that. But if you could only see how much good a physician can do, I know you'd be proud.

I'll have to tell you Jake's story someday. I'm sure you'll see that I am joining a noble profession and one in great need of morally ethical men.

I can't tell you how much it meant to me that you, Dad, and Emily Marie came to my graduation. I know it took a lot of sacrifice for you all to do that, with the farm and all...and for me to go to school.

Mother, I'll never forget what you and Dad have done for me. I swear to you that I will never do ANYTHING in my practicing of medicine that I know you'd be ashamed of.

> *Your Loving Son,*
> *Tristan*

Tucking the letter safely away, she thought,

"Even bad professions need good men."

Then she sat down in the quiet of her empty home, picking up her favorite book, and began reading: "Twelve Centuries of English Poetry," which had been given to her as a wedding present by her sister (her only sister, who had died six months prior of tuberculosis). *Maybe he'll be able to save...maybe someone else won't loose their sis...*

Her tears broke against her thoughts so she stood, went to the kitchen, and prepared supper.
***

"I sentence you...Bob..."

The judge whispered to the court attendant, "What is this man's full name?"
"We don't know sir. He didn't have any documents. There's no record of birth from where he said he was from. Ther're no living relatives as far as we can tell. He goes by the name of 'Big Bob.'"

The judge groaned.
"Sir?"
"Yes, suh," Big Bob replied.
"What is your last name?"
"I don't reckon' I knowed it. My ma always called me 'Big Bob,' so did my pa."
"Where are your mother and father now?"
"Both dead."

The judge looked at the report. He looked at the gallery.
Empty.

"Very well, Big Bob, I sentence you—
for the murder of Mr.____
—to be hung by your neck until dead. Court dismissed."

Big Bob was taken away by the sergeant and another officer.

Funny thing about life (or the loss of it)—it affects different people, differently.
And it
(Big Bob's life—and pending loss of it)
had affected the sergeant.

From the time he'd booked Big Bob to the day of his death sentencing, the sergeant knew (deep down in his bones—or guts) that that poor daffer was somebody's fallguy. Only, every time he asked Big Bob to tell him the truth Big Bob showed one characteristic: loyalty.
The sergeant wasn't a stranger to loyalty.
Like Big Bob, he'd taken what someone else had coming.

(One night his lieutenant's wife had come to the station to see her husband only to find a prostitute taking money from him—and when she threatened her husband with God only knew what, he said he was simply giving her the money that the sergeant owed her. When she asked to speak to the sergeant her lieutenant/husband said she couldn't, because he was "in the can getting cleaned up" [even though the sergeant was simply taking a crap]. So the lieutenant's wife decided that the sergeant's wife needed to know what kind of bastard she'd married. The result of the "revelation" led to the sergeant's wife speedy abandonment of him.)

It had hit the sergeant as hard as any death. But he never ratted out his lieutenant. The bitterness of that loyalty created something more. A desire...to believe in the goodness of humanity.

From then on the sergeant had searched, amongst the faces (and rubble) of what surrounded him for—exactly what? It was as if the searching had become near-biological: as if his very cells cried out for—an unknown...oxygen?souloxygen? and the not finding of exactly what kept him breathing belief that good existed.

Then Big Bob came along. Big Bob, "the innocent victim" (just like every big stupid guy who'd gotten roped...just like him): where the guy who should've been the one whose skull cracked the concrete got of Scot-free.

It just so it happened that on the night that Big Bob got sentenced, the sergeant was in charge. When he brought Big Bob his supper, he said to him, "You know, Big Bob. I know you didn't do it alone."

Big Bob's eyes got big.
The sergeant continued,
"Yeah...I knew it all along. You're not the type to cut people up."

Big Bob shook his head, "I hate blood."
The sergeant smiled, "So why don't you tell me who really did it?"
    Big Bob looked up with eyes near-child like,
"See, Boss, it don't make no difference now. He's long gone. He's the smart one. I done my part too."

72

"Yeah, what?"

Big Bob poked his food, then shuffled his feet,
"I...I knocked them out...and..."
"And?"
"...after he was done he'd tell me if I needed to pull the head off or not."

Big Bob took a bite then lifted his head up, smiling. "Oh, and I carried them everywhere we went. I'm real strong."

The sergeant smiled,
"Yes, Big Bob, I remember!"

They laughed.

"So, Big Bob, where did you carry them?"

Big Bob stopped swallowing.

The Doc who always gave me a lolly, I don't want nothin' bad to happen to him. It wasn't them that did those bad things...it was Roy...and me

"Big Bob?"
"Yeah?"
"Where did you guys carry the bodies?"
"To the river."
"Oh. Okay. So there was more than one of you *and* more than one body?"

I'm a dead man anyway

"We killed three. Plus I killed my pa."
"Food, right?"

Big Bob nodded and sat back down, wishing he hadn't said so much.

The sergeant watched him take a bite.
"Why'd you kill your Pa?"
"He killed my Ma."

The sergeant got real close to the bars.
"Big Bob,"

Big Bob stood.
"Yeah?"

"Promise me that if you get out of here you won't ever kill anyone again."

"I can't."

"Why?"

"Cause I have to stop Roy. He's real bad…I promise that I won't kill no one else. Ever…after him."

The sergeant breathed *that* breath—that needed vengeance that suddenly, but unexpectedly, clashed with conscious: "I have your word?"

"Yeah."

Somehow Big Bob found himself cloaked in dark night and walking alone on the street of that city with only one thing in mind…Roy.

***

It hadn't been but a week since they'd been home from Tristan's graduation in Des Moines when Emily Marie began acting strange (in the eyes of her parents, George and Elaine). For Emily Marie had taken to prancing around—dancing in a way neither her mother nor father had seen before—it seemed her bodily movements were exaggerated in a {rather obscene} way.

When George asked his daughter to pass him the salt she replied, "Yes, kind sir," handing the crystals over with sweepingly wide hand gestures (which were hardly required for the nominal task).

When Elaine asked her daughter to bring in the laundry from off the line she watched Emily Marie grab sets of shirtsleeves, swirling them around her (clasping them—of all places—to her blossoming breasts) while swaying   back&forth   to a crooning rhythmic tune that had certainly never been played at church.

And her clothes! One morning, before school, she'd come downstairs in her best Sunday dress only she'd cut the side seam—slit it clear up to her knee! Elaine switched her for having to spend the better part of her morning restitching.

When George was told what had happened he went to see Pastor Morgan who recommended switching. After being informed that had already been done, he said he'd pray for her. Those acts of intervention being duly done, George and Elaine figured their worries were over.

But one day Emily Marie did not come home from school. Near suppertime, George searched the barn, the fields, the neighbor's farms [] fields. He did not find his daughter.

It was well into the darkening night when George went to Chuck, his across-the-road-neighbor who acted both as peace officer/livestock auctioneer.

The two men continued their search until light from the next morning (Chuck had to leave in order to auction-call). George had chores... he didn't want to go...he wanted to find his 'little sunshine'...

Where have you gone? Are you hurt? God, please keep her safe!
Maybe she's come home while I've been out

George ran to his farm. The moment he saw his wife he knew…Emily Marie was gone.

The cows cried—some in need of food, others in need of milking.

The hens waited at the door to be set free from their egg-laden nests.

The wind had knocked a treelimb onto the fence tearing its wire from its rotting wood post—
(there were always things in need of fixing)—
and something always able to get out…

George did not care. He wanted his daughter…
his little Emily Marie.
"George," Elaine comforted, "You keep searching. I can tend to what's in need."

The husband—the man—looked to his wife, pulling her tightly to him. With his head buried into her neck he murmured, "Thank you, Laney. Thank you."
With that he left.
When he returned, well into the pitch of lateness, his face was silently haggard.
"Did you find her?"
"No."
"Did you look…"
"Listen, Elaine, she's gone."

Panic strangled Elaine's voice to a husky wisp, "What do you mean she's gone?"
"I mean she's gone and I don't want to talk about it any more."

Now Elaine Andersen was, perhaps, fairly open-minded and kind (gentle, so some of the women in the county said). What most did not know of Elaine Andersen was that she could put a badger to shame when it came to familial ferocity.
"You listen here, George, you better tell me what happened to Emily RIGHT now or…"
"Or WHAT!" George screamed, standing to face his wife's blearing eyes.

"OR…or…I'll…never forgive you!"

He knew his wife had a Christian soul; for her to say such a thing (such an utterly damning thing)—well, George just didn't have that kind of withholding heart.

"You'd better sit down," he said, returning to his gentle demeanor.
     She did as he suggested.

There, in those twining hours, she learned that her husband's searching led to one truth: their only daughter had run away.
***

Chapter Five

Back in Des Moines, back in time—back when Tristan had only just graduated with his Bachelor's degree of Science, back when Tristan and his little sister walked home from the burlesque theater:

"Did I ever tell you why I wanted to become a doctor?"
"No."
"Well, it all started…"

The story went:
> while finishing his last year at the Iowa Agricultural College (studying agriculture and mechanics with the full intention of returning home and farming) Tristan met Jake Kalmar (a young Iowan who'd originally come from—to Tristan's surprise—two towns East over from his. Though they'd never met prior).
>
> Jake was part of the newly-formed veterinary science program. Both (he and Tristan) were signed in Professor Heints' advanced biology class.
>
> On the first day of class, Professor Heints immediately informed that only half would be able to get a passing grade. "And," he said, "You must decide today which half you will be."
>
> Tristan turned to Jake, poorly mimicking his professor's German accent, "Und you . . . vich half vill you be in?"
>
> Jake laughed, which caught the attention of Professor Heints who glared at both young men. It was to be, for both of them, a shaky start with regard to their professor but the beginnings of a smashingly victorious friendship. For after that day, the two were inseparable.
>
> So it was not unexpected that Tristan would ask to tag along with Jake to his animal dissection lab (where cats were splayed and their muscles, bones, ligaments and arteries tagged). Tristan was so enthralled with the neatness of science that he decided (amongst the smell of preserved flesh) that the

79

life of a farmer was not for him. He thought that he—too—
might become a veterinarian (more specifically, a teacher of
science for veterinarians) however, this conviction was to
change in less than a fortnight's time. Specifically, on the day
Jake's instructor, Mr. Williams, said Tristan could observe
Jake performing an equine "tail bleeding."
Everything was going fine…
            Jake made the initial incision but
                at that very moment
                        a beautifully huge horsefly landed
                                on Tristan's neck. It bit him so
                hard
                                        Tristan screamed…
                                        poor Jake, well—

Tristan and Mr. Williams took Jake to the local doctor; both
explained how Jake's jolt made his scalpel slice his
pinky-finger's fingertip clean off. Unfortunately, during the
bustle of the severence, Jake's first digit had become lost
(somewhere on the barn's floor).

The doctor cut down to Jake's second joint (stating he needed
clean, uninjured tissue for it to "heal proper" and to steer clear
of infection). The doctor did qualify that Jake's wound might
still get infected ("Gangrene—risk…further amputation" he
added to the bill).
            Eventually, Jake healed and went on to become a
veterinarian.
            Tristan, however, had been deeply affected by his
friend's experience with that doctor.

One never quite knows how thoroughly the things that go
wrong affect those to whom the wrongs occurred (or the
wrongdoers). Or, for that fact, the wrongs themselves.
Therefore (logically) Jake's lost pinky finger digit became the
impetus for Tristan becoming a physician. It—
could have been no other way.

Tristan, still lost in reminiscing, hardly heard Emily Marie pipe, "You know, dear Brother, that sounds SO interesting, but what I'd like to know is…"

Tristan immediately snapped out.

"What did you say?"

"I said, my dear Dear Brother, …"

"Yeah that—you better stop acting funny like that or Mother and Father will know we've been up to something. I mean it, Emmy, if you tell I'll never…"

"Never what?"

She beamed her bright, straight teeth and fluttered her eyelashes like the diva she imagined herself becoming.

"I'll not take you to any more shows!"

"Oh!" She slapped his arm, "You're SO MEAN!"

He laughed, "Yep. That's why God gave little sisters big brothers."

She put her arm in his and they scampered to the hotel where their parents had already had begun to worry on their whereabouts.

Unbeknownst to George and Elaine (and Emily Marie and, for that matter, Tristan) they ALL were face-staring long, long journeys.
***

As she unlocked the door to her employer's office—that of Dr. Hill—Genevieve Pardieu wondered how a French midwife from Paris, such as herself, had come to be so busy bringing the decent, upright women of Ashland, Oregon to relief from hysteria through her European training in the use of vibrators and massage.

She'd already been working for Dr. Hill nearly five years when he announced he'd spent a great deal of money on something he was sure she'd find miraculous—a brand new item—the vibratory table.

She remembered laughing because Dr. Hill's new-fangled item was something that, in France, she'd been trained to use more than seven years ago, in 1880.

"But," she said to Dr. Hill, "I'm so glad you've gotten one. Perhaps it will save my hands."

Ever since Genevieve and her family had immigrated to the United States, she'd had to induce the hysteric patients to paroxysms—in order to expel the maleficent humours of the womb—strictly through massage.

Although her techniques were quite effective, Genevieve found that there were times (especially at night, after a busy or particularly rigorous day) that her wrists ached—badly.

So when Dr. Hill unveiled the new table Genevieve was ecstatic. She couldn't have known—as she'd merely been trained in France to use such devices but had never practiced in Europe as a midwife: mechanization meant production.

Dr. Hill, on the other hand, was quite aware of what potential benefits the scientific progress promised. According to some of his colleagues (two former medical school chums he'd kept in touch with) vibratory therapy was the heart | soul of private practice. With only one table, a single physician's midwife could treat as many as twenty-five women per day.

Of course Dr. Hill knew this estimate was variable. He knew there weren't even enough wealthy women in Ashland and Middleford (the nearest larger-sized town) combined to sustain a regularly filled schedule of twenty-five women per day (every day). Still, he was quite pleased when his investment paid itself off within six months of its purchase (and in addition+ his midwife's schedule was usually filled much more quickly—and densely—than even his own).

Through the window, Genevieve watched the sun crest the hilltops.

Delivery wagons passed by; though it was only half-past six in the morning they were already moving products /to\/from\ destinations: the horses' hooves only made thudding sounds on the still-damp dirt roads.

Genevieve re-read the most current newspaper in the office— dated April 19th, 1887 (the paper was already more than two months old) while she waited for her first patient of the day, Mrs. Warrant.

Mrs. Warrant was always Genevieve's first client of the day for Mrs. Warrant was the lumbermillowner's wife. Her husband was an important figure in the growing town of Ashland, ". . . with much to do," as she frequently told Genevieve, insisting on being treated for her hysteria early—and often.

The door swung open. It was Dr. Hill.
"Good Morning Dr. Hill," Genevieve chimed.
"Not for me!"
"Oh, how so?"
"I was up all night at the Svensen place delivering their huge baby boy," he gruffed, adding, "and guess what they named him?"
"Patrick?"
"Sven! Can you believe that . . .Sven Svensen!"

Dr. Hill put his hand near the height of Genevieve's face, wiggling his fingers, which meant he wanted to have a look at the schedule book.

Upon seeing his schedule (seeing that Genevieve's was booked solid until the afternoon) he smiled.
"I'm off to get some breakfast. I'll be back for Mr. Winston's rheumatism at ten o'clock."

Over the years of their working relationship Dr. Hill and Genevieve had become friends; he accepted that she was French (which meant—to him—that she had different ideas [about many things] than he did: as an American). In return, she tolerated his gruffness. However, she'd lately noticed (over the course of the last winter) that a fatigue was growing over him: that his hands trembled a bit (from time to time), that he often had dark circles around his eyes and she worried (not only out of her feelings of friendship for the doctor but also because her employment depended upon his). Without Dr. Hill she would have to find work elsewhere.

Finding work wouldn't be difficult (as there was always work for midwives with such skills as those she possessed) but she'd grown fond of Ashland and hated the thought of leaving it.

"Dr. Hill, have you ever considered a partner . . . I mean someone maybe to do jobs like you did last night so you don't have to work so hard?"

He smiled, "Everyday!"

Dropping his medical bag in the corner—intent on breakfast at the corner café—Dr. Hill was disappearing out from the door he'd just entered through: "Now remember, hysterics are our livelihood. Take good care of them."

Genevieve held her hands up, waving them both in a salutary goodbye, "They'll be in good hands."

What Dr. Hill had not told Genevieve was that he'd already written to the director of the new Pacific University Medical School of Portland, Oregon nearly three months earlier requesting a physician/partner for his practice (hoping, greatly, of hearing promising news at any moment).

On the street, Mrs. Warrant saw Dr. Hill however, when she waved at him (indicating she wished to speak to him directly) he responded by quickly averting eyecontact, pointing towards the direction of the café, smiling, and quickening his paces.

Mrs. Warrant walked into the office where she directly proceeded to the vibratory theater without so much as a feigned greeting of civility to Genevieve Pardieu.
***

Before:
that winter (the winter of Tristan's first year at medical school)
proved the worst George and Elaine had ever seen.

Perhaps, if her parents had been alive then Elaine could have
measured her beliefs against the past—still…would she have believed
that, in fact, there had been one worse? One so terribly awesome for
those first few
                    (many Scandinavian)
who'd settled in the colonies of America
                    (and who migrated out onto the plains of Iowa)
that it created a dead long silence.

Death, itself, was neither tragic nor fatal for George and
Elaine: spiritually speaking. Death was as much visited upon faithful
people as Life. But without history one has no bearing of relativity.
How could Elaine (or anyone) know how terribly awful that winter
was to prove?

Without history, and the bearing of relativity—no one (including
Elaine) could know that worse—so much worse—had been suffered
before.
***

It was nearing 7:30p.m. (well dark) when there came a rapping on the screen door of Jake Kalmar's family home.

"Who on earth could that be in the middle of the night!" his mother, Greet, exclaimed. Pausing the click of her knitting needles.

"I don't know," Jan Kalmar replied. Rising from his chair.

"I'll get it, Dad," Jake said, leaping up with the agility bestowed upon young knees (forcing Jan into a quick remembrance of his own once-lithe legs).

Jake opened the door to Emily Marie Andersen.

"Good Lord!" Jake exhaled.

"Watch your tongue!" Greet scolded.

"Sorry Mother. Miss Andersen, what are you doing here?"

The young girl did not enter the house, even though Jake offered—without words—with his sweeping wide arm.
He is so darned cute

"No," Emily Marie whispered, "I can't stay. I…must speak with you, Jake. A moment."

Jake's dad called out, "Everything okay, Son?"

"Uh, not sure. Be back in a few minutes to tell you."

Outside, on the covered porch's steps, Emily Marie sat. Jake stood, watching how she'd begun silently twisting a pleat of her skirt between her thin fingers. He tended to think that young girls were like young mares. Sometimes soft quiet compelled desired result faster (gentler) than brutality. She proved his theory correct, shortly thereafter.

"Jake, I came to you because I need your help."

"What is it? Is Tris okay?"

"Tris? Oh, yes. He's just fine. It's just, well…"

Jake waited.

Well what? Come on girl spit it out. It's the middle of the…

"…it's that I'm…"

Yes, yes, yes

"…I'm running away."
Oh dear Lord!

For a moment—with all his thought along with all his body—Jake Kalmar halted. It was as if, at Emily Marie Andersen's utterance, God had stopped the circular motion of the world. A quick stop, admittedly, for Jake snapped back into the moment only to find his knees knocking, giving way to the collapse of his attempted stance.

"Are you alright?" Emily asked, rising—she stood and steadied him.
Emily Marie thought, "Oh I knew I shouldn't have come here. He's going to tell. He's going to take me home. He's going to tell…"

Jake had seen enough life to know that there were certain times for certain young girls (nearing or at Emily Marie's age) that, in fact, had a better chance for a happy life (a safe life) by running away from the family they'd been born into. He NEVER thought it possible within the Andersen family! It was simply too shocking. Then again, he had never been able to imagine it in ANY family, therefore (in his youthful wisdom) acknowledged himself a poor judge in such cases.

But since Emily Marie remained silent, Jake decided questioning was in order:
"Is it…your dad? I mean does he…do things? Touch…such?"
"Pa? My Pa's the most decent man you'd ever want to meet! How dare you say such a thing! "

She stood, as if to leave, but remembered—she had nowhere to go.

"I'm sorry," she said, sitting back down.

Jake shook his head side-to-side a few times, then raised his eyebrows, "Well…uh…"
Jake rubbed the back of his neck.
"…are you beaten real bad?"
Emily Marie laughed.

87

"Why on earth are you asking me such things, Jake Kalmar? You know our family. I just can't hardly believe YOUR mind!"

Jake's hackles finally stood up.
"Now you listen here, Emily Marie…"

Jake's dad opened the door. "Everything alright?"
Jake turned, facing his father, "Dad…"
"Yes Son."
"I have to go to the Andersen farm."
"Right now? In the middle of the night? What for?"
"Well…uh…"
The father knew his son:
He's hiding something. Ever since he was born I could tell when he was because otherwise everything's a straight answer
"Yes. I'm listening."

"Uh…well…Emily Marie…"

Jake looked at her eyes, her blue eyes emphatically pleading…so silent…so beautifully quiet.

"…came…to get me. Be—cause……oneofherPa'scows…is……in trouble."

"Trouble with what?"
"Birth."
"Oh yes? Miss Andersen," the old farmer's eyes turned onto the young girl, "Is this so?"
She dropped her eyes from his, then nodded.
Something is wrong, that's for sure and I'm going to get to the bottom of this one way or the other

"Well, then," Jake's father said, walking down the steps past his son, "I guess we'd better get the wagon ready. Good thing it's near a fullmoon. Enough light, that is,"

He looked back over his shoulder at Emily Marie (who'd not dared raise her eyes to meet his).

"so you can drive Miss Andersen home straight away. Help with that…cow."

Jan, having already walked several paces, was waiting for his son to follow him (while Jake stood, seemingly transfixed). Finally he called out: "Jake, I could use some help hitching up."
"Yes, Pa."
The young man jumped at the chance to leave those steps, to clear his thoughts (or conscience, for there wasn't ANYTHING Jake Kalmar hated worse…than lying).

Greet Kalmar opened the door. "Come in child. No sense waiting out there. It will take the men a good bit to get things ready. I made some tea."

She'd known a thing (or two) about the precariousness of maidenhood. She'd had cousins who'd talked (confessed) unnaturalness. So she kindly put her hand on the young girl's shoulder, guiding her into the *warm* light.

"Do you take sugar?"
"Oh, I don't drink tea."
"What was I thinking? Of course, you're still a child. How about some milk?"
Poor thing. She's what…maybe 12, 13. I do hope she's alright.

"Thank you, Mrs. Kalmar," Emily Marie smiled, taking the translucent white.
What enchanting eyes she has

"You're most welcome, Child."
They both drank. Mrs. Kalmar her tea: Emily Marie her milk.

"So," Mrs. Kalmar began, setting her cup in its saucer, "Your Pa has a cow in trouble is it?"
Mrs. Kalmar's eyes watched Emily's every move like an osprey to a fish's spine.

"Yes," Emily replied, looking the woman straight in the eye, forcing her spine erect (forcing her body not to crumble beneath the weight of her own lie) and that rigidity made her think: *Maybe it's true then*

        Mrs. Kalmar sipped her tea.
"Well I hope Jake can help," she said, taking Emily at her word, "he's a miracle with our livestock. I'm so glad he became a vet."
"Really?"
"Oh yes. Ever since he came home from school he's been saving us money."
"How so?"
"Well," she said, lowering her eyes looking through her eyelashes at Emily, "as you well know, births can be tricky things. Now Jan, I mean Mr. Kalmar, he's really good with births. Still, there are just some of them that are so bad…well there's not much to do except pray that either the cow…or the calf…survive. Because you know it can't be both."

"Oh, yes. I suppose that's true."
        Emily Marie gulped then took a sip.
        Mrs. Kalmar knitted her brow.

"Yes…well. I'm guessing that's what's happening with your Pa's cow?"
"Oh yes. Yes…most definitely. I just, well…"
"Yes?"

"Yes, well, I just don't know much about such things. My mother keeps me inside."
        Emily Marie took another sip of milk, then added:
"You know learning to cook, such and so forth. Oh, and chores. And…school. Yes! School."

"Yes, but surely, you help around your farm?"
        Jake opened the front door.

"We're ready," he announced.
"Well then," Mrs. Kalmar replied, standing up from the table, "I suppose you two had better get going."

"Yes. We'd better go right away," Emily Marie piped (feeling a tinge of guilt for not having drunk the entirety of the glass Mrs. Kalmar had given her).

Mrs. Kalmar looked at her son's face. It seemed worried beyond what she'd seen it before, concerning cattle.
"Son?"
"Yes, Mother."
"Would you like your Pa to go with you?"
"No, Ma. I need to do this on my own."
The woman saw her son—not a boy anymore.

"Then," she said in a cracking voice, "be…careful."

Jake smiled. Rushed over to her. He held her close to him long enough for her to feel three beats of his young heart.
"Don't worry, Mother. I'll be fine."

It was the one line every mother dreads hearing. Jan (knowing this) immediately came to Greet's side. "He'll be alright, Greet. He'll be just fine."

She looked into her husband's eyes—eyes she knew never lied—and eased, waving goodbye to their son.
Back inside their home Jan explained to Greet what he'd learned from Jake. Suddenly Greet, again, grew very nervous.
"What's wrong with you now?"
"Oh Jan! You don't know anything!"
She was crying even before she'd made it to the sink.
As she scrubbed the glass that girl had used, Jan came up behind her, put his arms around her waist—gently urging her weight to rest against his chest.
"Come now, Greet. Jake's a good man."
"That's it. He's a man and she's…well she's…"
"She's going home. He's taking her home. He'll be back straight away. He gave me his word. I've no reason not to take him at it."
His large hands turned her round so that her reddened nose and wet eyes could no longer hide.
"If I know anyone, Greet, I know our son. He's no man to do what you're thinkin'. Shame on you."

Her lip quivered.

"Yes. Shame on me. I know I shouldn't think such things. It's just I know…"

He lifted her chin.

"I know what you know."

He kissed her cheek, softly.

"Not all men are…you know."

She smiled.

"I know, Jan. You're a good man."

Then she let all resolve (all fear) past her and she melted away, inch by inch, until her arms turned into sweet churns around Jan's neck and she kissed him…over and again for being tenderly.
***

The ride to town was filled, mostly, with silence as Dr. Hill drove Hannah Lee Watkins' wagon to town.

Though words were exchanged sparsely, thoughts flourished as rich as milkthistle and the quiets were, periodically, rippled by Ginger's (or Sliver's or Steel's) muffled nosings and snortings {soft fleshy sounds only horses can make}.

By the time they reached Ashland-proper the sun was already nestled behind the timbered mountain-cradle.

Dr. Hill opened his office door, lit the gaslight then led Hannah Lee Watkins to the vacant apartment upstairs.
"You can stay here while we tend to your arm."
"That's very kind of you but…"
"No charge."
"Thanks…but…"
"Yes?"
"I, uh…"
She seems so childlike…as if she's afraid of the dark…or being alone…it couldn't be—she's always alone

"Sliver and Steel…where will they be? My wagon?"
So that was it. I should have known

"Oh, Mrs. Watkins please don't worry about such things. I'll take them home to my barn. They'll be well-taken-care-of. I promise."

She smiled, sat on the small bed, and exhaled as if she'd been relieved of a great worldly weight.
"Wait here just a moment," Dr. Hill said, "I'll be right back."

Hannah Lee kicked her boots off then pushed them under the bed *if I can just put my head down for a moment…I'm so worn out…and it would feel so goooodddd…*

By the time Dr. Hill returned he found Hannah Lee fast asleep atop the quilt his wife's sister had given them as a wedding present (though his wife later confessed she very much disliked the colorpattern, thus it ended up at Dr. Hill's office).

Dr. Hill rolled the sleeve up on her uninjured arm, giving her an injection of opium.
Now, my poor dear...you'll rest tonight without pain. Sweet dreams

He turned out the lights. He drove home to find his wife, Margaret, quite awake and not likely to be wanting of sleep any time soon. For she was hotter than a July afternoon with wondering where on earth her husband had been (especially after hearing from Johnny, the Smith, that he'd been with the "widder" well-into night).
***

Chapter Six

When Genevieve Pardieu inserted her key into Dr. Hill's doorlock she was quite surprised to find it already unlatched.

In all her years Dr. Hill had never bested her with regard to early morning opening. In fact, if truth be told, Dr. Hill had a tendency to "sleep late" (at least until 7 a.m.) lending some in town (the ones who liked to speculate) the opinion that such leisure was the result of partaken "spirits."

However, Genevieve knew Dr. Hill was not a partaker of such things. He was simply getting old and (being the only physician in town) getting tired.

"Dr. Hill," Genevieve's eyebrows raised, "what brings you here at this early hour?"

"We have a patient upstairs."

"Really? Who?"

"Mrs. Watkins."

"The widow from the glen farm up past the mountain?"

"Yes."

"When did she come?"

"Last night, I drove her."

Genevieve grinned. "Reeeaaalllly?"

"Don't be silly! I'm a doctor. She's badly hurt."

Sensing the seriousness in his voice all fun went from hers. "Is there anything I can do?"

"In fact, yes. She has a badly fractured arm that's infected."

"Will she make it?"

Dr. Hill looked at the ground.

It's not good

"Well," he said, "we'll do our best. Right now she's sleeping. That's good. I gave her opium last night. When she wakes we'll get her into the surgery and begin treating that arm."

"My schedule is booked. First up: Mrs. Warrant…"

"Damn those hysterics! This is important."

"I'll let YOU tell Mrs. Warrant that."

"I just might…I just might!"

"I definitely want to see that."

"Oh leave me alone, Genevieve. Honestly, I don't know why I put up with your…"

Just then the door opened. A young man, dressed in a cheap (but clean) suit, carried in a medical satchel.

Both Dr. Hill and Genevieve stared as he removed his hat to reveal golden blonde silk. His blue-blue eyes shimmered as he announced himself:

"Hello. You must be Dr. Hill."

Tristan stretched out his hand to the gawping man.

"My name is Tristan. Dr. Tristan Andersen."

Dr. Hill remained blankfaced.

"I have, here," Tristan continued, reaching into his attaché case, "Your letter requesting a physician—a partner—for your practice."

Genevieve smiled ;(ear to ear);

Tristan responded to her, equally linearly.

"Excuse me," Dr. Hill stammered, "May I see that letter?"

"Certainly," Tristan replied, handing it to the graying-haired man.

After a few moments Dr. Hill burst, "Ah yes, now I remember! I'd pretty much given up hope. Thought maybe my letter'd gotten lost or something. So the medical school sent you then?"

"Yes."

"Just graduated then?"

"Yes."

"Thought you'd set yourself up in on a good practice, eh?"

Genevieve widened her eyes to the young man, confiding to him a secret warning of ware.

"Sir. I came because my advisor, Dr. Mereth Hague…"

"Dr. Who?"

"Dr. Mereth Hague."

"I don't know any such person."

"Well, Dr. Hill," Tristan intimated as if to leave, "I apologize. Apparently, there's been a mistake."

But before Tristan could exit he felt the old man's hand brusquely patting his back.

"Now, now. I didn't SAY there'd been a mistake. Come sit. Wait here a moment. Then we'll talk."

Dr. Hill exited onto the street.

Tristan Andersen waited in Dr. Hill's front room for nearly half-an-hour (which gave him time to begin second-guessing the "ethicality" that Dr. Hague had so generously bestowed upon the older doctor).

The time also allowed Tristan to watch Mm. Pardieu escort two women patients
>(of upper-class—as Tristan determined by the style/expense of
>their clothing /jewels)
to=from a room that sat just off to the side of the front waiting room.

During one of the interchanges Tristan snuck a glance past the room's threshold: the walls were nearly as richly appointed as the women who entered therein.

However, for Tristan, it was Genevieve that made the environment absolutely enchanting. Even her simple condolences for Dr. Hill's tardiness, when expressed with her velvety voice, stirred him.

And the stirring felt deep—like dormancy—like seed birthing in an alfalfa field. Every time she entered the room his heart leapt into his throat. Every time she left it…he felt joyless.

Finally the front door opened. Dr. Hill re-entered and trained his eyes on Tristan. "Oh yes. I forgot about you. Well. I've a serious case to attend. Come with me."

Dr. Hill opened a door that opened to a stairway. The narrowly steep steps led to a small studio apartment where a woman lay in bed. The back of her head faced the approaching men. Her hair spread over the pillowcase in dark brown waves. Tristan noticed the profile of her ear~cheek. It seemed, to him, to shimmer by the light teeming past the sashes|through the tall windows.

"Mrs. Watkins," Dr. Hill nearly whispered.

Tristan watched the woman's singular eye open.

When she tried to roll over (using, by instinct, her broken arm) in order to face the voice that had addressed her she suddenly cried out in pain, collapsing. Then, using her other arm, she struggled but finally managed to sit herself up.

When Tristan saw her face he was taken aback:
Those eyes! Those cat-like blues and that hair...her mouth...

"Good morning Mrs. Watkins," Dr. Hill said, emphasizing "MRS."

He kept a watchful eye on Tristan.
"This is..."

Tristan didn't say a word.
"A...hem...this is?"
"Oh, yes. I...I am. I'm Dr. Tristan. I mean Dr. Andersen. I'm Dr. Tristan Andersen."

Dr. Hill grinned
Oh to be a young fool again.

"Dr. Andersen is going to look at your arm and tell me what he thinks we should do about it. Okay, Mrs. Watkins?"
"That's fine Dr. Hill. But you know I can't..."
"Free of charge," Dr. Hill smiled at Tristan. "Right, Dr. Andersen? You'll examine Mrs. Watkins free-of-charge."
"Of course," Tristan smiled.

Hannah Lee smiled too. For it was no secret that Tristan Andersen was, himself, a most-handsome young man.

When Dr. Hill and Tristan returned back down the stairway they both went into Dr. Hill's private office (where the old physician explained to Tristan that he'd, in fact, changed his mind about the partnership. Instead, he had a paid apprenticeship to offer him).

Tristan emerged from that den red-faced with frustration only to face a most-beautifully curious Genevieve.

Genevieve, in turn, turned pensive when she watched the young man walk to the front door in, what seemed to her, a state of anger.

Dr. Hill strutted behind Tristan like a tail-inflamed peacock (holding the door wide for the young man) and said:
"After all, with times being what they are. The financial crisis in our country and what not, you should be quite happy just to have employment in what you've trained in."

"Good day. Sir. I'm sorry to have wasted your time."

"Very well then. It's settled!"

"Fine!"

Tristan exited onto the street.

Almost immediately Dr. Hill called out, "Dr. Andersen! Come back in."

Tristan looked, observably, confused but re-entered. Dr Hill began to give him the following instructions:

"Go to my stable. Fetch Mrs. Watkins' wagon, her two horses (Sliver and Steel) then take this road to the old tree that's been split by lightening, veer to the right and head up the mountain. It might take you well into the early evening."

Dr. Hill could see that the young man was listening attentively. He liked that. But Tristan would not be budged. He was not going to be wrangled into an apprenticeship position (if he could help it). Still, he went along with the older doctor knowing (as some wise young men do) that sometimes one gets further by yielding (within reason) than resisting.

"Who will I be attending?"

"Mrs. Watkins' cattle, my dear boy."

Dr. Hill laughed.

Genevieve tried not to laugh, but did...a little.

Tristan did not laugh but stood, dumbfounded.

"Listen, Dr. Hill, I don't know what you think you're pulling here but I..."

Dr. Hill collected himself explaining that, as he'd already observed, the widow's arm was a badly infected compound fracture. And that he'd only been able to get her to accept medical attention on the condition that arrangements were made to have her cattle cared for.

Tristan listened.

"You see, Mrs. Watkins—Hannah Lee..."

Dr. Hill looked at Genevieve (who quaintly raised her eyebrows, miming: 'Hannah Lee?').

"...is a widow. A poor widow at that. If she looses this herd she'll be done for. She needs to know that her cattle are well-cared for while she's recuperating. Which, frankly, might take several weeks. If I were to hire a young man to tend to her cattle, well, I'd be done for—because I'm a married man of modest means."

Dr. Hill nudged Tristan's arm.

Tristan found himself warming to the older man's appeal. "Okay," Tristan said, "on one condition: partnership—NOT apprenticeship."

Dr. Hill thought for a moment.
"You'll get no extra pay," the older man sized up the younger man hoping he'd hedged his bets wisely.
"That suits me fine."

Dr. Hill found himself warming up to the young man (who seemed to him—at that very moment—a near perfect image of himself…at that age).

As they shook hands on the partnership Dr. Hill said:
"Oh. I forgot…"
Tristan braced himself.
"…you'll have to live in the apartment upstairs. Physician on-call and all that."
Then, as if trying to sweeten a sour deal he added:
"Rent-free, of course."
"That would be fine."
"Oh. And if we have to have someone stay with us…a patient…then you'll have to stay somewhere else."
"Naturally."
As Tristan exited (again) Dr. Hill called out:
"Oh. I probably should've asked if you know anything about caring for livestock?"
"My family has been farmers in Iowa for generations."
"Still farming?"
"Yes."
With that Tristan disappeared into the sunlit morning leaving Dr. Hill and Genevieve to wonder why on earth such a, seemingly, fine young man had become a doctor.
***

Emily Marie Andersen sat beside Jake Kalmar as he drove his team of horses through the moonlit night.

Though it was spring, it was cold. She snuggled to his side:
for warmth, he thought
for love, thought she

and the wagon swayed rhythmic-steady for a long, long time until Emily Marie breeched her own romantic folly, asking, "Where are you taking me?"

They were headed to her father's farm. Emily Marie clutched his arm. He could feel her shivering hands on his sleeve.
"What's wrong?"
"If...if you take me back there. I'll...I'll...kill myself."
"Oh don't be silly!"
"I mean it Jake Kalmar! I can't go back there."
Jake wasn't listening. Already he could make out Emily's father's figure shuttling between house {} barn.
"Something's wrong," Jake said.
"That's what I've been trying to tell..."
"No, not with you," he said, "with your Pa's...livestock."
Jake snapped the leather against the horses' backs.
Time got fast—all of a sudden.

Then the young man stopped. Looking Emily Marie in the eye, "Now you listen. You're being a silly little girl! Your Pa looks real worried about something that's going on in his barn. So you just stop all this foolishness you've been talking about."

Her body heaved. Snot (as if previously damned) burst free. Jake put his arm around her shoulders.
"I don't mean to be mean, Emily."
She turned her wet face to his only to find his profile as he was, once again, staring at her father's barn.
When he quickly returned her glance...
My God...he's absolutely beautiful
...he fumbled to hide his thoughts with words:
"It's...well. We can talk about whatever's bothering you...after we find out what's going on at your Pa's. Okay?"

She sniffled, "Okay."

"Who's that?" Jake asked, pointing to a tall, stocky man brusquely walking into the barn.
"Oh that's Mr. Stonewall, our neighbor to the East."
"And him?"

Jake pointed to a man (nearly half the height of Mr. Stonewall + more than half his width): "That's Mr. Blackson. The blacksmith."

Jake scrunched his eyebrows. "Yeah right."

Jake 'snutched' his tongue between his teeth. The horses plodded on. When they reached the house, Jake tied the horses and braced himself. Though not very old there was one thing he knew: unattended daughters meant a lot of trouble (especially when brought home by a singular young man).

However, Jake was pleasantly surprised when he met up with Mr. Andersen, saying, "I want to explain about your daughter..." to which Mr. Andersen interrupted: "Forget about all that right now son. Something's wrong with Bessie!"

From there the men traveled to Jake's comfortable topic: talk of how the cow'd gone down would not get up.
Whether from her calves growing (thick*fat) for eating or her becoming {again} fresh with milk, Bessie held a good portion of the Andersen family's survival betwixt her bony hips and cleat-feat. So seeing her down set Mr. Andersen stammering, "I don't know what we'll do if we loose our Bess. I don't know what we'll do..."
Jake (who always carried his veterinary bag with him) listened to her heart, her lungs, looked at her tongue, her eyes, her vagina, her teats (testing the milk), and took her temperature. After pulling his hand from her anus@manure duly shaken from his arm, he said, "She's got mastitis."
"Is it a serious case of it?"
"Could be. How long has she been down?"
"I brought her in the barn tonight. I bring her in every night."
Mr. Blackson winked^jabbed Mr. Stonewall who sniggered. George heard %saw it all.

"Now it's not like I'm a daftie or anything," George said loudly, "it's just…well…I figure it's best, you know, considering how much we rely on her."

>*George did not tell that he'd been treating Bessie with his remedies, for days.*

Mr. Blackson laughed, "Oh yes, no one gets treated like good ole Bessie."

"Ah shut up, Smithy!" George yelled. "Can you help her, Jake?"

"I'll do my best. A lot will depend on you keeping her teats well-drained and…"

In the meantime Emily Marie sat on the wagon waiting, wondering whether she should go in the house and face her mother or not. Emily Marie opted for not. So she waited with hope. Hope that her presence would go unnoticed—and it did…for ten whole minutes.

Elaine came out of the house, heading toward the barn, when she happened to glance at Jake Kalmar's wagon. That's when she noticed a figure atop it that, upon closer examination, proved to be her very own daughter.

"My God! Child, where on Earth have you been! We've been worried sick about you!"

After Bessie had been tended to (after Mr. Blackson and Mr. Stonewall had returned to their homes) George and Jake stood alone in the barn listening to the recovering cow begin to quietly chew her cud.

"Is her calf still on her?" Jake asked.

"He's strong enough to be weaned. Mind you, I like to keep them on a little longer—seems to help them grow bigger in the end if they nurse a little longer. You know what I mean?"

"Yeah. Dad does that too."

"How is your pa?"

"Good. Good. Your wife?"

"Good. Good."

Silence

"So you think Bessie's going to be alright then?" George asked.
"She looks good now. Just remember. You have to get all that infection out of her teats. Make sure to throw the milk out. Don't feed it to anything."
"Yeah. Got it."

Silence

"Mr. Andersen…"
"Listen Jake…"
"Sorry Sir, you go ahead."
"No, Jake, you first."
"Well…if you're sure?"
"Yes, please. You first."
"It's just kind of awkward."
"It's Emmy isn't it?"
"Yes."
"She ran away?"
"Yes. She says…well…I don't really know how to put it…"
"Just spit it out is the best way."
"Well I didn't really take her seriously, but…"
"What?"
"When we pulled into your farm she said she'd kill herself if I brought her home."

Silence

"She said that?"
　　Jake looked at the cow. He knew she was recovering. *Why can't people be more like animals: eat, breed, sleep, live, die…all natural*

"Yes," Jake replied.
"Well then, Jake. It seems we have some things to discuss."
105

Inside the Andersen family home Emily Marie sat quietly with her mother. Elaine waited for her daughter to offer an explanation for her behavior. Emily Marie sat—stone.

Elaine finally just had to begin it:
"Well, young lady you've got a lot of..." though she was not even given a full sentence of wrath before George and Jake walked through the front door.
George looked at his little girl...
She is growing up

...and said, "Emmy,"
Emily Marie couldn't bear to see her father's eyes. She looked at the floor instead.
"Yes, Pa?"
"It's time for you to go."
"What on God's green Earth are you saying George!" Elaine screamed.
George used the same deep, kindly voice he used on his livestock when they got fired up (or scared): "Elaine...sit down."

Elaine obeyed her husband, sitting.
Emily Marie's first impulse was to run. Her pa had said she could go so she'd better skeedaddle before he changed his mind. But when she crossed her home's threshold, stepping into the dark of night without the spirit of rebellion to fill her with courage, she knew she needed something more. She looked at her mother, whose face had fallen into the palms of her hands.
"Mother?"
Elaine could not raise her face, but replied, "Yes?"
"I love you."
George's eyes tingle-burned. "You'd better go now," he strained to say.
Emily Marie threw her arms around her father's neck.
"I love you too Pa."

Still hoping.
"Maybe," the father said (his voice breaking every now and then) "you'd like to get started... first thing in the morning?"

This time Emily Marie followed her urge to run (for she knew, given a night to think on it, her parents would change their minds).

"No Pa. Jake has to get back to his farm as soon as he takes me to the train station. Don't worry. I'll be alright."

From the wagon, from the dark, Emily Marie waved goodbye. Even in the night, the mother and father swore they could see their little girl blowing kisses to them on the increasingly sultry wind.

Alone, again, George turned Elaine's face to his.
"Love," he cooed; her body trembled as he held her close to his chest, "It'll be okay. I have much to speak with you about."

That night, in the quietudinous comfort of their bed, George and Elaine spoke of their children. They asked each other all the questions parents ask of themselves when children make their first attempts to live their own lives. Hours passed with wondering why. Hours were spent with how. Those were the hours in which the man of George held the mother of his children and the woman of Elaine cried her fears into the night.

Sometime, perhaps just before the sky purpled with the yellow speckles of oncoming dawn, George
        (holding Elaine, who'd tucked herself into the fold of where
        his arm met his chest and had fallen asleep)
allowed a man to weep.
***

Chapter Seven

The train
      ga-jiggity jugged
         ga-jiggity jugged
            along
            the
            tracks
                driving   Roy   west.

"West…always west," he thought. "If I keep going west one day I'll
end up home."

Then he smiled a rather sneer for, once again, he thought on those
early days \ those first days of slitting / throats for fun.

Roy shifted himself in his seat. Having been lost in virginal thoughts
he'd inadvertently erected.

Rows down from Roy a young girl sat with a young man.
Their sounds (whispers more than talk) were as if of two small

children secretly planning a raid
of their mothers' kitchen pantries.

They were unaware of being much-scrutinized.

Every so often—
when train's sway swung a certain way
(when traversing a slightly misaligned tie)

      —they would lift their eyes from their laps
        (each's hands within the others')
        and look at each with a set of not-child eyes.

Those crossovers of time revealed.

"Next stop San Francisco," the porter hollered.
      Roy smiled.
*The great San Fran. The infamous city…not quite Sin City…but it'll
do. Wonder what to be there…doctor…lawyer…minister…*

"We're almost there," the young girl beamed.

"Yes. Listen," he said, watching the browns and green passing the train's glass, "We need to talk. My parents are expecting me home…"

"Now don't you go spoil it for me Jake."

Emily Marie nudged him (while practicing the winking she'd seen the actresses do when they flirted with descents from their stages).

> Jake turned quietly serious.
> Emily became seriously quieted.

Neither knew their past.
Their long-past.
A past that had proved bittercruel / deathlydangerous.

For the Kalmar and Andersen families had been no strangers
> (though one had immigrated to America from Sweden, the other from Norway. Yet even *they* put those historical feuds aside—in the spirit of America. After all, they were both Scandis and Scandis needed to stick together).

***

The Kalmars and the Andersens, upon reaching the "land of opportunity," settled in far Northwestern Iowa. That very first year on their new soil...the Kalmars and Andersens would come to view each other unforgivable.

You see, the Kalmars had a beautiful daughter named Ida, Ida Kalmar had been chosen (by populous rather than from Ida's vocational conviction) to become the settlers' schoolteacher.

Ida was fourteen years old.
The Andersens also had a fourteen year old: his name was Tristan.

That first Northern Iowa winter there came a blizzard like none either Scandi family had ever seen (and both—from their homelands—had seen fierce cold).

There was something ominous about that storm. It was a thing that got born out of nowhere and, once it had been delivered, departed just as it had come except it took bitted fractures of life alongside it.

Before it hit, Ida went to the schoolhouse (as did all the children). The morning of that day came with such calm beauty—no one even bothered bundling up. Within an hour of starting her lesson, the temperature outside dropped more than twenty degrees.

When the cold began setting in, Tristan and his father feverishly worked to get their just-bought livestock (purchased with every bit of wealth they'd brought from across the sea) to safety inside the barn.

Then the temperature dropped so deeply that Tristan no longer thought on beasts. Nor did he think of the father he was leaving behind (alone) to do more work than was possible for a singular soul under those conditions.

[He couldn't have known that his actions would cause his own father to give up his flesh in an eventual black sacrifice.]
The only thing Tristan Andersen could think about was Ida Kalmar.
Ida, overriding her conscious' protest that the children would be safer with her, allowed some of the kids (the ones who lived closest to the schoolhouse) to go home.

111

When those children stepped outside the cold proved unmerciful. Some ran back into the schoolhouse. Some, like animals, panicked # running into the onslaught of white. For not only had the snow begun…but the chilling sweep of torrential freeze.

Tristan had run from his farm as fast as he could, but by the time he'd reached the schoolhouse (which was nearly a mile from his home) frostbite had already set in about his face, hands, and toes. Inside, Ida and Tristan held the remaining children close…to themselves and to the pot-bellied stove whose redness comforted (though its heat proved no match).

The Storm raged on…on…until

there was no more burning. The air had gotten too cold.

This was when the wind seized its opportunity—in the darkness of pure white—it ripped the little schoolhouse's roof from its nails. The wood disappeared into whirring milk frozen into shards turned razor blades: all spinning round at 70 miles per hour.

No one survived within the school.
None of the students who'd left the school survived either. Their frozen bodies would not be accounted for until spring.

Mr. Andersen's leg was amputated from the knee down (due to the frostbite). All of his animals died, bankrupting the family.

Mr. Kalmar (who'd decided he'd wait for the next calving season before sinking his money into livestock) ended up being, consequently, more affluent than Mr. Andersen. Plus, during the storm, the Kalmars had remained inside their home beside a fire that also fought, eventually succumbing to the bitter cold. Huddling together for warmth, they waited for their daughter to return, safely, home.
Of course, she never did.
That winter—during *that* storm—everyone suffered.

112

Death proved as rigidly fixed as the ice upon which the people's shoes shorn. The Kalmars and the Andersens were no exceptions. Only, there was …something.
When Ida's mother was preparing her daughter's body for burial she noticed…something.

"How did you find Ida's body?" she asked her husband.
"Well," he replied, "That Andersen boy, God Bless him, seemed to be trying to cover her…"
He teared up, "…like he was trying to save her or…"
"Protect her?"
"Exactly!"
That was when Ida's mother knew: Tristan and Ida had been lovers. From that discovery was born a bad blood. A venomous hatred within Mrs. Kalmar towards the Andersen clan
(though she never shared her discovery with a single soul—not even her husband)
that made the fact that her husband felt compelled to help the Andersen family in their time of need
(and through that "difficult" winter by way of settling their bills at the general store)
an even more bitter poison for the mother to swallow.
Mind, poison hardly ever remains contained forever.
Sometimes the most deeply buried darkness finds its way to birth.
***

The train
        ga-jiggity-jigged

Roy fingered the medical bag he'd stolen from Dr. Hague and
laughed, pleasantly amazed, at how easy it was to become a
physician:
all one had to do was to raise a framed
certificate—hanging it
for all to see.

"Dr. Hague," he chuckled, "That's me. San Fran. And Dr. Hague,
wherever you are by now: the hangman's tree ?] perhaps a jailcell []
...I'm free free free!"
***

Big Bob looked over his shoulder.

It was only a cat rustling scraps of garbage.

He thought it was Roy—he thought everything was Roy, so he followed the sound down a dark alley (thinking it was Roy); rats clawed bits of rotting meat from behind a café. The prostitutes (with moaning patrons groaning inside them) made Big Bob hopeful he'd see Roy.

He didn't.

Big Bob was on a mission. Big Bob thought God had saved him that night—the night the sergeant freed him (him being a guilty murdering sinner)—for a special purpose. And the only special thing he knew he could do was to kill Roy.

However, logistics came first. Big Bob needed money. *Doc has money. Doc might help.*

Then Big Bob thought:
Maybe Doc knows where Roy's gone. Maybe Roy went to the docs for money? Docs' where I have to go...

Hidden in what shadows he found (hoping to be hid) Big Bob crossed town.
***

When Jake Kalmar agreed to escort Emily Marie to the unknown (out West) George Andersen gave his word that he'd help Jake's dad run his farm. He assured Jake that everything would be alright.

So, every morning (come first light) George rode over to Jan and Greet Kalmar's farm. Every afternoon (sometimes quite late) Elaine watched his hunching shoulders ride past the house, into the barn. That's when George began his own chores. By the time he'd be done it'd be welldark. Elaine grew worried for her not-young-husband.

Day after day George rode to Jan's farm and each sway of the horse's hips made George more anxious how much longer his own farm could suffer his absence.

Elaine (who worried how much longer their farm could withstand George's absence) assumed George's chores. But it was wearing on her also. For she was a not-so-young wife and George had noticed that Elaine had stopped preparing proper suppers.

A boiled potato.

Vegetables—raw!

An egg and a slice of day-old-bread.

No more yellow butterpats in the shape of roses. She said she could not be bothered to add carrotcolor to the cream and when George continued with his complaint she quipped, "It tastes the same, God Bless it!"

It seemed this went on for a very long time…until, one day, George went to Jan's farm only to find Jan in his barn. He was wearing a worried frown.

"What's wrong Jan?"

"It's Buttercup. She's got the mastitis again. I'm sure of it. We can't afford for her to loose another teat. She's already on three even though last time I'd drained every last bit of puss out of 'em. One still went blank. I wish Jake was back."

That hurt George—on many levels—so for a long while he simply watched a man gently stroke his beloved beast's flank without saying anything. Finally, he spoke, "Jan. I've some remedies from our homeland."

Jan grinned. "Now George Andersen. Don't tell me you go in for that nonsense do you?"

George frowned. He usually didn't tell people about his family's beliefs in herbs, poultices, and tinctures (ancient remedies) for his animals (for his family as well). Such practices (in their new country) weren't usually well-received but he thought it might be different with Jan Kalmar because they were both Scandis. So George stiffened up: "As a matter-of-fact, Jan, I do."

Jan looked side-to-side, whispering, "So do I. What should I do?"
"Well I'd start with goat's milk butter and marigold on the utter…the entire utter…then give her some red clover. Do you happen to have any of those wildflowers around—you know, the ones that—when you cut the root—the root bleeds like real blood?"
"I've never seen such a thing."
"That's okay. I'll go get some."
George was walking out the barn when Jan called,
"Do we need anything else?"
"A needle."
"A shot-needle or sewing one?"
"Sewing."
Meanwhile, back at his own farm, Elaine was busy. She'd milked the cows, fed the hogs, and gathered the eggs. She was in the middle of mending a fence that one of the yearling horses had managed to tear through the night before (during a warm thunderstorm) when George came galloping to her (their poor mare all in a sweaty lather) yelling:
"Laney, bloodroot! I need some bloodroot. And some of those mushrooms we use when we're really ill."
"What for?"
"For Jan."
"When did he fall ill?"
"It's not for him it's for Buttercup."
"Buttercup?"
"His milkcow."
"George Andersen. I will not use those medicines for his co…"
"Stop right there. Jake's family is just like ours."
"I doubt that. I'm sure they're not needing their Buttercup the way we need our Bessie."
"Now Elaine. Judge not. Besides, I think that crunch everyone keeps talking about's got the Kalmars' too. I think their Buttercup keeps

their family fed, which means they need their dairy cow every bit as much as we need ours."

Elaine softened. She usually did…when she knew George was right. She soon returned with a small medicament bundle.
"Do they have a proper needle?"
"Of course."

But before George hurried off he leaned down and kissed the top of Elaine's head, "I love you, Laney."
"Oh go on…"

Then he was gone.

After her errands to town had been run, the potatoes boiled (for George's supper), the household and farm tended to—as evening was falling—Elaine decided it was time to do what she could not do when George was home: read.

She'd sneak to read all kinds of books every chance she got: soft novels (those society deemed appropriate for women), agricultural texts, history, and current events (much to the chagrin of her fellow churchwomen to whom she'd made the mistake of confiding her reading list in). Naturally, her most recent subject of interest was Oregon.

Oregon's been a state since February 14, 1859. Our own Iowa is only 13 years older; we got our statehood December 28, 1846

Outside she heard hoofclops so she discreetly replaced Oregon in its proper place, hurrying to the kitchen to prepare George's supper plate.

When he finally came through the door he was unable to eat. In fact, he looked so haggard, Elaine feared for her husband's very well-being. She was not, therefore, surprised when George picked at his supper.

That's not like him. Something's getting at him

"What is it George?"

He sighed, forking a mouthful of potato. He stared (at her) past her…past (—to where…she did not know) until, finally, he spoke:
"Did I ever tell you how the Kalmar and Andersen families met?"
"Tristan met Jake at university."
"Yes. That's true. I mean…before that."
"I didn't know there was a 'before that.'"

George's head fell; he looked at his supper as if praying.

"You see, my family's been here—in America—three generations now."
"As have mine."
"Yes, but yours have stayed in the same place…right here."
"Your point, George?"
"When my family came from Sweden…we settled up north."
"I know this George."
"What you don't know is that the Kalmar's also settled there."
"Okay."

Elaine changed her tone as if she were talking to a small child—a condescending tone that usually drove George to moderate rage (when he was in a normal mood—which he wasn't, therefore he did not rage) when she said: "You do know, George, that it wasn't TOO uncommon for people from Scandinavia to settle around each other when they came to America."

George didn't even huff.

This frightened Elaine more than any of his rages: this growing absolutely silent—still.

"Listen, George, I'm sorry. Okay?"

still—silent

"Laney, you just don't know when to be quiet."
"I'm sorry. I promise. I'll listen. Without interrupting."

"It's just that this is very hard for me. I don't know if I can finish telling it…"
"Please, George, I'll be quiet. I'll just listen okay?"

"Okay. So our families settled around the same town. Difference was…the Kalmar's had come from money. We didn't. My grandparents sold everything they had. They came with just enough…to buy a few beasts and build a sodder. The Kalmar's had enough to buy a whole herd as well as build a nice house."

119

"I see," Elaine said as nicely as possible.

George smiled, "You're really something, Laney."

Elaine smiled, "You're really something too. Now, tell me more."

"The story went…"

***

Chapter Eight

Curt Bell compared the shipping receipt to the delivery. Everything matched up. No overcharges. Only Wendy Waeh's almond oil had not come with the shipment.
She will not be pleased...nor will her father

You see, Curt Bell knew, full-well, the extent of the relationship between Wendy Waeh and her father. Such had been the case ever since that afternoon...when Wendy'd deflowered Curt Bell's innocence. Ever since...they'd become secret lovers.

The only one who even suspected them was old Mrs. Bell. When she confronted her son with the affair, Curt —bluntly, succinctly—demanded: "Shut your mouth, Mother, and don't you dare speak of this again to anyone."

Mrs. Bell was horrified that her only child—her beloved son—was nothing at all like her dearly-departed
(beloved-because-obedient)
husband. After that, she hardly spoke a word to anyone (including Curt) unless it was regarding her receipt of more medicaments.

It was near about a year after the affair had begun when Curt asked Wendy to marry him. She refused (of course in an attitude of pleading) for she knew her father would never let her wed.

Another year continually filled with Wendy's confidences to Curt about her, her life, her father:
> (having a father that demanded satisfaction from her without "traditional" deflowering; having a father that preferred taking her "not in her womanly way," having a father that even, sometimes, told her that having her that way made him feel more of a man. That it was even more pleasurable because there could never be a child).

One day, at the creek, Curt asked Wendy:
"Does it hurt?"
"No, not really," she said, picking a dandelion. "Well, I suppose it did. At first...but," she smiled, grabbing Curt, "it caaannn feel good too."

Curt's face flushed. He'd never known her in the way she'd known him.

"Mind you," she continued, looking away (far—at nothing), "it all seems a bit unnatural."

Again, Curt blushed.

She sensed it, retracting, "Not you, my sweet love," she cooed, "not you. Not us. Or ANYTHING we do with each other. Him I mean."

"Unnatural? He's a sodomite! I say he'll rot in bloody hell!"

"Now, let's not spend the few moments we get, fighting."

He pulled her face to his, kissing her so tenderly that he wept, "I love you Wendy. I love you more than you can know. Please marry me. I'll take you away from here I promise. He'll never touch you again...I'll...I'll..."

"Shhhh, my love, shush. There are things you don't understand about my father."

Curt wrested himself from her arms.

"I don't want to hear you say that."

Wendy stood to go.

Curt looked up from where he sat.

"I love him," she cried.

As she walked away he watched her right hand's handkerchief gently kiss the corner of her eye (over^ &^ again^) until she was gone out of sight.

I hate him

So, when the almond oil did not come Curt stood, alone, lost in his thoughts, knowing that Wendy would suffer for it. Because whether or not the oil came for her...her father did. The oil simply gave her pleasure...by saving her pain.

So he hated and loved it and hated him and loved her and felt his own being unraveling his hand-hooked-rug-soul between claws on one side and wings on the other.

***

At the table, over another dinner, an exhausted George bowed his head and prayed his usual prayer:

Lord, Father, Master: please give me strength to do what You want me to do. Forgive me my sins because I know they hurt you and I don't want to hurt you...if I can help it. Please bless Tris, Emmy, Laney, and everyone I know and love. And baby Ida.

Then he, unusually, added:
Please bring Jake home soon. Amen.

Elaine waited in the silence until he un-bowed his head. He said, "Did I ever tell you how the Andersens got to know the Kalmars?"

Elaine thought, "Dear Lord, he's losing his mind," but said, "Yes, George, you did."
"I mean about how we settled up North?"

Give me strength. It's the same thing every night now. I don't know how much more I can take.
"Yes, George, about the sod house and so on."

"I did?"
"Yes George."
"And about..."
George looked side-to-side, as if someone might overhear, "...the baby?"

Elaine's eyebrows perked:
This is new. He's never mentioned a baby before.
"You mentioned something about a...feud. A secret. But I didn't know what it was."
"Well the only thing scandalous about the whole thing was the way Old Kalmar didn't think the Andersens were good enough to marry one of them."
"What do you mean?"
"I mean Tristan."

"What about Tristan?"

"Not OUR Tristan...back then, you know, with Ida."
"Okay. I'm with you."
"Well, they'd been in love from the time they laid eyes on each other.
Times were hard then. I know: you're going to say that time's is hard
now, but they were really hard then. Everything was, well maybe
things seemed less permanent...everything was new. Whatever the
reason was, Tristan and Ida became lovers."

Elaine, growing frustrated: "George, I know all this!"

"The point is," (he drawled out 'iiiiisssss' just to annoy her), "Tristan
asked Ida, over and over, to marry him...so the story goes...but she
said no."
"Why? You said she was in love with him?"
"Yes, she was," George inched his face close to Elaine's as if he were
sharing one of the infamous tales of M. Sherlock Holmes, "and he
was an Andersen."
"Yes. That's obvious."
"And she was a Kalmar."
"Obviously. Please, George, please!"

George leaned back, patted his belly, sighing.
Elaine waited...tapping the table with one of her fingernails.
A fingernail, she noticed, that had a black-half crescent lying beneath
it   *I'll clean them after supper*

"And..." George continued.
Elaine thought: *Oh yes more*

"...the story goes...she said they could be lovers, in the Biblical
sense, until they were old enough to run away."
"No!"
"Yes! They were going to run away as soon as they had a way to do
it."

Elaine leaned back in her chair.
"You said there was a baby?"

George leaned across the table and kissed his wife's cheek.
"You don't miss a thing, do you Laney? Sharp as a tack, you are."
"Oh don't be so silly!" she said, but smiled.

It made her smile…to see that part of her husband resurrecting before her eyes.

George, seeing flickers of his 'old Laney' filter through the tough façade she'd adopted (because of the burden he knew he'd placed upon her). It was relief to see her bald-faced: he wanted more of it.

"Are you sure you want to hear…huh huh huh? Sure you want to hear," he tickled her side, "a little more???"

She laughed/giggled:

"Silly old man!'

"Okay. Well it happened that they were actually running away. On THAT day. The worst day in the whole history of the world. That blizzard day that hit so hard and fast the cows froze standing up."

"Which one? There've been lots of blizzards."

"There's never been a blizzard like THAT one. It was so bad…"

Elaine laughed {partly because George poked her arm—mainly because she just couldn't resist not playing along}:

"How bad was it?"

George gave a great big bellylaugh.

"I tell you, Laney, that was the real reason I married you."

"Because of a bad blizzard?"

"Because you have a sense of humor."

"Oh go on."

It's so wonderful to see him like this again. Thank you God!

"Ah, yes. The blizzard. THE blizzard. Well the thing about this blizzard was that there wasn't any real warning about it. Mind you, northern Iowa didn't even get it as bad as other places…"

"Like where?"

"Well, like…Minnesota, I think."

"I have an aunt in Minnesota."

"We're Swedish. We're required to have at least one relative in Minnesota! But back to the story. The blizzard came so quickly and so…hard. 40 below, it got!"

"That is bad."

"Yes. And no warning. Those kids that left the schoolhouse froze walking home."

"And Tristan and Ida froze at the schoolhouse. I know the story, George."

"Yes…and no."

"Oh Good Lord! What do you mean, 'yes and no'? It's either one or the other!"

"Meaning they COULD have survived."

"Oh George!" Elaine cleared his emptied plate.

Then George just echoed (like a lost lonely cavern): "Could have…could have survived…survived such a terrible storm…could have…"

A small tear escaped Elaine.
Lord. Lord? Please help him
***

Chapter Nine

"More?"

"No thank you," Mr. Isaac Inns replied, "Lily...I mean Julie."

The young woman scowled.

"You really MUST keep that straight! If we're going to manage this arrangement there can't be any mistakes."

In the background a baby cried out, like a cat.

"She's hungry. I have to go feed her."

"Yes...Julie. I have to go into town."

"For what?"

"Supplies."

"I thought you just went."

Isaac Inns was not the smartest man. He was also not conniving so he 'fessed up: "Mr. Warrant asked to meet with me."

"Oh dear Lord why?"

The baby girl whined. Julie looked toward the sole bedroom in the small shack of the house that the Isaac Inns's family had called home for generations.

"You wait. I'll be right back."

She returned without missing more than a three-count, dipped her finger into the honey jar, letting the baby suck.

"Now why does Mr. Warrant want to meet with you?"

"I suppose he wants to discuss your wedding to Mike."

The baby slurped%gurgled.

Julie got lost—for a moment—in the warm flesh of her baby girl's suckling mouth.

Jake

Returning, she mused: "Okay. So we need to have a reason why haven't I come to see Mike since that day I slapped him."

The corners of Isaac Inn's lips curled down. Whereas his eyebrows curled up from the nasal: "Because...he got fresh?"

"Exactly! He can't suspect my innocence—or lack of—or the marriage would be off."

Now, as said previously, Isaac wasn't the sharpest man but he still remembered the day he'd met Lily (though she'd confessed Lily had merely been her stagename. She wove a story for poor Isaac Inns on that fateful day when he'd lost so many four-footed beasts. Her story (+ his recollections) soldered in his mind an interconnection that went as such:

She'd been traveling with a troupe of actors.
"Poor thing," he thought when he saw her. Even the whiskey couldn't make her act, sing, or dance—well.

There was a young man in the audience watching her with eyes ablaze.
"Ah," Isaac thought, "young love." Not that he'd known such-a-thing himself...still, he'd heard. At the end of the show, as he was climbing onto his wagon, the stagegirl and audienceboy got into a row.
"Funny," Isaac thought, "it almost looked like the boy was getting down on his knee. Marriage?"

Suddenly that young girl ran directly towards him:
"Sir, " she said, with such urgency in her voice, that Isaac found himself quite mesmerized. "May I entreat upon you?"
There were tears in her eyes.
"Most certainly," Isaac replied, "how can I help?"
"Take me away," she said...climbing atop Isaac's wagon.

Isaac looked towards the young boy (whose eyes looked horrified—) just before he turned and ran away. "Young love," Isaac thought. Then thought, "Now what?"

The young girl looked at him: his worn boots, frayed pants, stubbly face, holey hat and said: "I believe, kind sir, that you and I might be able to strike a fair deal."

To this Isaac—of course—being a respectable man, replied: "I think you've mistaken me..."
"Before you continue...I can cook, clean, mend...I can take care of you."

Isaac let out a breath: "Oh...I see," he said, "well..."
Lily didn't hesitate: "It's obvious you have no one to care for you. All I ask is that I be given a roof and food for me...and my child."

Isaac's eyes grew saucers: "Child?"
Lily rubbed her stomach: "Yes, sir. Child."

Now, the Inns men might have been called scoundrels by some with regard to acquiring land...but none (at least none that Isaac had been aware of) had ever been named thusly for the way they'd treated women. "Okay," he replied.

And that was how Lily
(also known to some as Emily Marie Andersen)
became Miss Julie Inns.

Isaac sipped his coffee.

The baby'd had enough of honey. She wanted milk.

He wanted outside.

Things had changed since the baby'd been born—not that Isaac didn't love the little girl—but Julie had changed…and not for the better.

She no longer wanted merely a roof and food. She wanted money which='d clothes, glamour, respect. She obsessed on making a profitable marriage to Mike Warrant (for the Warrants—if richness can be measured with clothes, glamour, and respect—were very, very wealthy).

Julie wasn't the only one who wanted the union between Mike Warrant and Julie Inns: Mike Warrant Sr. wanted Isaac's land: and Mike Warrant Jr. wanted Julie Inns' hair however Isaac only thought he wanted the Warrants' money (money Julie promised she'd give him after they married) for as time wore on he suddenly began to feel that he was losing everything. Because, to his deep surprise, he'd grown quite fond of Julie and her little girl's company. He liked the way they flitted around the house. He liked how Julie picked wildflowers to "brighten the sty" (as she'd say). Most of all he liked Julie's little girl, Ida May.

You see Isaac Inns had never even seen a child born (let alone been the one to deliver one into the world) so it was in that very moment—when he laid his hands on that tiny wet red body and his own eyes welled up such that his heart beat clear through his entire self—that, with every second he'd known of love, he loved that child. And so (hoping for humanity) he wished for nothing greater than Julie to forget her grand scheme and for her to simply stay—at home—with him…and Rusty (the Shepard).

***

At City's medical school:

"Hello. I'm Dr. Pruesst. What can I do for you?"
"Big Bob's the name."
"Okay…Bob. How can I help you?"
"Well I'm looking for the doc who…" Big Bob looked around then whispered, "you know…used those people's bodies."
"Oh."

Dr. Pruesst also looked around but said nothing.
So Big Bob continued:
"You know. The one with the lollies?"

Dr. Pruesst then looked Big Bob up^down.
"Why don't you come into my office," he said, averting is eyes from those of the department's receptionist.
"That'll be real fine," Big Bob beamed.
He treats me nice too. I wonder if he has any lollies

Dr. Pruesst pointed to a chair. "Please, have a seat."
"Don't mind if ah do."
"I think it was Dr. Hague that kept 'lollies' in the lab. Perhaps he's the man you're looking for. Might I ask you why you're looking for him?"
"I need his help."
"With what?"
"Well it's like this…"

Big Bob told the whole story.

Dr. Pruesst's squirming in his seat progressively intensified. Dr. Pruesst, being a researcher, was no virgin in procuring bodies. Everyone in research had the same waking nightmare: one day they'd come face-to-face, in plain daylight, with the men who found murder easy.

For Dr. Pruesst it was the worst thing he could imagine: a brute (Big Bob) holding a physician's livelihood on the tip of his tongue. A man who seemed to feel absolutely no compunction about reiterating every detail of how he'd delivered murdered men to science.
To him I'm a complete stranger and he's telling everything! Who else has he told? My colleagues? Police? I must get rid of this man!

"…and then we'd come to the university-here…"

"Yes, yes. I see. Well Dr. Hague is DEFINITELY your man and I'm sorry to say that he has left the university."

Big Bob's face actually looked visibly sad.

"Well…where'd he go?"

"Oregon."

"Oregon! How on earth can I get to Oregon?"

"You…uh…need…money?"

Big Bob sat for a moment. He didn't even know where Oregon was.

"How much it cost to get to Oregon?"

"Don't worry about that," Dr. Pruesst said, standing up from behind his desk.

I never rode on a train before

Then the doctor handed Big Bob an undisclosed amount of money.

"Wass' this fer?" Big Bob asked.

"For whatever you might need in order to find Dr. Hague…in Oregon."

Dr. Pruesst exerted effort to emphasize

"Hague"

and

"Oregon."
***

"Hello Mrs. Andersen. How are you today?"
"Well Pastor Morgan. I can't really complain."

Pastor Morgan, being somewhat perceptive, could see there was—in fact—something troubling Elaine Andersen and (having previously gained George's confidence—and confession—that the Andersens were upset over their son's occupation) he, preemptively, aimed towards that target.

"Is it about Tristan's vocation?"
"Good God no! Sorry Pastor. That just slipped out."

Sometimes I feel as if everywhere I tread is sheershardglass that I tread upon. Best to be silent. She'll come out with it...eventually

Elaine twiddled a thread on her shawl. She twittered her eyelashes feigning the perusing of Pastor Morgan's bookspines.

Dear Lord, she's tough. I wish she'd just let...
"I'm worried about George!"
"George? Why?"
"Well..."

She fell quiet again.
Wait. Patience. Virtues and such. Wait. Like fishing...

Patience wasn't one of Pastor Morgan's strongpoints.
"You're worried about George because?"
"If he keeps going on like this I think it will kill him."
"Kill him! Surely, Mrs. Andersen, you're exaggerating."

Her quiet unnerved him.
"Is George really in danger?"

She twaddled her thread.
Wait. Oh to heck with waiting! I just can't sit around her and wait for a silly lady to tell me what's going on when somebody's life may be threatened. And she's, SHE'S, sitting there PLAYING with her silly thread

Elaine voiced up: "Do you know the Kalmars?"

"I've heard of them. Two towns over?"

Elaine nodded.

"Has one of them threatened George? Is he in…some kind of…debt?"

"I suppose you could call it that."

Pastor Morgan let out an emphatic draft of air out his nose. "Now listen, Elaine, you must come to the point. I might be able to help George BUT I must know what's going on!"

"Oh. I'm sorry Pastor Morgan, for troubling you." Elaine stood to leave.

Pastor Morgan's eyes flared

Nononono don't let it out…don't let it out…keep the devil off your tongue, old boy, say something nice…quick…something inspirational…

"I'll pray for George then?"

"That would be great."

"Just a general prayer…then? Nothing specific you want me to pray for?"

Elaine thought for a moment—holding the door wide—

"Could you pray for a baby that died a long, long time ago?"

Pastor Morgan told himself that he couldn't help it: such frustration finds ways out (ways that led
>   his head
>   to wagging—slowly—side-to-side,
>   like an old dying dog).

If there was one thing Elaine Andersen understood, it was exasperation—so she gave the pastor a bone (so to speak):

"The baby's name? Ida…Ida—Andersen. Could you pray for poor little baby Ida who died long ago?"

"Yes, Mrs. Andersen. I can do that. And about George?"

"Don't worry yourself about that. You were right. Too much imagination," she said, rapping her knuckles—hard—upside her head.
***

It—
>   can be interesting
— experience.

Being in the home of a stranger.
Being alone with knowledge.
Knowing to notice
>   —things:
>>   little things
>>   big things.
>   One can hardly be faulted for curiosity.
Investigation—speculation.

Tristan found himself (while performing his first "official" act as a medical doctor) in just such an ethereal situation. It had been nearly two weeks since he'd come to Hannah Lee Watkins' farm (to tend to her livestock). Two weeks without a word (or the replacement Dr. Hill had promised to send when he "had time." And Tristan had wondered why Genevieve had laughed when she heard Dr. Hill say that. For if there was one thing Dr. Hill seemed never to possess—it was time).

Tristan's first duty was to the animals, naturally, and he had performed his duty proficiently (which meant he, unlike Dr. Hill, had time left over after it
was done).

The widow's house wasn't fancy. It was rundown…neat/tidy but dirty: there were unclean dishes left in the sink so Tristan washed them. He could not bear such messes. If there was one thing Dr. Tristan Andersen cared deeply for—personally and professionally—it was cleanliness.

You see Tristan'd become enamored with the rather controversial methodologies of a physician/scientist named Lister. In fact, after the very moment he'd finished reading Lister's text, Tristan decided that there was absolutely no other way of going about things than antiseptically.

Fortunately for Tristan (and Hannah Lee Watkins) his concern for cleanliness and aversion to infection in no way interfered with his reconciliation to duty. While wallowing in cattle manure he treated (to the best of his medical abilities) minor injuries to the cattle. He did, however, isolate two heifers that seemed a 'bit off' and was glad

he'd done so. Later they both died. Naturally, this afforded Tristan's analytical mind much to feed on as to what might have been the causes of death. It also concerned him about his own safety so (via harsh soap, stiff brush, and alcohol) he meticulously disinfected himself with vigorous scrubbing each and every time he handled Mrs. Watkins' cattle (needless to say, he'd quite chaffed
his skin crimson-red).

  The widow's herd was respectably sized. She had what all poor farmers had (chickens, hogs, dogs, cats—of course mice and rats). Tristan cared for them all (minus the rodents). His favorites were Sliver and Steel (the two horses Tristan had brought back from town). Whenever he came to their field they'd use their warm muzzles to gently nuzzle Tristan's pockets—for he'd decided to sacrifice the little lumps of sugar he kept in his medical bag

  (sugar doubling as an antiseptic—like salt—and used for
  treatment of sugar sickness)

to the sweetness of those two lovely equines.

  Beside the house was the widow's vegetable garden bed. It looked dead so Tristan performed triage (he tended what seemed most likely to survive…giving them water from the well between the sparse rains. The rest he let full-stop die).

  Down the hill from the house twisted a little creek. To the best of Tristan's calculations, the farm must have encompassed near to 150 acres. After the first week passed, Tristan thought: "It is, most certainly, an isolated place."

  During the second week, Tristan thought: "Beautiful, definitely. The mountain crags, like a huge castle, to the south. The creek, on the west with rows of tall pines. The almost-prairie feel to the loping hills around. 'High desert,' some call it. It doesn't seem like a desert to me. It is a little browner, and drier, but at the same time somehow feels like home."

  Yet when the day drew its curtain closed around the fourteenth fire of his fourteenth night {and the light outside had died away} Tristan found himself disquieted. Perhaps it was that his back was getting tired of sleeping atop the bed of blankets he'd laid upon the living room floor

  (feeling it improper to sleep in the woman's sole bed)
  [plus he also liked going to sleep by the fire because it made
  him feel less lonely—most times]

for whatever reasons, this night…disturbed him.

Doubts raced (had being a doctor been a dream?).

He watched the firelight flicker the browning pictures—
> [photos, obviously, valued by the person who'd hung them
> that they'd been willing to pay what dearness framers
> charged].

He recognized Hannah Lee, smiling, as she looked at the man beside
her. He knew, too, that she was a widow. And he mused:
*Death. So many ways biology ends. Those heifers—thank God
whatever it was that killed them didn't spread. Yet. That's it.
Disease. He looks so young and strong. She looks younger than me
and I've never even been in love. What have I done worthwhile with
my life? At least she had love. What do I have? A license to doctor?
Despised? Caring for someone else's cattle? I should be home
tending my own father's farm...I've been a fool!*

There was a rattle at the door.
Tristan grabbed Hannah Lee's rifle.
The door latch lifted.
He cocked the trigger. Aimed.

It was Dr. Hill and Hannah Lee.
"Thank God! I..." Tristan stammered.
"Put the rifle down, son," Dr. Hill commanded.
"Oh yes. Sorry. I wasn't expecting...and you're here. It's the
middle of the night and...oh. Then good news is it? Your arm,
better?"

Hannah Lee smiled, nodded. "Thanks to Dr. Hill's kindness
and your caring for my farm."

Hannah Lee held her arm out for Tristan to see.

Dr. Hill's cheeks flushed.
"Now you just rest up. I've got to go," Dr. Hill made for the door,
"Another baby. You'd think there'd be a slowing sometime or other
but no! More and more babies. Marge (my wife) says it's like dishes,
(or laundry): just when you're sure you're done out come more." And
with that he closed the door behind him leaving Tristan speechless
and alone with Hannah Lee.

An actual moment—only—passed before Tristan ran out after
the older doctor, out into the blackened night.
"You're not leaving right now are you?"

"Sure. You heard me didn't you?"

"Yes I heard you. But it'll only take me a few moments to gather my things."

"Son, now you listen to me. That woman is our patient and she's been through a great deal. We darn-near lost her."

"From what?"

"From INFECTION! Don't you remember?"

"Yes, but I thought…"

"Listen, I'd love to chat but I have to go."

"So what am I supposed to do?"

"You take care of her until she can take care of herself," Dr. Hill boomed his voice as his wagon pulled away, "oh, and don't let that wound get re-infected."

There

   it

     was.

It made Tristan
  more than a ranch-hand…more than farmer
  or abandoning son: he was needed
  in the very way his idol,
  Lister, needed him to be needed.

It

   was

apropos.
***

Having failed attaining Emily Marie's hand (at the Greensprings Inn) Jake found himself returning home, on the eastbound train, when he, naturally, began dreaming of her (though quite awake and literally staring out the window's sunlit warmth).

The vision felt like her,
that heat, like the night
they'd landed at the City by the Bay. San Francisco.

Neither imagining.

Jake (having made arrangements to stable his team of horses at the train station in Iowa for only a short time) operated under the assumption that neither he—nor Emily Marie—would stay in that city by the sea for very long. That they'd return to Iowa, to their beasts in Council Bluffs, to their homes, married.

That had been the bargain, that night, in George Andersen's barn. That night when Jake had tended to Bessie's mastitis.

That night
(after everyone had gone, leaving George and Jake alone)
when the deal,
(equally strenuous for both in hopes of promising outcomes)
surrounded by dark flits amidst haydust such that the light shimmered softbrown, was struck...it—

didn't seem so large.

His family—her family.
After all, Tristan was his best friend.

Though Jake had never even had a girlfriend, he fancied Emily Marie (perhaps not nearly as much as she'd fancied him but he knew love could grow). And even though he hadn't been thinking on settling down (wife...children...and such) he knew he wanted to— someday...and somedays come one day...still...

George (sensing what many older men sense in younger ones when cusping abysmal choice) watched the young man balk (like a horse...or mule) so he put his strong arm round the young man's shoulder:

"She trusts you. So do I. I know you'll do the right thing. Maybe along-the-way you'll see it like I do: sacrifice to save life. Because, I fear, if you don't wed her and bring her home she'll die. Physically or spiritually, San Francisco is no place for a young, impressionable girl. She'll never make it alone; too many predators."

"You've been there?" Jake asked.

"No…I imagine. It's like a swoon of hawks circling over just one field mouse. A mouse like Emily Marie doesn't have the common sense to hide."

On that eastbound train, George Andersen's words ("…doesn't hide…") reverberated in Jake's head like a refrain from a worship hymn at church. Only with each reverberation, Jake cringed.

He had tried his best to keep his end of the bargain. He even did something he knew he shouldn't (something sinful that would damn his soul) just to secure the deal

But she wouldn't have me. Why? And after that night, together, and…oh my God, please forgive me, Lord, for I have sinned. And I'm sure…leaving then, well that has to be a sin too and OH my God! What will Mr. Andersen do when he finds out!

I can't…I can't face him. What am I going to do? I can't go back there without her. SHE doesn't want ME! She ran off with a complete stranger, a MAN. What kind of a monster am I that she'd run from me when all I wanted to do was marry her?

She's young. So am I. Maybe she just needs time. I know I could use some. Just to sort all this out. I'll just tell her dad she wanted time to think on it and that I'll go back. Then she'll be sure to accept my offer. Her dad can't fault me for that. After all, I can't FORCE her to marry me.

The train's engineer announced:

"Council Bluffs, Iowa. Council Bluffs, Iowa."

Jake was happy to be away from machines. Within an hour he'd harnessed his horses, stroked their soft throats, and felt an utter sense of relief to be amongst animals—them…he understood.

"People don't make sense to me like you two," he whispered and began his solemn journey back (to home…and to George Andersen).

***

141

"Dear Tristan,

I hope this letter finds you well and that you're finding whatever it is you're searching for out there in Oregon.

I am writing you because your father is not well. Shortly after you left for medical school Emily Marie ran away. I know...I should have told you earlier. It's just that I didn't want to burden you and I thought she'd come home. I kept waiting. She never came. Now (as you well know) it's been two years since you left. In that time I've received a single letter from her postmarked San Francisco. She went there with Jake Kalmar.

Well, the long and short if it is this. Jake came back...but Emily Marie did not. It's a long, long story and I've not much time to write so suffice it to say that your father nearly worked himself to death on the Kalmar farm waiting for Jake to bring Emily home. And when Jake came back without her...it was as if someone took your dad's life right out of him.

I've been doing all of the chores and have, lately, been feeling my own health begin to suffer. Of course, we're doing our remedies but, as I said, I fear for your father's health. And my own. Is there anyway for you to come home?

Love to you and God Bless, Mother"

Tristan had wondered why he'd heard so little from his family. He'd written skeins of letters without receiving in turn. He'd assumed the lack of correspondence was due ostracism (for his career choice).

I had no idea. What on earth got into Emily?
And Jake, what's all this got to do with Jake?
I wish I could go home but I can't leave the practice. It's not so easy as to just up-and-leave. What would Dr. Hill do without me? He's come to rely on me.

Poor Mom!

I know what it's like to be overworked. I'm carrying more than 75% of the patient load (I never have much time). And now Emily. Where on earth are you, Emily Marie?

Tristan set the letter, and his responding thoughts, aside. He had "Professional" duties to perform. Dr. Hill had made arrangements for him to meet with Mm. Genevieve Pardieu—at her apartment—in order that she should teach him how to effectively treat hysterics.

***

Chapter Ten

"That's an interesting painting you have there," Tristan said to Genevieve, pointing to the (black/white/gray) gouache painting hanging on her bedroom wall.

"Oh yes. I got that back home, in France, when I was working in a small hospital."

"A patient's artwork?"

"A patient's lover's artwork."

Tristan raised his eyebrows, "Really?"

Genevieve smiled.

"You Americans are so prudish. Where are your people from?"

"Iowa."

"I mean originally."

"Oh, sorry. Sweden."

"Well, then, I can't understand you being priggish. Swedes are known world-wide for rather 'open' ideas regarding love."

"True. That was only because—and, mind you, only in certain parts of Sweden—being open to 'love' as you put it was the only way to ensure survival."

"Ah yes. Come now. Surely such understanding of the nature of 'openness to love' must translate to open love making?"

"My parents became Methodists."

"Not Lutheran?"

Tristan shifted his weight.

"Long story, anyway, back to the picture."

Genevieve giggled.

My God. Genevieve's the most beautiful creature I've ever seen

"Oh yes. The picture. You see, there was a woman at the hospital who was lying-in with her second child and her lover...well, he was very poor."

"So not a successful artist?"

"Success is arbitrary."

"That's what every unsuccessful artist claims."

Genevieve squinted at his skepticism. "He was very concerned for the woman, Sien. You see, Sien had been... well let's just say, very poor and living by whatever means she could..."

"You mean, a prostitute?"

Genevieve tilted her head, looking at him through her thick black eyelashes before she continued, "Her lover was a religious man."

"Ah yes. The religious who take up a lover then get her into trouble."

"I beg to differ. The child was not his."

"Oh. Really?"

"No, I mean it. The child was not his. So the lover, Vincent, had found her (from what he described to me) near the point of taking her own life and decided that even as poor as he was that he could at least offer her a roof over her head …and perhaps kindness."

"So did he?"

"Did he what?"

"Give her kindness?"

Genevieve sighed.

"After I came to America I received one letter from Sien. She told me that he'd left her. She said, however, that he'd been good to her and her son because he sent them money…when he could."

"So how well did you know this artist?"

Genevieve changed the subject.

"Sien was a patient—for nearly a month."

"A month? For having a child?"

"She was also being treated for hysteria."

"Hysteria, I see. Rather expensive treatment for a woman of no means."

"Yes. And neither she nor Vincent had any money. So that," Genevieve pointed to the painting, "was how they paid me for treating Sien's hysteria."

Tristan looked at the painting of a naked woman resting her head upon her arms; arms that rested upon knees and read the scrawled title, "Sorrow."

That poor woman. Poor child…poor man. So much sorrow.

"Is that," Tristan pointed to the painting, "Sien?"

Genevieve looked at the painting and, without taking her eyes from it, replied: "No…it's me."

Tristan's eyes grew wide and took renewed interest in the painting. Then, for reasons he could not understand, he found himself becoming extraordinarily critical: "It doesn't look anything like you!"

She smiled, "Artist's license I suppose," then snickered, "I, too, thought the same as you."

Tristan looked at the woman, who was looking at art, and couldn't help but wonder.

Genevieve knew: "Yes, Tristan," she preemptively said, {sitting on the bed and patting the empty space beside her} "I've had lovers."

Tristan, obeying her physical request, sat beside her on her bed. He remained silent. He'd suspected as much. For her knowledge (of herself—of men—of women) was far too advanced to be intuitive (though it comforted him, at times to believe it so).

Genevieve, sensing Tristan's discomfort, continued: "Should I lie to you?"

"No. I want you to always tell me Truth."

His lips acted a man's part—:his eyes
wore a boys' woundingly brave.

"Then the truth it is," she said and told him another story. A story it seemed to Tristan to be that of another woman (—not the Genevieve he knew, and was falling in love with—). It seemed of a far away place—and of things that must have been—like history—yet felt contrived (like Grimm):

> While Sien was recovering, from what Genevieve thought to be mostly a severe case of fatigue and malnourishment, and receiving treatments for hysteria, Sien's mother cared for the little baby boy.
>
> Sien's first child, a girl, had been sent into service for a wealthy family. Nobody really knew much about where she was or what was happening to her.
>
> Vincent, the artist, came and went throughout each day: always claiming to have worked ferociously feverish and always covered in paint.
>
> One day, after Genevieve had just finished giving Sien her treatment and was leaving Sien's room (in order to let her rest and recover), Vincent stopped her in the hallway and asked to speak with her.

Genevieve agreed and they walked out into the hospital's gardens, which (as it was a fine spring day) was quite beautiful. All the trees (that had it in their nature) were budding. They sat.

Vincent asked:

"How is Sien? Really?"

Genevieve hesitated

(knowing that the physicians hated when midwives gave patients and/or their families such answers even though many patients (and/or their families) felt more comfortable asking the midwives),

"She's doing well with her hysteria treatments."

"Good. Good."

He poked the ground with a stick: making circles and lines. Genevieve shifted her weight in order to go.

"No, please wait," Vincent said, grabbing her elbow.

They were, as Genevieve then noticed, quite far from the hospital.

"Please, Sir, let me go."

"Oh," he said, as if coming to his senses, "I'm terribly sorry. It's just...I've had no one to talk to...and I've been terribly...ah well...it's not for you to...I'm sorry."

And he rose up, springlike, to his feet.

Genevieve looked at his strawberry hair, his weak chin and wide forehead. She knew human suffering and never thought it a gift that she was empathetic (rather a curse). Especially for a girl her age (16). Out of compassion she stayed.

When the man saw that a very young girl could burthen such kindness something flooded over him. Something, which seemed to Genevieve, almost as if unadulterated joy. At that moment he told her everything he'd ever done and dreamed to do. Flamboyant—animated—like a guitar whose master's fingers had finally come to life after an eon of dying:

"When I was at Zweeloo at six o'clock in the morning, it was still quite dark; I saw the real Corots even earlier in the morning. The entrance to the village was splendid: enormous mossy roofs of houses, stables, sheepfolds, and barns. The broad-fronted houses stood between oak trees of a splendid bronze. In the moss are tones of gold green; in the ground, tones of reddish, or bluish or yellowish dark lilac gray; in the green of the cornfields tones of inexpressible purity; on the wet trunks tones of black contrasting with the golden rain of whirling, clustering leaves—hanging in loose tufts, as if they had been blown there, and with the sky glimmering through them—from the poplars, the birches, the lime and apple trees. The sky smooth and clear, luminous, not white but a lilac which can hardly be deciphered, white shimmering with red, blue and yellow in which everything merges into the thin mist below—harmonizing everything in a gamut of delicate gray..."

Then, suddenly, he stopped telling her about Zweeloo and looked away, somewhere beyond the images of his mind...beyond where they were sitting beside each other...and grew very, very sad: "The artist's life," he said, "And what an artist is, it is all very curious—how deep it is—how infinitely deep."

And when he, once again, looked at Genevieve he saw that tears were streaming down her tender-yeared cheeks.

He wiped them from her—and began his own lamentation: "My dear, that my heart knoweth its own bitterness is a thing which I think you understand,"

Genevieve nodded.

He kissed her, "and in consequence will pardon," pressing her there, for the first time, amongst the strong scents of blossoming.

"We were lovers only a few weeks."

"Did you love him?"

Genevieve smiled. It wasn't a joyful smile...more one to cover contemplation...and it took her a few moments to respond, "I did not love him. I pitied him."

"Pity?"

"Yes. Because when I looked into his eyes I saw torment...

149

…well…" Genevieve changed the topic, "Shall we get back to work."

"Yes.　　　　I suppose we should."
"I'll just lay back. And we'll start with the basics."
"Very good. Thank you for helping me with this."

Genevieve let her robe fall open.

Tristan, reacting to her nakedness, felt a surge of energy shoot throughout his body…particularly the tips of his ears, his eyeballs, and…

This is medicine. This is to help people who are suffering. This is for poor souls like Sien…and Vincent…and that poor little girl

"Ready?" Genevieve asked.
"Yes," Tristan replied, "You?"
"Yes. Okay. Give me your hand. I'll guide you through it."

And so Tristan's education in the manual treatment of hysteria had begun. There, in a small let-room where the sunlight beamed through milk-filmed glass and the smell of chamomile seduced sense…

the smell of the flower

—and the flower—

and the germination of something extraordinary.

***

Julie Inns rocked her baby girl back and forth/ \back and forth (though the infant had long since fallen asleep clinging to her mother's nipple only to—every so often—gently nuzzle her infantile lips when arising from—ever so slightly—the rhythmic rolling of the sea she dreamed upon). Julie did not notice. She was lost. Remembering her past as if it had been a stageplay she'd landed a part in, her lips mimed the words of all the elements she knew by heart:

the train stop in San Francisco.

the hotel room.

making love for the first time ("Emily don't," Jake murmured, "please don't...")

touching him against his will

kissing (pretending to be a shimmering star)

stripping

(clothes) standing above him

making a bed of a floor

She remembered his eyes darted

from her

to the wall

to the ceiling

to her

to the bedspread

to her

to her   to her.

She remembered lying beside him on the floor

and his body feeling as rigid as dried lumber

and how he gasped

when she pulled his hand to her small

breast. And then she remembered

him...

surrendering...

and how wonderful

it   (surrender)

felt: like the sweetest thing she'd ever tasted...

better than milk...

or sugar...

or anything...

and how warm his naked body felt when he pressed

151

against her…
and how she bled. Feeling
           suddenly
no-longer-a-girl but equal to every woman she thought of whose
images came like echoes…or church gongs…or dinner bells…and a
mourner's wail):

"We can get married here in San Francisco!" Jake, near joy, cried.
        To Emily Marie his voice reverberated: *married*
                                    married
                         married
                 married
         married
        the image replayed: *Mother*
            Mother
    Mother
Mother
        the horror set in:
life is over
over
over
        So Emily Marie ran.
        She ran frighteningly disorientated. Unable to realize to what
extent a price would be exacted from her for naked skin's folly: in the
hallway her naked skin hardly noticed
        where it had fallen against the wall.
It
did not notice much at all
after she'd slammed her head to her knees
(though her tongue did bleed). Under her cascading hair—she began
to uncontrollably heave (sobbing—grieving).
        Jake, having clothed himself, sat by her side:
"What's wrong? You love me don't you?"
"Yes," she sobbed, without raising her head.
"I wasn't…a brute was I?"
She sniffled, "No." She did not raise her head.
        Jake felt every stranger in that hotel burning their eyes (like
sulfuric coal) into both of them, particularly him.
        He touched her arm, "Let's go inside."

She pulled away.
He looked around.

A whisper: "Police."

"Emily. You can't sit out here naked. They'll haul us off to jail.
Listen," he touched her arm again. This time she did not flinch, "you
go in the room. I'll wait outside. When you're dressed…and ready to
talk…you let me in. Okay?"
Emily rose, without seeing a single soul, re-entered their hotel
room, locking the door.
Jake waited.

And waited.

And waited.

He slept with his head pressed against the door.
It never opened of its own accord.

Jake, eventually, used his key only to find Emily Marie still naked,
sleeping atop the covers.
She stayed asleep for most of the next day. When she woke
she woke and spoke only (as if an emperor's songbird) of the
THEATER!
Jake, naïvely in love, agreed to take her.

The woman remembered it all…remembered and determined
never to feel that sort of drowning gooey ecstasy
(like tar),
that sort of slow sucking down into pleasure
(as if metaphysical laws of gravity);
and that one should never have
(so physically and emotionally keenly)
what one does deeply desire. Which was why she wanted to marry
Mike Warrant.
Julie placed her finger in between Ida May's lips and her own
nippleskin (breaking the infant's suction) then placed her in her crib.

153

Isaac would be home soon from checking the cattle and the fences in the south fields. He was always particularly hungry when he came home from the south—for it was so far from home.

As she peeled potatoes she thought of the next time she was to meet Mike. Isaac had had his meeting with Mr. Warrant. It had gone well. Isaac conveyed Julie's concerns that Mr. Warrant's son might prove a brute, to which Mr. Warrant countered with the proposal of a pre-marriage financial settlement. Isaac, having been thoroughly [discerningly] coached by Julie, bartered her chastity's value up. Mr. Warrant negotiated skillfully by leveraging each dollar he pledged (premaritally) against increments of Inns's land. When the whole arrangement was settled: Julie and Mike were to be wed within the year.

There was only one small hitch: Ida May. However, the little child posed no insurmountable impediment to the arrangement (not in Julie's mind that is). Julie had worked it all out: Ida May was simply to become her much-younger-(but equally bastard)-sister.

Of course the ruse meant that poor Isaac Inns (being SUCH a lonely man) had to have been—once again—"in the family way" with yet another stage-girl thus creating ANOTHER unwanted child (as if actresses existed simply to abandon their infants). Julie assured him that it was not as absurd as it seemed and could happen—perhaps— quite...sometimes, maybe.

Isaac didn't particularly care for this portrayal of himself. He'd always considered himself a decent man. He wasn't much of a drinker. He didn't whore around (much). God forbid if he had actually gotten a woman "in the family way" then he would have done the honorable thing (marry her or, at least, not have gotten himself into the same bind twice).

But in the two years Isaac and Julie had lived together, Isaac had learned one thing: once Julie made up her mind there was no resisting. Besides, Julie had thought of a backup plan for her daughter. If the Warrants wouldn't allow her to "raise" her little sister then Julie would simply have Isaac keep ^raise^ her. Isaac didn't put up a fight to that idea, for secretly he wondered if it hadn't been God's hand that'd brought the little girl into his world in the first place. "Maybe that's what this is," he'd think to himself, "Maybe God heard my prayers to end my lonely life...and sent this precious baby-child. Time will tell."

Still, every time Julie talked of her grandplans concerning the Warrants, Isaac would whisper—in his mind—

> *time will tell*
> *time will tell*
> *time will tell*

It was at those times (times of planning schemes) when Isaac longed for Rusty to, even-slightly, whimper
{or

> wag

his

> non-tail

nubbin}
so that he could respond to the dog's hindquarter request by filling his, usually empty, food dish. The man thought it slightly sad, that it was
at those moments with Rusty
he felt—

> useful,
> needed,

and to which the animal reacted by curling saggy lips, licking his master's hand, and hungrily taking that which had been given him.
***

For Roy, nothing piqued his appetite more than a young woman swooning over a man. Something in that feigned vulnerability, faintly veiling deepseeded desire, absolutely intoxicated his senses. So it should prove nothing remarkable that Roy noticed the young girl and young man
>   (whom we know to be Emily Marie Andersen and Jake
>   Kalmar)
riding on his train.

As it should be no surprise that Roy
>   (because of his very nature)
made them—specifically her—his mark.

Once in San Francisco Roy followed the couple to the hotel. He was, in fact, one of the people in the hallway. Unbeknownst to Jake
>   (or, obviously Emily Marie—who wasn't aware of much of
>   anything as she sat, naked, in the hotel's hallway)
Roy was the very person who'd whispered, "police."
>   (Having that delectable young girl arrested for indecency
>   would have interfered with Roy's plans: plans, which included
>   precise whispers, suggestions, and furthered implications.)

For if Roy was anything, he was convincing. That was where the theater proved providential. Roy had specifically requested (taken) the room adjoining Jake|Emily's. He enjoyed listening. Roy believed much could be learned
>   from it—
such as the precise moment when the young girl
(precisely: Emily Marie)
lost her virginity.

>   Roy was not one taken to self-acts of gratification,
>   but (after partaking :- however vicariously, in the
>   deflowering of a young maiden) he felt a desire
that needed fulfilling. So he, briefly, left his hotel room, traveling to the district of town where red met red throb&pulses that could only cooled when settled with cold, green. Even in the rush of it—

Roy's passion was particular. That night he hunted—quickly, deftly—for a prostitute with the same colored hair as Emily's. (After settling her fee and securing his release) he returned to the hotel where he found Jake sleeping against Emily Marie's room-door.

He quietly entered his room. Through the divider, Roy listened, hearing nothing within. Recalling her nakedness:
> the curves of her young body:
>> her apricot-breasts,
>> her summer-gourd abdomen,
>> her tender-meaty legs,
>> her buttery-complexion; Roy's hunger for her grew by
> the seconds
so he whispered through the thinness between them:

"theater."

His pressed ear heard no reply.
He whispered
$$it—$$

again.

Then, ever-so-softly, sounds began.
A click.
A deeply-toned murmur:
> Jake had re-entered.
> Roy was sweetly consumed between his vision of young
Emily Marie and his torment of wondering whether or not she'd heard his beckoning—and if she'd obey.

When Jake~Emily left their room, Roy followed—his heart nearly burst when their four youthful feet crossed the streets to the destination of…the theater.

Roy's excitement solidified then. He knew—
she was his: he knew
(beyond a shadow of doubt)
he'd be unlike her young lover.

For Roy knew exactly how to rein her in—like a wild-eyed beast—and she would do exactly that which he'd willed her to.

Inside the gaslights
(a not-quite-burlesque-theater-but-near-enough)
Roy sat directly behind Emily Marie.
He watched the two young heads.
He longed to touch the softness of her neck's nape—he didn't dare…not until the lights went dark. Not until he was sure she'd not be scared by a man's touch. Discernment was in order, so he leaned forward, whispering
(gently—hotly—) atop her ear's curve with his anise-spiced breath, "You like the theater?"
His lips quivered
(ever-so-slightly)
when Emily Marie's posture froze beneath it—
the licorice of it
as if she'd become a seated statue. Stone.
Roy reclined himself, in that dark, and smiled.

For the young woman of Emily Marie had done exactly (couldn't have done it more perfectly)
what he'd needed her to do. She froze. From terror? No. She never once turned to her lover
(to anyone)
for help. Roy knew her type. Willfully separate. Experience had taught him that nothing tamed easier than a beast turned independent from its herd.
***

Training Tristan in the techniques of hysterical evacuation took time.

Time—passing
        such that we, but fares…

"Yes, that's it…there…very good, Tristan, very good. Okay, do you feel that?"

"Uh…I think so."

"That there," she put her finger over his, pressing it gently down on her genitals.

"Uh…I'm not…"

"There! That bump. That hardened feeling there?"

"Yes! Yes, I feel it."

"Good. Good. Now keep touching it. Gently, at first until I tell you to you apply more pressure."

"Okay."

"Gentle! Not pressure yet."

        Tristan pulled back his hand as if he'd burnt it on a stove.

"It's okay but you MUST be gentle. One slip like that one you just gave me and you'll not only end your clinical treatment of a hysteric but I can almost guarantee that the woman will never come back."

"Why?"

"Because, well," Genevieve sat up, pulling the robe she'd cast aside, across her naked body, "I'm not sure exactly why."

        She poured a glass of water from the pitcher. "Would you like some?"

        Tristan shook his head, looking out the window. The whole experience of evacuating hysterical women repulsed him. Sure, he'd learned about the condition in medical school and the treatment protocols of manual stimulation, vibratory therapy, and hydrotherapy. However, he found the thought of touching women's genitalia, in such a manner, disgusting.

"Why do I have to learn this?" he asked Genevieve.

"Because Dr. Hill says you must."

"That doesn't make any sense. You're the best," he smiled…curtly.

"Flatterer. But I *know* different."

        Tristan blushed (briefly).

"Okay," she smiled, "back to work."

He went to her. She put her arms around him, kissing him. He grew beneath his clothes.

"Now…none of that, Love." Genevieve teased, "Strictly business."

"Yes. Yes. Business. But I hate it—"

Tristan removed Genevieve's loosely-fastened robe/sash and kissed her breasts.

"How am I supposed to do it—"

he spread her legs,

"you know, pretend that"

he tasted her,

"you're merely a,"

then raised, slid his slacks to his ankles,

"patient…"

and penetrated her.

***

Chapter Eleven

"George you must drink your tea."

"I don't want any tea."

"I know but it's Remedy."

George sat up, begrudgingly, sipping. It was the least he could do, he thought, since he'd taken to his bed (after Jake Kalmar had returned…without Emily Marie).

When he'd finished, Elaine took his empty cup from him but when she began to leave, he called out, "Laney?"

"Yes George?"

He patted the bedcover.

She returned, sitting beside him.

He looked at her eyes: eyes-once-blueblue-turned-gray…and wept.

Laney set the service on the floor and pulled her husband's head to her chest.

Finally, Lord, he's breaking. Break him Lord…so You can raise him back from the deadland. Amen.

George wept
    and wept,

for how long Laney did not know
except the shadows in the room had grown taller
and her stomach felt sharp pinching when…suddenly…
George cried out: "Well that's enough of that!"

He stood, dressed, stormed out of the bedroom (stormed out of the house) scurrying to the safety of his barn.

Elaine Andersen, cleaning her kitchen, began to feel (for the first time in more than the year's time since Emily Marie had run) hope that things might mend.

George, alone in his barn, fell again to weeping. His journey to optimism would prove much like those of sailboats maneuvering the choppy waves of San Francisco's bay.

***

During the show's intermission Emily Marie excused herself to the lavatory.

Roy watched Jake stand outside the restroom's door and waited, knowing he wouldn't have to wait long because he knew Jake was a proper young gentleman. Proper young gentlemen quickly grew uncomfortable when standing in front of the women's toilet, particularly when those entering (and exiting) repeatedly gave him remonstrative side-glances for his presence there. Understandably, then, he excused himself for the needing of 'air.'

Roy assumed Jake's exact spot. In stark contrast to Jake, Roy felt absolutely no discomfort whatsoever at the women's admonishments—merely sweet, thrilling anticipation as he waited for Emily Marie. He knew she would, instinctively, return to it—the very spot he held—as it was where she'd last seen (expected to find) her lover.

When Emily Marie laid her eyes upon Roy a sensation coursed her nervous system that she'd never felt before. It— was a sensation that thrilled her to her very core.
     It—
was a feeling that most would know
(most, that is, who are knowledgeable of the world)
    fraternally twinned with fear. But Emily Marie wasn't going to be bullied by her own twitterings so she approached the man and was just about to say, "Have you seen my friend…"

    when Roy whispered
    (first and only this):
"You belong in the theater. You are beauty itself."
    before he vanished.

Emily Marie searched for the mysterious man but found him nowhere. Just then, Jake touched her arm and told her that they needed to return to their seats. He wondered what he'd done that had gotten her so upset that she would so agitatedly pull her arm from his fingertips, "Fine!"

Roy didn't return to the audience. He cared not-a-bit about the theater…his audience had been received : he'd successfully planted a very (and singular) intentional seed.
***

A development arose in Ashland. Mike Warrant took (one fine Spring day) a stroll. Strolling along
—through the town—
he'd found he'd fallen deeply in love the very moment that Wendy Waeh exited Bell's Apothecary because at that very moment a fine gust of Springish air happened to ruffle the fringes of her hair
(ringlets, specifically. Ringlets she'd purposefully displayed below her hat's rim for she knew—as only lovers can of each other—that her lover, Curt, could not resist them)
which, complimentarily, accented her coquettish charm.

To Wendy's chagrin, however, Curt was not in a "ringlet" mood. Rather he was wrangled,
refusing to indulge, even a glance,
at her playfully hair-enhanced frivolity. He simply told her that her almond oil had not come. When she winked {Gomorrah-like} (using her muskiest huskiest voice) whispering: "That's alright, Mr. Bell,"
flapping her eyelashes,
"I've brought some…of my own…for us to share."
Curt downright refused to accompany her (suggestion) to his backroom. Stating, matter-of-factly, "I'm sure it'll be in the delivery-next. Have a good day."
She huffed.
She puffed.
A ringlet fell askew.
Her peachy-creamed cheeks turned a purplish hue.
Still, Curt Bell refused.

Love must be excused, sometimes, for on *that* day
(the day they'd met as lovers by the creek)
Curt had waited for miles-of-time for her to return to him…to speak those two words he'd longed
(with all his hearty being)
to hear. Wendy Waeh never returned. She never said those two words. She only walked and walked. It—
seemed to Curt, she was always walking away from him, which pained him dearly. So that Ringlet day had been *the* day that Curt had determined that it—

would not be "any-day" ever that she would say "I do," and so left
him no other option than to shut his heart to hers
(or rather his body…on that particular afternoon)
amidst bottles of Dr. Pepper tonic [||] Coca Cola remedy…amidst a
plethora of ointments, salves, concoctions and "must haves" people
claimed needed in order to make it through the hardness of their
lives…amidst his inability to look her in her eye—to say
Goodbye:
those dreamy, dreamy lapis lazuli eyes…and when she'd gone…
                                    and he went back…
                          …alone…to where he'd known her
and touched
          like she'd done
(crying salt tears he was sure should have tasted bitter)
          he involuntarily came from crying out her name.

Mike Warrant had determined to have her just the same.
Wendy (being of a needy nature when it came to the attentions of
men) appreciated the young Warrant's blatant affection. In fact, she
didn't hesitate one bit
          —quite the opposite in fact—
when Mike Warrant asked if she'd allow him the pleasure of touching
her hair to which she replied by quickly removing her covering of it.
          Fondling her ringlet (staring into her purplish-eyes) he sighed,
"My God," murmuring, "your…your…"
"Yes, yes?"
"Your…your…"
"Yes? I'm…what?"
"Your heeehhheehhh…eyes. Yes. Your eyes," he recovered.
"My eyes?"
          Stroking her ringlet, staring at it–not her eyes at all,
"…are absolutely exquisite!"
          Wendy brushed his hand from her locks.
"Well thank you. You're too kind."
          Mike, looking as if he'd been bitten by a wasp, recoiled,
"May I call on you sometime?'
"Surely," she smiled.
          But, when she looked back over her shoulder (hoping to find
Curt raging redred with jealousy) only to find the Apothecary's shop
window empty-dark, her imp-sparkle visibly dulled

165

(for everyone knows it's no fun to play when others won't).
"However, *you* must be proper." Wendy qualified to Mike, "Get permission from my father."

If there was one person everyone knew it was Mayor Waeh, including
(perhaps especially)
Mike Warrant
(for it was no secret that Mayor Waeh possessed a shroud of business savvy + economical sound).
That's what those
(in that town)
who wore such businessmen-acumen-swatches gaggled when they secretly valuated what richness abounded around them. If there was one thing Mike Warrant suspected, it was that the mayor would deeply appreciate what the Warrant-family assets valued.

So that night
(after Mike had told his parents of his meeting with Wendy Waeh)
the father—perched
above his dinnerplate—envisioning, with delectable pleasure, the union-potential between his son Mike and the mayor's Wendy. His mother, however, (being as many mothers are) knew her son: *Damn that hair on her head.*

There was only one hitch to the Warrant's potential\conglomerate wedding feast: Julie Inns.
How could any of them have known the depth, the extent, of that young woman's intentions?
No one did…except—Roy.
***

Inside his apartment (above Dr. Hill's medical office) Tristan arranged his multi-colored glass:

tinctures,

extracts,

essences,

dried herbs, and

salves.

He kept them hidden in a closet. For he knew (all-to-well) what the views of "modern" medicine were regarding "folk" remedies. He'd made the mistake, early on in medical school of suggesting women consume additional red meat when wanting to conceive a healthy baby…

"…because there seems something in the meat that helps the baby and," Tristan continued, "I believe that same thing helps women to conceive when having troubles getting with child."

Dr. Hague
(who was lecturing on issues affecting women…including hysteria) smirked.
"Well, Mr. Andersen. Thank you for clarifying for us what it is you *believe*. Are you going to continue your oration…perhaps on divination this time…or may we return to the facts of medicine?"

Yes, Tristan had learned a lesson that day: do not to share (with medical professionals)
what had been
(with him)
family-practiced for as long as family. Better to hide it away, he'd determined…in a
[cupboard]
closet.

Of course, secrets kept tucked away in closets are like little bits of gold
(or poison)
waiting for pans to lift them from
{river}beds.
As such, Tristan's treasure was to be discovered one day (this day) by Genevieve.

Tristan hadn't even heard the door creak open. He knew his lover's schedule was full for the day and that Dr. Hill had gone home to lunch with his wife. His presupposition: no one would be coming to his room.

It's amazing how one's beliefs determine reality: Tristan dismissed the just-audible scraping/shuffling as being...unimportant...insignificant...a mouse, or nothing.

However, Genevieve's hysteria client had come down with severe bronchitis. Dr. Hill cancelled her appointment for vibratory therapy and went to see her at her home. This was Dr. Hill's least favorite thing in all the world: being cooped-up with bronchitis patients in small, warm rooms while they barked, hacked and gagged. For he just knew somehow...(if one didn't escape such environments fast enough)...one day he'd fall too: victim (to what he'd always suspected had it's connection to grippe).

When Tristan heard his door creak wider still—he suddenly turned to face Genevieve (who'd been trying her best to sneak, carrying her tinyheeled shoes in her hands, creeping along on her beautifully bare feet). Instinctually, he slammed the cupboard shut. Unfortunately a jar (containing bloodroot) smashingly shattered. The deep red root (its juices bled) onto the bare woodgrain floor
where it—
immediately soaked itself into a grand,

permanent stain.
"Oh no!" Tristan shouted, trying to recover the precious root (without a single effort to address the floor's reddening for he knew what bloodroot touched stayed stained forever).

Genevieve (whose plan to pleasantly surprise her lover with an afternoon lovemaking) could see that Tristan was upset. She rushed to his side to help, only he told her to stay back (for fear she'd wreck her only good working/goingout dress. As she stepped back towards the door she noticed the closet ajar. Shimmerings of glass. "What's in your closet?"

He stood, looking at her dumbly, like a sheep or steer. "Nothing."

She smiled, coyly. "Ah. Nothing is it?"
"Yes. Nothing."

For a moment neither moved. Like cats on a lawn...waiting...every nerve on the verge of firing...muscles

tensioned to stone…as statuesque as flesh will allow:
until…until…POUNCE!

She darted for the closet.

He automatically thrust his arm to prevent it.

It was all very natural…
(so very innocent) that Tristan found himself coming into
(out of) a fog, horrified to see that Genevieve lay sprawled on the
floor.

She held her face, crying: "You bastard! How dare you! You
bastard!"

When he crouched next to her, she cringed, pulling her body
into a ball (like a pillbug. She'd known men's fists before).

When he touched her she slapped his arm. "Don't you touch
me ever again!"

He immediately recoiled. Then freely opened his closet for
her eyes to see (though through one eye her vision was impeded by
swelling). She stopped cursing him. And when he knelt beside her
again, she let him cup her body to his. And when he swore that he'd
never meant to hurt her (that it was a terrible mistake)
and that he loved her beyond any secret he could ever keep…she
believed his eyes: for they were crying
(tears less like tears than deep fissures from the bottom of the ballblue
where all eyes first begin to see)
from a place where none could ever lie.

Tristan lifted her in his arms.

She laughed. "I'm not crippled you know."
He didn't laugh. Didn't even smile. He was full of hatred of himself
for what he'd done. And when he set her upon his bed and she began
to playfully tease he responded stoically: "Your eye needs tending.
Lay still."

She obeyed.
"Whatever you do, do not open your eyes. Do you understand?"
"Yes, but…"
"No buts. Don't open you eyes. I'm going to treat this bruise before
it makes you unable to see. Hopefully, we'll keep the swelling down
enough for you to work."
"Oh God! I forgot. I have Mrs. Warrant! She needed an additional
session. You know, an *emergency* paroxysm."

She laughed: Tristan did not.

"Anyway," Genevieve continued, "she's scheduled right after the bronchitis-lady's appointment. How long have we been up here?"

Tristan looked at his new watch (the one he'd ordered from Curt Bell out of the new Sears & Roebuck catalogue): "Thirty-five minutes."

"Oh Tristan," she sat up, "I can't...I've got to go!"

Tristan pushed her shoulders back.

"You can't go like this. Now stay still. The more you rush around the more swelling you'll get."

He closed both her eyes with the tips of his fingers. He put cloth pieces over both eyes (placing additional things on her injured one). At first she thought she recognized a scent, but then lost sense of everything except the burning sensation on the tissue around her swelling eye. "Hey, that hurts!"

"Can you stand it?" Tristan asked.

"Yes but..."

"Whatever you do, do NOT open you eyes."

"I know. You already said that."

"In fact, don't talk. The more you move your facial muscles the more chance there is of it— getting in your eye."

"It?"

"I'll explain later. For now lay still. Rest. I'll tell you about my cupboard until Mrs. Warrant comes."

"And then?"

"I'll treat her."

Though Genevieve knew Tristan was ready to treat hysteric patients (as they'd certainly practiced enough) it took every ounce of restraint for her to keep from rising up. For Genevieve also knew how much Tristan detested even the thought of *it*— but she also knew Mrs. Warrant. She thought, "Mrs. Warrant has had so many treatments, she can probably treat herself."

Tristan removed the first substances (wet tea leaves mixed with a fraction of crushed cayenne pepper) carefully wiping away what was left clinging to her skin. He washed the skin surfaces with clean, gentle soapy water.

"Now, then..."

"I go back to work Doc?" Genevieve grinned. The swelling was already making her face look disfigured.

"No, my dear." Tristan murmured, quietly kissing her uninjured cheek. "Now then, for the second phase."

This time he showed her what he was preparing in his mortar. His pestle ground:
bright yellow flowers,
a whitish bark, and
a few dark colored dried fruits.

Setting the mixture aside he said to Genevieve:
"St. John's-Wort,
White Willow bark,
Bilberry,
Calendula, and
Comfrey."

When he put new pieces of cloth over her eyes she grasped his wrist. "How long will I have to keep this on?"

"Fifteen minutes. Rinse with cool water. Lay back, rest with your eyes closed for fifteen minutes. Repeat."

"Repeat! Am I supposed to be here all bloody day then?"

"Yes," he smiled, teasingly, and kissed her pouting lips. "At least until you've done it four times."

She added in her mind for a minute...or two...

"That's two hours!"

"So it is," he laughed.

Glancing at his watch, he became aware of a painful looming: his first encounter with a hysteric patient was to occur within the quarter hour.

"And then," he cooed, "it will be time to close shop."

Genevieve lay back against Tristan's pillow. "Yes, Doctor. And then what?"

He placed a basin with clean, cool water on the bedside table along with several clean towels. He gently placed the cloth over her closed eyes and applied the poultice.

"And then, my love, I'll show you just how very, VERY sorry I am for ever hurting the one person I adore most in this world."

She listened.

The door closed.

Her lover's feet tread down the stairs.

***

Julie was humming a tune
(scrubbing dirt off the potatoes planted the fall prior that she'd dug up
out of the newly-warming soil of spring).

Rusty lay at her feet. Asleep: dreaming. His feet twitched.
When he'd whine Julie would tap him with her toe, "It's alright
Rusty. You're alright." Then she'd get back to her potatoes—and her
hum.

The tune was one Isaac thought he knew but couldn't quite
place. So, on that potato-day, he asked: "What is that you're
singing?"
Julie snipped: "Humming. Not singing. Singing goes like this:"

Ida May, you're growing tall
All along the beech tree—ees.
How I wish I'd known it all
When you were a baa—aaby.

Ida May, you're growing tall
Though winter came and took you away
And I never knew you at all
Since you were a baaa—aaaby.

Isaac's eyes teared. "That's a very sad song."
Julie stopped scrubbing potatoes.
"Well, now that you mention it, I suppose it is a sad song."

Isaac stared at the young girl's profile. She really was very
young (so young to be a mother—out of wedlock). He'd heard stories
of young women doing horrible things
(hanging themselves from rafters, drowning their unwanted babies)
awful things. A shudder telegraphed down his spine.
"Yes that's a sad song. You're not thinking anything terrible are
you?"

Julie scrunched her face at him but continued peeling potatoes.
It—
was enough
to ease Isaac Inns
(he preferred people not speak—it seemed to him, Truth was easier
without words).
"Where did you learn that tune?" he asked.
"My dad."

"Who is Ida May?"

    Again, Julie stopped her chore.

"You know," she said, turning to look Isaac straight in the face, "I don't really know."

    For a few moments she stared off into space, pondering. Yet (as it can be with the young) she quickly returned to what she'd been doing (as if nothing had happened) and recommenced her humming.

    Isaac, however, was unable to extricate the tune from its lyrics. He called Ida May to come sit with him. The toddler had been playing in the one bedroom of the house (Julie [_] Ida May's room: Isaac had taken to sleeping in the barn, not that he minded). Truth told, to Isaac his house no longer felt his. It was theirs...the two young girls.
    Though Ida May livened up the place | Julie doilyed it (making curtains and a tablecloth to cover the planks Isaac'd nailed together with square-head nails and always setting out freshcut Spring\Summer wildflowers). Such things had made the small cabin feel homey but there was more...Julie did strange things (like making concoctions).
    Isaac remembered his mother telling him stories of witches (and gypsies). About how they made brews and cast spells. Sometimes (when he'd watch Julie doctoring: mixing flowers with roots—turning water bloodred) he wondered if Julie hadn't been raised by a witch (or gypsy). Like when Ida May had gotten grippe. Julie (using a rolling pin to crush the purple flowers growing wild around the place with the bark of a white willow tree, licorice root, elderberries, garlic and something he'd never heard of before: she called it 'boneset') forced poor little Ida May to drink the brew.
    Ida May protested every drop and whined (fiercely) every time she had to put her head over a steaming hot bowl of water (filled with lemon balm and peppermint leaves). Ida May, however, didn't seem to mind the baths of rosemary & thyme. Then even Isaac had to admit the scent was sublime. In the end, it seemed Julie's remedies worked: little Ida May's grippe went away (and she never got pneumonia—having been sick for less than a week).
    When Isaac asked Julie where she'd learned such things she simply replied, "That's the way it's done in my family." Leaving

Isaac none-the-less wizened whether it was a witch or gypsy she'd lived with.
***

Ever since the day Wendy Waeh's hair had been discovered (by Mike Warrant, Jr.) outside Bell's Apothecary, the courting was on. He made no small business of letting everyone know he was determinedly bound to marry her.

There was only a little bit of scandal that
(Mike Warrant having jilted Julie Inns)
> scarcely passed the lips of Ashland society for, if Truth be told, Society preferred the likes of Wendy Waehs. Society always prefers the known to mystery.
>
> However, what Society

(Mike Warrant Jr. |his family included|)
could not know was that a fierce [deadly] battle had begun (although not unique, as courtship tends to proffer such things),

because neither Julie Inns nor Curt Bell were going to be put off so easily:

[neither Curt
> (who knew Wendy's heart and knew she loved him beyond any love she could profess to the insipid insolent progeny of industrialism: Mike Warrant Jr.)

nor Julie
> (because her designs for the Warrant fortune had not been constructed by herself alone)].

You see, ever since Julie had come out West from Iowa (Iowa and being Emily Marie) she'd felt a presence…sensed a spirit that pushed her to things she hadn't thought of before.
> First, it was deciding to join the theater.
> Second, it was denying Jake's offer of marriage.
> Finally, it was determining to become Mrs. Mike Warrant.

All these decisions had been drummed into her head by some force she couldn't quite place…though it was nothing as dramatic as ephemeral: nothing so unique or haunting as specter…it—
> simply put,
>> was the suggestive power of a man. A man who'd
taken fancy to a young girl riding upon a train (pursuing her thenceforth—relentless).
***

Chapter Twelve

Big Bob's trainride ended with his brain's amazement. He
could not wrap himself round the idea that one could be in City
then
(in—what seemed to him—a 'blink ah the eye')
in Portland.
> The days of the stage
> (coach)
wcrc numbered in aught
> (when it came to travel between metropolises)
and to antiquation was relegated
> (the unsophisticated, the isolated, the poor working)
those who lived outside the cities in
> (cities-too-small-to-be called cities)
…towns.

> Ashland was a town
(by the aforementioned standards)
though it rested alongside the two great lines
—the Oregon Express & the California Express—
>> [who'd found themselves joined in matrimonial ceremony on
>> December 17th through the power vested in Charles Crocker
>> who symbolized their union by a golden spike driven down
>> into the earth].

Ashland's neighbor, Middleford
>> (later renamed Medford because a man with power vested in
>> him to name Ashland's neighbor and co-profiteer of the
>> newborn railway had originated from Medford, Maine),
was also a town.

> Of course, in between, betwixt and beyond were other towns
like Talent and Prospect

(oh the gold gold gold)

> and Jacksonville
> (with its Vaudeville & musical shows)

(oh the gold gold gold)

and there was a feeling of promise that something good was
about to come round so everyone wore on their faces
optimism tender as privileged women afforded powder-scent
to their slender*stout necks {&laces}.

Sure…the nation had its problems.
     Which nations didn't yet?
     And sure there'd been a
     (national/global) economic crisis
(oh the gold, gold gold)
     with bankruptcies, divorcees, suicidees.

     Progress does come at a price—everyone knew that.

And certainly there had been quarrels over land
     (particularly if it—

          belonged to the Indians—
          whites always quarreled over Indian
          land).

But with Manifest Destiny on a country's side,
     what truth does
          genocide ring
(a distant tolling like a rolling buoy on a not-yet-raged sea)?

And wasn't it just the way things had to be that the weaker
succumbed to the stronger
     (according to *Man's Descent* as extolled by a man standing
     next to a man, who in his very next breath cried out, "Down
     with the Capitalists")?

It did not seem a time of reason
     (though plenty of espousals declared themselves reasonable)

and it was not very difficult to see that Man
        (then—now…always?—)
     (merely acted)
…agreed (?).

It was just this sort of legacy left to men like Isaac Inns, men whose family had "claimed" ancient lands.
Legacy left
to Indians when left
nothing
but bullets
and tears
that lent to a speech that rent a young, French woman's ears:
"I am tired of fighting. I want to have time to look for my children, and see how many of them I can find. Maybe I shall find them among the dead. Hear me, my chiefs! I am tired. My heart is sick and sad. From where the sun now stands I will fight no more forever."

and made her weep:
for the miners
and strikers
and Indians
and the French
and the Chinese
and the poor Americans.
Genevieve clutched two of the few books she'd brought to America from France hard to her chest: *Kapital*…and the *Bible* knowing them both, Truth.
***

Once in Portland, Big Bob asked around: "Where's the medical school?" The bums on Burnside didn't have a clue. They said there was a Red Cross somewhere and Salvation's Army...beds and soup. Big Bob wasn't hungry. He'd eaten. His pocket even jingled a bit—he noticed that some bums had noticed it—"Now don't you get any bright ideas," he menaced.

Still, he watched his back as he walked. Walking, asking until, finally, someone said: "Yes, it's over there."

Big Bob craned his head to see where the man's index finger pointed. All he could see was the

gray

gray

gray of a sky getting ready to rain.

It was Springtime.

The man's finger pushed in and receded...pushed in and receded within the air as if it were pushing against some invisible force... "there there there," he insisted, "see?"

Big Bob nodded to save the man's finger.

He walked

(without seeing the 'there') in the general direction of the pointyfinger's insistence.

***

Roy had become (assumed) a physician. He handed Dr. Manfred his credential (Dr. Mereth Hague's credential) clarifying that although he was a practicing physician he'd specialized in surgery. "How odd," Dr. Manfred replied, "Here in Oregon you must be either a physician OR surgeon. One can't be both."
"Ah yes," Roy recovered, "in City things are different. Besides, it should prove beneficial to you that I am quite skilled with a blade..."
oh yes I am
"...because I can be of assistance with all of your duties."

Dr. Manfred pondered. It was true: he needed the help. Ever since the railroad had come
(and the gold and the women)
people were sicker than ever and always getting hurt.
"You have references from..."

Roy smiled, doing his best not to sneer: "You'll see...my work is my best reference."
Dr. Manfred looked at the medical certificate, reading silently, thinking:
Harvard Medical School. Better than I did. I went to Salem.
Still...there is something about this man that just doesn't sit right

"I'll tell you what," Roy interrupted the silence, "You just give me any job you don't want to do. I'll do it. You can keep your eye on me. See if you like how I handle myself. If you like what you see, we can talk, okay?"
Roy'd used THAT tone.
Commanded, Dr. Manfred nearly agreed: "Only I don't have much need for surgical skill. You won't mind then?"
"Mind?"
"Working with hysterics?"
"Uh," Roy shifted in his seat, "No sir. You just show me your procedures. I'll be glad to do them."
Dr. Manfred's eyebrows knitted.
Certainly he's dealt with hysterics in City so why is he still
enthusiastic. No man in his right mind wants to deal with hysterics.

He shrugged his shoulders

Ah well. Better luck for me then. Saves me from that NASTY work!

"Follow me."

Dr. Manfred led Roy into the hydrotherapy theater. "Stay right here, beside me." Dr. Manfred instructed Roy where to stand. "The patient is Mrs. Bigewol." He leaned closer to Roy, whispering: "She's a widow of just three months. Very bad case I'm afraid."
Roy replied, "Ahhhh."

The woman entered,
       stepped behind a dressing screen
         and emerged fully naked.
"Please take your seat," Dr. Manfred instructed her.
"Yes doctor," she replied, sitting
(instinctively covering her breasts with one hand and her pubic hair with the other).

Dr. Manfred leaned over to Roy: "She's still nervous with the process. You being here probably doesn't help." Then Dr. Manfred addressed the lady: "Mrs. Bigewol please don't worry. This is an associate of mine, Dr. Mereth Hague. He'll be observing today. So just go ahead and let your arms rest on the chair's arms, okay? Good. Now spread your knees:
    a little wider apart...

    Good...
    a little wider...

    Good...

    and just a little more...

    That's just right!
Okay, Mrs. Bigewol I'm going to begin your treatment. Just stay nice and still. Relax. Let the paroxysm happen as quickly as you can. Okay? Good."

Roy couldn't believe his eyes. Here was a beautiful young ripe woman willingly spreading herself for a man
(who seemed not in the least-bit-interested that he was spraying a jet of water on her most private parts) AND ***paying*** him to do...it.

"Very good Mrs. Bigewol. You're keeping quite still…
    and that's very good…
    but it's okay for you to move a little now…
    go ahead and move your hips a little so that the water stream
    feels most intense…that will be most effective in bringing on
    the paroxysm."

Roy smiled:
*I don't know what this paroxysm thing is but I know exactly what's
happening to her*

    And then it—
happened:.
    her tender body began quivering,
    her knees (beyond-her-will) lifted towards the ceiling,
    her toes stiffened,
    her pink soft nipples hardened

Roy's smile remained rigid:
*Oh yes! Oh yes I know full well what you're feeling dear Mrs.
Bigewol*

"Very good Mrs. Bigewol. Now you may dress. Oh, and don't forget
to schedule for your next appointment. Have a nice day. Okay?
Okay."

    Dr. Manfred led Roy back into his office.
"Och. I do hate that. Hysteria is such a cruel disease. These poor
women."
"Yes, I see," Roy parroted his tone, "she seemed to have a
nice…*paroxysm.*" Roy tried hard (very hard) not to laugh.

"Ah yes. She's young. The young ones do. Only. We must be very
careful. They can get dependant…this treatment is quite strenuous on
them and must not be given more than…"
I'd love to give it to her

"…twice, weekly."

183

"Ah yes. Twice-a-week. I see. Just how many hysteric patients do you have?"

"Och, you wouldn't believe me if I told you."

"Try me," Roy grinned. His eyes sparkled. He could see Dr. Manfred was already warming to him.

"Nearly three-fourths my practice."

"Really!"

"Yes. Sad to say. You see. It's that hydro-theater. That did me in. Not that I'm complaining mind you. The money is good…but the work…"

"Since you brought it up," Roy never missed a beat, "I'll require a salary of X."

Dr. Manfred waited, silently. Roy could read the dread on his face. He knew he had him. The man actually hated what he'd just done…that gave Roy strength.

"I can't pay you more than Y."

Money settled (at Z), Roy began working that day. Quickly, Roy discovered that there were certain women
  (those who didn't achieve their 'paroxysm' from the hydro's
  jet as quickly as he thought they should)
that he was more than happy to offer alternative services
  (those of his experienced surgical hands)
to which many responded quite favorably.

In fact, Dr. Manfred was surprised to see just how eagerly his new associate had taken to such a detestable job. (Plus, it seemed to Dr. Manfred that the # of women being treated for hysteria was actually increasing ever since he'd hired Dr. Hague.)

However, Roy's work at the clinic
(though quite profitable to himself and to Dr. Manfred)
was not his primary passion.
It—

was Julie Inns
and he had plans for her:
  her wedding Warrant,

184

her becoming heir, legally, of the Warrant estate,
her 'administering' the tonics he'd prescribe to the family
(certain untraceable poisons) and inheriting the entire Warrant
fortune (upon their deaths)
and, finally, her succumbing to his will: surrendering
everything (money: herself) to him.

      Big plans
(Roy liked big)
      take time
(and much hard work behind scenes that eyes of common men—and
women—never see).
      Naturally then, the engagement of Mike Warrant to Wendy
      Waeh ran counter to Roy's big plans

      so Roy determined the best way
(his own special way) of ending it.
***

The night Roy watched Emily Marie climb aboard Isaac Inns' wagon was the night he began writing her. After Isaac and Emily Marie had left, Roy has asked the bartender where Isaac lived. After getting the man's address, wrote her everyday (knowing, full well, that Isaac only picked up his post once a month). In fact, that lagging delay was exactly what Roy banked on:
a slew of letters—her reading
(page-after-page)
his voice,
emersion in his words—the words of a man
(a lover)
she would know only as "Your Faithful Admirer."
Over time (and writing her thusly) Roy:
courted her,
wooed her,
stroked her foolish, childish pride and
urged her to marry for money
(swearing one day they'd be together. Richly happy).
Emily Marie soaked in every syllabic promise.

Nothing took away from his daylight hours of giving women climactic pleasure and his nighttime hours of learning the Warrants'…and
(after the engagement announcement)
Wendy Waeh.

Every evening, after work, Roy rode to Ashland to study. He finally found his Trojan horse (of all places) at the local apothecary.

For weeks he'd been watching Wendy Waeh. One evening he saw her coming out of Bell's Apothecary. Under a ruse
(it seemed to Roy)
of having forgotten something, Curt rushed out to Wendy, taking her hand in his. It only took an indiscreet second for Roy to pin the two as lovers.
"I can use that, " he thought.
He followed her to the flat she shared with her father. He listened to the noises they made, the muffled nuzzling and knew.
"I can certainly use that."

It wasn't, however, until he (contrivingly) befriended Curt (a frantically distraught Curt who'd been unable to persuade Wendy to call off her engagement to Mike Warrant. To marry him)

that he discovered a man in need of a confidant. Roy gave him that. In return, Curt gave him the full account of Wendy's situation with her father.

That wasn't enough for Roy. He needed more. He had to have that one final detail—that special hint of color that finishes a great work of art—a small yet critical piece of a well-conceived scheme. He knew he'd know it when he found it (heard it, saw it…)

It came one day,
while Curt stood behind the counter of his empty shop,
when Curt said: "She just can't marry Warrant! She doesn't even LOVE him. Besides…she says he has some kind of hair fetish. I mean what does that mean anyway? I don't care what kind of money the family comes from, that's weird. And after all she's already been through…"

That's it

Roy heard nothing more: "Now now my good friend," he, briefly, consoled, "you shouldn't let yourself get so worked up. You'll make yourself sick. Hysterical even."

Roy sneered.

Curt stopped short.
He knew how male hysteric patients were treated: it was torture (absolute, gory torture).
"You're right, Dr. Hague."
"Mereth. Please, call me Mereth."
"Mereth then. I shouldn't get myself all worked up but…"
"No buts. Don't worry.
        It
                will work out fine in the end. I promise you."

For some strange reason Curt believed him. He believed that (somehow) everything would work out for him and Wendy.

That night Roy orchestrated a grand finale.

He sent a note to Wendy
(writing as if he were Curt)
 asking her to meet him at the creek
(even though it was already twilight evening)

because
　　　　　　it　　　　　　　　　　　　　　　　　　　was absolutely urgent.

　　　　Roy waited for her to go (timing Wendy's departure—
perfectly—with her father's arrival home to an empty flat where a
note would thence be delivered: "Must speak with you. It's an
emergency! Signed, Mr. Mike Warrant"). Then Roy rode to the
Warrant family home, introduced himself as Wendy Waeh's attending
physician, and requested that Mike Warrant come with him
immediately (stressing that his young fiancée was desperately in need
of her betrothed) as she was suffering from an acute fit of hysteria.
"Of course," Mr. Warrant consented, "whatever we can do for the
poor girl."
Mrs. Warrant, however, (upon recalling how hysteria was treated)
cried out: "Oh no! No!" But Roy was already hastening her son
away (riding double upon Roy's very swift horse).
　　　　On the ride cross-town Roy told Mike a ghastly tale of a father
who'd been molesting his only daughter (since, relative, infancy) in
the most vile way: sodomy.
He then told the young man that the only way a sodomite will ever
stop sodomizing is that they, themselves, must experience being
sodomized.
"You see," Roy stated, matter-of-factly (in his bedside manner) "Then
they know how it feels to be violated."
　　　　Though Mike Warrant listened he couldn't help wondering
what on earth the doctor's story had to do with him. This was Roy's
cue: "That father, that man…is Mayor Waeh."
"Excuse me?"
"Yes," Roy re-stated, "Wendy's father."
"Who the hell do you…"
"No need to be angry with me. You see, Wendy's under my care and
I firmly believe the reason behind her (adding—with melodramatic
intonation—"quite") serious hysterical episode is that, for all these

years, she's been being raped by her father. You're going to marry this woman? You love her, correct?"

"Uh...yes."

"Well then. You must do everything in your power to save her."

"I will. But what can I do?"

Upon reaching the Waeh residence Roy reined his horse to stop. "I have your confidence then," Roy whispered.

"Yes."

"Well then. You have mine also. We must do what must be done."

With that he led Mike Warrant upstairs where the two men fell upon Mayor Waeh (who'd been sitting in his wingback chair, sipping whiskey while reading the San Francisco Chronicle) and they:

gagged him,

bound him, and

Mike

(in the process of raping him)

did not notice Wendy opening the flat's door

[because in spite of Mike being a braggart, he'd never even kissed a woman—other than his mother]

(Roy knew this)

and was engorged with the sensation of his erect penis going in and out of a warm body and the, theretofore unknown pleasure, shooting through him with every thrust

(Roy knew this too)

so that when the door handle shimmied

(just when Mike felt the intensity of his pleasure becoming stronger and stronger—so strong that he longed for it to never stop)

he was unwilling to stop.

And, when something shot out of the end of his penis, releasing wave after wave of quivering pleasure throughout his entire body...

(Roy knew this would happen)

only then
> (…after a few spastic movements…)

was Mike able to make himself see the horrific repulsion crossing
Wendy Waeh's face.

Roy watched them both…hungrily
(for if there was one desire he loved most to indulge in it was making
a human's face contort just as hers was…horrified, terrified,
putrefied).

> Mike guiltily withdrew
> buttoned his pants
> and tried to explain why he'd done what he'd done.
Desperately he pushed Roy towards her: "Your doctor said it was
what I had to do to make him stop molesting you."
> Roy just shook his head as if he, like her, was appalled.

Mayor Waeh stayed:
bent
> over a table
with semen
and blood running over his testicles.

"Get out!" Wendy screamed.
"But…"
"Get out Mike Warrant! I never EVER want to see you again!"
> Mike looked at Roy. Roy nodded his head toward the door.
"I think we should go," Roy finally said. Mike was beyond subtlety.
Roy grabbed his arm and led him down the stairs.   Outside Roy
climbed on his horse. "You want a ride back home?"
"No," Mike replied, "I think I need some air."
"Right."
> As Roy rode away Mike hollered: "She didn't act like you
were her doctor."
"I suppose it was the shock of what she'd seen. But you did the right
thing. Believe me."
> With that, Roy rode into the darkness of waiting
> (grinning all the way).
***

Chapter Thirteen

Meanwhile, back at the farm (the Andersen farm) George made an emotional exodus.

Otherwise, things went as things most often do
(—on farms that is…)
in the lives of regular people: day begun at sun (ended by it too) where [inbetween is] much work's done.

Yet, something changed between George and Elaine. It seemed (during George's hiatus from his life and being in servitude to the Kalmars') he'd altered.
Not objectively.
Not tangibly.
Naturally
when one of a pair is altered…the other is altered also this was how Elaine found her life slowly changing.

At first it was the, "Can you help me with the fences?"
and then it was the, "I think Bessie likes your hands best. Will
you milk her?—I'll get down hay from the loft while
you do."
Until (time after time) it became clear to Elaine that George didn't want to be away from her side.

In fact, she was shocked (to say the least) when (after assisting him with *all* of the outside chores) George followed her into the house and ACTUALLY asked to help her with her household.

Elaine's initial (kneejerk) reaction was to assume George thought her incompetent but before her pride forced her mouth to rant she took a long glance at her husband's sad

bowed

stance
and knew that (for whatever the reason) he needed to simply be.

So she hugged him, kissed him and suddenly the two found themselves making love. It's often amazing how truths come to bed. For that afternoon, as Elaine circled George's ringleted hair round her finger, he rolled to his side, whispering, "Laney…"
"Yes George," she smiled.
"You're wonderful."

He kissed her and told her all about the journey he'd just come home from.
***

192

"I'm looking for Dr. Hague," Big Bob said to the girl at the front desk of the medical school's administration's office.

"He's in office number…"

"Thank you Ma'am."

The girl grinned sweet because she was sixteen and this was her first week at a job (other than her daddy's cattle ranch). Plus, she couldn't help grinning whenever someone called her Ma'am (because it always automatically made her think of her mother. Then she'd fight from crying) "Darned tuberculosis!"

The phone rang.

"Hello. Pacific Medical School."

"Hello Doris. It's Dr. Jones."

"Hello Dr. Jones. How may I help you?"

"Oh nothing. Just wanted to see if this thing worked."

The telephones just-installed-the-week-prior were "the latest greatest." The only problem was that the faculty had only the one person (or place) to call: the secretary/telephone operator (meaning Ma'am Doris) because no one knew whom else in Portland had a telephone.

"Very good Dr. Jones. Is there anything else?"

"No, that's it. Goodbye."

"Goodbye."

Dr. Jones was contemplating the lightening speed with which technology seemed to be racing

(candescent lightbulbs and wax cylinder Victrolas)

and the ever-widening spread of its applications

(like ripples from rocked water).

Dr. Jones was the antithesis to "naysayer" when it came to technology—he loved it. He'd even traveled to the World's Fair in Chicago just so he could see all of what he was sure he'd never seen before

(nor—was convinced—likely would thereafter).

He was, of course, much impressed with:

Britain's replica of the warship, *Victoria*,

the Sphinxes and Mummies,

and the ostriches

(he'd indulged himself a visit to Buffalo Bill's Wild West

show though it wasn't part of the Fair)

and the food.

193

"Lovely," he thought when reminiscing tastings of:
>Juicy Fruit gum,
>Cracker Jack carmelcorn; and
>Hires Root Beer

[however he'd conceded that his favorite flavor had been]
>Pabst's Blue Ribbon.

With regard to Melvil Dewey's vertical file, he just knew it would come in handy for every secretary (someday, though he couldn't imagine when).

He was sure that the executioner's electric chair might change the face of justice but...
>(he had to admit)
>he'd been quite smitten with

Ferris' gigantic wheel—for it was a feat worthy of Physic.

A close second was Edison's first moving picture— the Kinetescope:
>an ominous presence thrilled—
>>chilled him. He thought,

"This will prove important, I don't know why."

Then came the lighting: everything incandescent and on
>(which really excited Dr. Jones)

Alternating Current!

He was pondering these very things while hanging up his telephone, when he heard a knock on an office door. He went to see on whose door it was, only to be quite shocked to discover that, in the hallway, a very shabbily dressed man knocked upon door belonging to the newly-installed Program Director of the first (newly-formed) medical school in the Northwest: Dr. Mereth Hague.

Dr. Jones found it quite odd that when Dr. Hague finally opened his door [upon seeing the man standing before him] the doctor's face went quite white.

"Interesting," Dr. Jones thought.

Dr. Hague quickly ushered the man (Big Bob) into his office, brusquely shutting the door behind them both.

***

When Dr. Hill came through the front door of the office Tristan was flipping through the pages of a text he'd ordered (through Curt Bell's Apothecary) on current medical conditions and their corresponding treatment procedures.

"What do you have there?" Dr. Hill asked (smiling for remembering that he, too, once youthfully\voraciously consumed "the new").

"Oh nothing really."

"You don't say."

Tristan put the book down, sighing.

"Something troubling you?" Dr. Hill asked.

Tristan patted the book. "It's just that I paid quite a lot for this book with the belief that it was as it claimed to be: 'new procedures' and…"

"Let me guess: nothing new."

Tristan nodded. "Yes! It's so frustrating because I just know there HAS to be something new. I mean listen to this…"

He read aloud to Dr. Hill:

> For persistent offensive feet take one part muriatic acid to ten parts of water. Rub feet with mixture every night before bed.

Dr. Hill replied, "Sounds good to me."

"Yes," Tristan said, nearly slamming the book back down upon the scheduling desk, "It's just not new! That approach is as old as the sky."

"I see," Dr. Hill grinned. "You'll find, my boy, in this profession there are lots of things claimed 'new' that are as you say "old as the sky." The point is that you're trying to learn new things. Don't give that up."

Tristan hoped Dr. Hill would not ask for Genevieve (who was still upstairs in his apartment with her eye swollen shut). The old doctor did not. He simply walked back out of the office. Not because he had somewhere to go (or something pressing on his attention) he just needed air. Needed an open space to grieve that he was getting too old (too cynical) to care what was (or wasn't) new. All that his years had taught him was that

people were born,

they lived the life they lived (some grandly: some horridly)

and they died.

Tristan watched the aging doctor walk outside, stop, and look up at the sky. He wondered what Dr. Hill was thinking of…but only for a moment…before determinedly returning to his disappointing book. For, frustrated as he was, he was going to make his hardearned money give him at least ONE bit of news.

At that moment the door opened. It was (you guessed it) Mrs. Warrant.

"Hard earned money," he thought.

"Come this way, Mrs. Warrant."

"Where is Genevieve?"

"She's unavailable. I'll be treating you today."

"Well," she looked the young man up^down (her hazel eyes swilling pleasurably, feigned disgust).

At first the hysteria treatment session seemed to be proceeding well, then for some reason Mrs. Warrant seemed unable to expulse the necessary humour and was growing quite vocal about it.

"Dr. Andersen," she reprimanded, "this just isn't working."

"Just relax Mrs. Warrant. You've been through this procedure…
so MANY times

"…and you know that it can take varying length of time…just breathe…"

Mrs. Warrant, piqued, "But Dr. Andersen…"

"…and try to relax."

Tristan tried using his very low-quiet voice, the 'soothing' voice Genevieve had taught him to use when treating hysterics.

"But Dr. Andersen!"

Perhaps it was her tone (an indignant, insistent tone—like a whiny mosquito) that irritated Tristan's vocal chords so harshly. For both (he and she) shocked when his voice expounded, "What do you need then!"

Mrs. Warrant's lower lip began to quiver. She was, after all, {near-naked|quite vulnerable} being treated for a cruel-heartless disease. What right did that young, beast-of-a-doctor have to raise his voice at her

Well! That's enough of this
and she began to rise

Tristan, recovering his composure, replied, "Dear Mrs. Warrant, please forgive me for raising my voice to you."

"It was quite cruel of you."

"Yes I know. Let's work together now to try to help you through this treatment shall we? After all. We're both here for the same reason."

"We are?"

"Yes, my dear Mrs. Warrant," Tristan smiled benevolently, "to help heal you from your disease."

"Yes, yes, that's right," she sobbed.

      Tristan wiped her tear with his index finger.

      She sighed. Her body relaxed a bit.

"Now, are you ready to continue?"

"I think so," Mrs. Warrant replied, "only…"

"Yes."

"…what I was trying to say was that…"

"Yes."

      He could see she was uncomfortable to talk about
                    it—

"It's okay," Tristan reassured, "You can tell me."

She smiled, "You are very kind."

"Thank you. You were saying."

"It's just that…I was getting…a little…uh…uncomfortable."

"Oh. Would you like another pillow? Are you cold, do you need a blanket?"

"No, that's not what I mean."

"I don't understand."

"You know," she pointed to the machine, "un—comfortable."

      Tristan must have looked bewildered.

      Mrs. Warrant was internally battling what to do. To tell him what Genevieve already knew to do or to simply give it all up and go home.

      Then she thought about the other women. All the women who suffered

      (like she was suffering)

and if she didn't prove herself brave enough

      (even though it was entirely humiliating and terrifying for her,
      personally)

then who would stand up for the betterment of those poor timid women who came for help from Dr. Andersen in the future?

No.

She determined: it was her duty to all womankind to tell young Dr. Andersen just what his job was. She swallowed a gulp of air first. "It's that I need…now…'manual' stimulation."
"Oh…yes…certainly…"
Oh no! Genevieve! You never told me!

"I'm so sorry Mrs. Warrant. I should have known that. Please forgive me. Let's do begin."
With that, Tristan turned the vibratory table off and [in the silence of that room]
tried to remember what Genevieve had taught him about inducing paroxysm in the hysteric.
"Forgive me if my hands are cool," he said, as he began massaging the Mons.
Mrs. Warrant was quiet.
Then her body stiffened…and relaxed. She looked away {at the wall where Genevieve had strategically hung a lithograph of one of Mary Cassatt's paintings}
"Very good, Mrs. Warrant," Tristan affirmed, "good engorgement. Lots of fluid. We're making progress."
Mrs. Warrant's body stiffened—then loosed.

She's getting closer. I can feel her clitoris rising…now falling…okay that should be just about it
Mrs. Warrant's body stiffened, shook and quivered, then relaxed. Tristan withdrew his hand, immediately washing it with soap and water from the basin.
"Very good Mrs. Warrant. I'll leave you to dress. You can make your next appointment on your way out."
Mrs. Warrant lay still.
Staring at the painting, she wondered what it would be like to make love in the colors of what hung before her eyes:
bright green
gold mirrors of
life
upon
life
into rows of eternity…
the sunflower…
the nakedness…

she'd nearly forgotten
        (or dismissed the fact) that
the picture was of a child—and its mother.
It was a reverberation to reality…recovery…slow
resignation…resistant acceptance.
"Thank you Dr. Andersen."
        Tristan nodded before quietly leaving the room.
***

Though he'd entered his home quite late
(crossing his threshold: tossing his riding cape)
   Roy poured himself a rather large glass of quite-fine whiskey.

Then he set
   (immediately)
upon his next logical step:
        My Dearest,
   (he wrote)
I have great news for us. The engagement between Mike Warrant and
Wendy Waeh is
   Most definitely
called off so we can proceed just as we'd planned before.
   I am so clever
Be brave my darling beauty. I know it is hard, not being able to be
together, but the world is cruel to lovers who are penniless and though
I am a physician I make hardly enough to live on…

   He sipped long on the amber…*now that's good whiskey*

…and could not bear seeing you suffer…going without…or
worse…starving your poor little daughter. Please don't be shocked.
I've known all along. Your secret is safe with me and we can live
together, the three of us, as a happy family. No one will ever know
except us. I DO adore you! My sweet, tender love. How could I not
but adore her too.

   Perfect. Her secret. Her fear. My forgiveness…now my
       command
So you know what you must do. Beforehand, Isaac did well in
arranging financial compensation for the indecency Mike Warrant
displayed. Now, because the Warrants have caused you social
scandal, it is urgent that he insists upon your wedding taking place
immediately! Time is of the essence.
   Then, my lover, you shall meet me and it will seem to you as
if we've met before. It will be as if our love always was and is
ethereal…that is ours, my dear Julie. That is ours.

Your Devoted Admirer

Then Roy wrote:
> Dear Mr. Mike Warrant,

It is most unfortunate that we met under recent circumstances. It is regrettable that Miss Waeh has broken off her engagement to you. That is not why I am writing you.

I can't, in clear conscious as a doctor, not forewarn you about the current danger you are in. You see I never would have suggested your assistance in remedying Mr. Waeh's sodomy if I had known that you had not known, prior, the comforts of female companionship. I deeply regret that I have put you in such peril.

Oh yes, quite enough to frighten that boy right off

You see, when one's first experience, such as the one you experienced while assisting in Mr. Waeh's treatment, is with a person of the same sex...it often leads to a pathological lifestyle. In other words, you will become just like Mr. Waeh. Except he sodomized a female. You will prefer sodomizing males.

Good and scared...to death. I wonder if he'll be the kind to hang himself after reading a letter like this. Letting Daddy down. Poor hysterical Mum. I bet he would...I bet I could make him...but back on track Jack...Now give him his lifeline

There is one way. Though not guaranteed. It has been fairly successful in these kinds of cases. You must marry a woman IMMEDIATELY and know her, in the Biblical sense, as quickly and frequently as you can in order to reverse what you've done!

He'll be running to Mum, I have to get married. I have to get married. Fucking lot o' them. Sometimes I miss the whores. Honest, dirty, near-dead-enough no one cared so much about living...Mary...

That is my professional advice.

Sincerely,
Dr. Mereth Hague

Pouring
      himself
            another
     (shallower).
Sipping   slowly.   Letting his eyes linger,
        seductively, over the cleverness of his craft.

"It all feels

      like velvet," he thought—fall
                   ing
                      exhausted
                          into bed,
   "My whole life as if caressing crushed blood-red velvet."
***

John Thompson rushed through Dr. Hill's office door. "Where's Doc?" he panted.

Genevieve, sensing the urgency, ran upstairs and knocked on Tristan's bedroom door.

"Yes, what is it?" he asked, in a faraway voice: entranced in what he'd only just assembled—was admiring and caressing—

      atop his desk

     (his brand new purchase he'd been waiting, patiently, to test: his eye already poised above the smooth rim of a Charles A. Spencer Standard Microscope No. 1 that had cost him dearly)

      and was adjusting

     (swooning over the rack and pinion system)

      when Genevieve intoned:

"It's an emergency."

"Oh, damn!" he said, putting the slide he'd made of his own blood beside the iron treasure. "Who is it?"

"John Thompson."

"Who?"

It would have been odd for Tristan to know that name, for the Thompson family never went to doctors. They doctored themselves as best they could then left the rest to God. Had statistics been factored for both encampments' successes

     (the Thompsons versus the Medicalmen)

they'd have come in close neck and neck.

Tristan followed Genevieve down the stairs. Holding out his hand to the man. "How can I help you?" he asked.

"Me? Oh not me, it's Widder Watkins. She's poorly."

Tristan narrowed his eyes, "What do you mean by 'poorly'?"

"I mean she's got bad fever and is in a lot of pain."

That's not good

"I'll come straight away."

     Tristan took his bag upstairs to stock it—

his private medicinals

     [his secretly closeted trove of tinctures & herbs]

as well as the profession's standards:

a bottle of little white pills that made stomachs bleed

     (of course:

bottles

needles,

opium,

bromide): the regular barrage.

He was following John Thompson out the door when Genevieve chimed: "What about the wedding?"

Tristan looked over his shoulder to see if she was serious. Her grin gave her away

(and made his heart flop for her because he knew that she knew him that well. Well enough to know that there wasn't a single thing in the world that Tristan hated more than "Social Events of the Season").

"It will just have to go on without me."

They smiled each other the smiles of lovers
(smiles which—in the anonymity of the space traversing air—

kiss goodbyes).

***

It was the social event of that summer (particularly because
it'd been seasoned with scandal):
     one minute engaging one woman,
     the next another,
     then back to the first.
     And then there was the speed of the thing
(it was hard to order (and receive) proper gifts on such short notice).

Some whispered, "shotgun"
     (like the kinds of weddings miners typically had when they'd
     gotten young girls in "the family way")
and paid close attention to Julie's abdomen
     (commenting on its size and/or lack thereof).

Though the society women speculated—
the society men hesitated—
     both were—equal-gendered in detestation of change:
     (particularly of the abrupt kind) for its

rapidity…always was carried upon suspicion, like waves of winged
butterflies pounding the Amazon air. Besides…the color
     for the year was aquamarine.
     It was the latest greatest. Even women from New York City
were dying for it
     (so the Sears Roebuck advertisement said)
which meant, of course, the women of Ashland wore it to the town's
most important wedding to date where Industrial Wealth bound to
Land in a massive asset union

(and the women speculated) while the men hesitated=both
                wondering which side of the equation
                realized greatest benefit.

However, the ceremony itself could only be discreetly described as:
fast fast fast:
"Do you Mike Warrant…"
"Do you Julie Inns…"
"I now pronounce you…"
     Some were shocked
(putting it delicately—or repulsed, when put honestly)

by the overt affection Mike Warrant displayed towards his young bride. Even though the women didn't really know Miss Julie Inns (with her mysteriously enigmatic background/life) they thought it poor taste indeed that the Warrants' son should behave so animalistically. For some, it sent shivers down their spines in remembrance of their first times with men like that (who couldn't seem to wait—who had no patience—who were brutes). These were the women who cried when the wedding photographer said, "Smile."

The photographer was the town's first (being a relative novice with a relatively novel technique). He tried very hard. However, capturing little bits of the townspeople's souls (hoping to preserve those special moments (some even lurid ones) forever) proved more difficult than he'd anticipated: only one photo succeeded (the bride|the groom with the entire wedding crowd). It wasn't very good for, with such large scope, people other than the frontstaged

bride & groom

looked like tiny gnats set against a wide waving societal sea.
Yet, the photo had managed to expertly capture Mrs. Warrant's haggard expression (as she stood pressed to her son's new bride). The poor woman looked on the verge of hysteria (some Society whispered, "Again") as she, wide-eyed, watched her only son (who was nearly ravaging the poor young girl after they'd entered the carriage) drive away.
Mrs. Warrant cried into her handkerchief, "He didn't even say goodbye."
Standing as invadingly close to the bride|groom (as Mrs. Warrant had been) was someone else…someone in the background of the two newlyweds…a well-dressed man (to be sure). It was not, however, his clothes that drew the eye.
It was his smile.
A sneerly, snarly grin
like a Komodo dragon   having already bitten his prey
and so waiting   for the essence of him
[the exogenous poison of him]
to make it die.

The couple had decided against an exotic honeymoon in lieu of getting "home."

       In the week it had taken to throw the wedding together, Mr. Warrant had evicted one family (of his many tenants) from a house: the house was his wedding gift to his son and his new wife.
The carriage driver whipped the horses.

       The tingling bells nearly drove the driver crazy
             but not near as much as hearing the young man say,
"Speed up Man. Can't you see? We're in a hurry!"
       Then.
It—

       the moment of truth…the moment when all one plans,
                                   hopes for,
                                   dreams

tip reality…
       when Julie—
as if waking from a fog to find her beacon of Emily Marie—
       watched the young man tear {claw}
her beautiful white (so-ever-expensive wedding) dress to shreds.
"Can't you get out of this thing any faster," he desperately cried.

Her terrified eyes looked
for his terrified eyes:
he was not looking at her eyes.
He was unhooking,
       unlacing,
       uncorseting,
       unbracing. He was trying to save himself
and did not care
              for moony eyes or tears.
He had to have her then^there.
He had to be a man.
A man's man. He had to be right.
He thought, "She's no right to keep me from what's legally mine."

       Only, sometimes…when one is in such a hurry:
Frantic.
Panicked.
It seems that's when it all goes terribly wrong.
Formidable knots become tyrannous.

Challenging courses, treacherous.

Such that when the fervor finally expends itself…like a flame without oxygen…it simply burns out.

This was the fate, that day, for poor young Mike Warrant.

He flat gave up.

He fell to the floor, sobbing:

"I'm lost. I'm lost."

He kept repeating.

Emily Marie straightened what remained of her coverings. She thought of Jake.

Tenderness

Then she knelt beside the shuddering young man. "Is it so bad?" she asked.

"You don't understand!"

She wondered how Isaac was getting on with taking care of Ida May

He can't hardly cook. I've spoiled him. So he says

"It's just…" he interrupted her thoughts.

"Go on."

He broke down into an even fiercer convulsion of agony.

"Oh never mind!" he cried and cried and cried.

Emily Marie scrunched up her nose. She never liked men who sniveled.

There was a knock at the door.

Mike did not care. He would not raise his eyes to see.

Emily Marie opened the door to a handsome man with steelblue eyes. "My Darling," he said, bowing, removing his hat to let loose darksand curls. She instantly knew it was him—her lover.

"Let me introduce myself," he began: Mike looked up/^'. Upon seeing the man, ran to him, clutching at him as if a child to its mother, "Dr. Hague thank God you've come! I'm desperate!"

Roy smiled at Emily Marie but rightly sensed something in her demeanor had changed.

"She's just not going along with it!" Mike cried out.

Emily Marie looked at the two men,

Going along with it. Is this some plan between them?

"I mean, those things she's wearing! All that…that…stuff…I just can't seem to get it off!"

Roy looked at Emily Marie.

Emily Marie squinted her eyes raccoon. If her brief time with the theater had given her anything at all it was the gift of recognizing a mesmerist.

This could be a problem. If only this damn FOOL would stop howling!

So Roy slapped Mike. Mike, looking shocked but began again to whine (he was not used to stopping what he wanted to continue regardless of what others insisted upon). Roy slapped him again, only this time with enough force to ring his ears, causing him to stammer. This time Mike stopped.

"Get hold of yourself man. I must speak with your wife."

"My wife?"

"Yes. The young woman you just married."

"Oh yes. Yes."

Mike slumped to the floor. Quiet.

"My Darling," Roy began again, trying to touch Emily Marie's elbow but she withdrew it as if his touch ate her flesh.

"I know your type." she sniped.

"Really," he sneered, "I quite doubt *that*."

He raised his hand, landing it square on her jaw.

It cracked.

She fell to the floor beside Mike.

Horrified, he screamed, "Dr. Hague!"

"Dear Sir," Roy spat the words, "You must complete your treatment right now or it will be too late! Do you understand me?"

He grabbed the young man by the shoulders, shaking him to dizziness. Then Roy fell upon Emily Marie, and deftly (expertly) removed
every string,
every hook
and eyelet,
every layer until she was—albeit softly…crying—quite naked.

"There she is, for you."

Mike's eyes bleared.

Roy spread Emily Marie's legs:

"There," he pointed, "that's where you need to be right now boy. Right now!"

Mike stood petrified, frozen like rocktree.

Roy grabbed him by the ear (pedantically), pulled down his pants and shoved his body between Emily Marie's sprawled legs. "There Boy! There!"

Mike remained flaccid.

Yes yes yes! It's going just to plan!

"Fine," Roy's voice resonated, "then you've resigned yourself to your fate. You stupid stupid boy! I pity you both."

With that, Roy left the two lying naked together. Both sobbing quietly for fear that that horrible man (Dr. Hague) would return at any moment. Every noise:

"Is that him?"

Mike looked over his shoulder.   It was nothing.

Every noise:

"Is that him?" Nothing.

Roy was already long on his way home. His job was done…for that day.

Emily Marie finally broke the tenseness: "I have to go to the bathroom," she whimpered. Her face was swollen. Mike touched her cheek, softly.

"I'm sorry," he said.

"Me too."

"For what? You've done nothing. It's all my fault."

"Another time," Emily Marie whispered, then left to relieve herself.

"I have to too," Mike said coming into the toilet, relieving himself also.

Then they sat next to each other, still naked, both wondering what they were going to do about the fine messes they'd gotten themselves into.

That was when Emily Marie really looked at Mike and when Mike really looked at Emily Marie.

He said, "You're quite beautiful."

She said, "You're quite handsome."

In their nakedness they both blushed.

"Kind of funny," he said.
"Yes. Funny."
"Being naked like this."
"Yes. Naked."

Suddenly, Emily Marie remembered sitting in the hallway at the hotel…naked…and frowned.
Mike touched her abused cheek
"Does it hurt?"
"Not much," she replied, pushing his hand away.

"Okay, then don't tell me. But I know it does."
Then Emily Marie smiled. For something in the way he said "it" reminded her
    of being small
            of being in school
of being—long
long ago—innocent.

So she pulled his hand back to her,
    letting him cup her breast
    and he was tender
(so very tender) ever-repeating, "Thank you
                        thank you
                                thank you"
every time he thrust his hips between her legs;
she couldn't help but sense
    she was
    somehow…saving him.
***

Chapter Fourteen

Meanwhile, while lurking in the hallway of Pacific Medical School, Dr. Jones could only make out low-tones coming from within the office of Dr. Hague.

The doctor had been in the company of the 'beggar/poor' man for nearly an hour, Dr. Jones mentally noted (which was quite long…on academia schema).

Oh how Dr. Jones longed to be a fly on Dr. Mereth Hague's office wall. If he could have been, he would have heard Big Bob tell Dr. Hague how Roy had set Big Bob up for murder.

He'd have listened to Dr. Hague's asking questions (like whether Roy had provided the police with evidence such as a body…or a head…or gold teeth). To which Big Bob replied that he'd assumed they had a body and a head. The teeth question puzzled him. But Dr. Hague did not elaborate.

Dr. Jones would have heard Dr. Hague say,
"Unbelievable"
and Big Bob say,
"He must be stopped."
To which Dr. Hague replied,
"Of course. What can I do?"

Then there wouldn't be any sounds at all.
For Big Bob wasn't the what-can-I-do type person. He was an I'm-gonna'-do type person: so he says,
"I'm gonna' kill 'im."
And Dr. Hague would be thinking,
"I hope you do. I hope you do. For all our sakes, for
Humanity—I hope you do."
And Big Bob would be thinking,
"I just don't know how to find 'im. Where do I go?" (only he'd say it out loud because he did that a lot—talk what he was thinking).

So Dr. Hague would sit and ponder, in a pondering pose…
what to do…
what to do…
where to look…and then!
"What does he do?" Dr. Hague would ask.
"Kills people."

"I mean for a living. You know, for money."
Big Bob would flatly say, "He kills people."

    Dr. Hague would return to pondering   pondering
    then! "Did he ever say a place to you?"
"'E said lots o' places. What's that got to do wi' it?"

    Back to the pondering...
          pondering...

"Well," Dr. Hague said, "I just can't think of anything. And I'm
afraid, Big Bob, I must ask you to leave. I'm due to give a lecture on
anatomy."
"Anata what?"
"A class for students."
"Oh. Well," Big Bob stood, "Doc, I don't suppose you have any of
those...lollies about ya?"

    Dr. Hague smiled. He couldn't help but like Big Bob...like a
dumb child. "No, Big Bob, I don't. Sorry, but here." Dr. Hague
reached into his desk, handing Big Bob an envelope before the two
said goodbye.

Outside the office [that which Dr. Hague locked behind him before
scurrying off down the hallway] Big Bob looked inside the envelope.

Money.
    "Funny," he thought, "these doctors always give me money.
Ah well."
    Big Bob went back down to Broadway with the bums, waiting
outside the Salvation Army for a warm bowl of watery soup and a
chance to get out of the cool winds of Spring.
    Winds that blew strong...
        from all kinds of places...
           like newsstands
              and garbage cans. From where
              (or what) one never knows how such
           wind blows except suddenly Big Bob found—
          in the palm of his hand—the Society page.
It was a miracle.
    Big Bob prayed (or at least said—aloud), "Thank you God."

For there, clear as day, at some Society wingding, stood Roy grinning that sneery grin. That very grin Big Bob had sworn never to forget.

"Ashland," he asked the bum next to him, "how far's that?"

"I dunno."

Back to the train depot Big Bob went.

Out came the envelope. Ticket paid.

Chugga chugga woo woo through:

Salem,

Eugene,

Roseburg,

Medford…and a carriage ride to Ashland.

***

Chugga Chugga Woo Woo
                            from
                    Sioux City
        on   through
Wyoming,
        the Dalles, Portland
        and
down
down
down to Ashland
        Jake Kalmar rode the train.
It's time to bring Emily Marie home.

        That long, long time at his family ranch (vetting cattle, sheep,
hogs, poultry and every living thing) let him become what it meant to
be a man.
He'd have to assume
        an immovable stand to get the one
                        (love) he wanted. He wouldn't back down.
        He was the male…she…well…wasn't
(at least that's how it went with animals)
so he figured the territorial way was best and determined he'd not let
her refusals sway him. For she'd accepted him that night in the hotel
and that was Nature's contract. She wouldn't default on something as
immensely grand as the whole world of things. How could she?
***

Soon after Jake left Iowa, his mother (Greet) fell ill. Jan (her husband) got Danny Smith (the barber/doctor). He said it looked like nervous exhaustion. He gave her the latest greatest:

'brain|nerve tonic'
(guaranteed to restore your [or make your]:
health
vigor
hair grow longer
hair be shinier
and keep you
as fit|trim as Spring chicken).
"It's called Coca Cola," he said, handing Jan the bottle, "but be careful. This stuff's mighty potent."

Jan looked back and forth between Greet
(who looked as washed out as a decade-old sheet) and Danny.
"Is it...dangerous?"

Danny, capitalizing on suspense (he loved drama) looked back & forth between Jan and Greet: "Well...it...could be."

Jan threw his shoulders back (indignant that Danny would mock his beloved wife's condition.).

Danny threw his shoulders back too.

Jan scrunched his eyebrows.

Danny scrunched his right back.
Finally Greet hollered, "Will you two knock that off! Just give me the bottle. I'll take care of myself."

That very evening she'd:
done the laundry,
ironed,
mended,
cooked one of the fanciest roasts Jan had remembered eating (EVER, except maybe on special holidays—and if so, only once) AND she sat cross-stitching into the wee hours of the night.

The next day Danny came back to check on his patient.
"So Jan," he grinned, meeting Jan at the front screen, "how's Greet?"
"Well," Jan rubbed the back of his neck, "come see for yourself."

Jan led Danny upstairs. There was poor Greet lying in bed moaning~groaning
(she did—however—have good color to her cheeks).
"So what's wrong with her now then?" Jan asked Danny.

"I TOLD you to go easy on that stuff. It's MIGHTY potent I said. Didn't I say? Where's the bottle? I need to see how much she took."

Jan handed the bottle to Danny. Greet had kept it on the bedside table.

"Good Lord! No wonder! It's near-gone."

Then it was Danny's turn to knit his eyebrows at Jan.

Only Jan wasn't playful; he didn't like being teased so he hung his head a little, saying, "Is it dangerous?"

"Dangerous! Dangerous! Yes it's dangerous. I said a LITTLE! Not the whole bottle! Now it's up to you, Jan. You can't trust Greet to do this herself. You have to give her just a bit at 10, 12, and 2…THAT'S IT! You hear me?"

"Yes Danny."

"10, 12, and 2. No matter what she says or how she asks…maybe even begs. No more than that."

"Okay Danny."

As he was leaving he gave him a small bottle of white pills, Aspirin, it said on the label, "Give her two of these right now. She'll feel better in a while."

Jan hollered out, "Do I give those to her too at 10, 12, and 2?"

"Good God NO Jan! What are you trying to do? Kill her or something? Just the once, just 2 pills right now. That's all. Och!"

Then Danny was gone. Danny had a full schedule: a big family was riding in to have many teeth pulled. One even had a wonky eye they said needed out.

"I've never pulled an eye," he thought, "I imagine it can't be much different than a tooth."

He also had 3 shaves = 5 cuts.

***

Mike went to work (the next day) a new man. His step telegraphed what the experienced men sniggered at (for almost all of them knew what happened on wedding nights, what had happened for them…long ago…when their wives would).

Inside the office:
"Son," Mr. Warrant beamed, "I'm so glad this all worked out as it has. You've made us proud. So," he nudged him; winked, "how's married life?"
"Uh, fine. I don't want to talk about that. I want to talk business."
"So, you get married and it's like this is it? All business now?"
He was teasing his fledgling
          (however Mr. Warrant Sr. was no ornithologist:
                    he couldn't know birds get viscous
          at the sight of blood).
"Yes. Business."
          Mr. Warrant sat behind his desk. It felt necessary to have a barrier between them. "Fine. Talk."
"I want to handle the business…not lumber."
"But you don't know…"
"Yes…I DO know! I know that you wanted this marriage. That you sent that maniac into my life. So now I'm married. You got what you want. So now it's my turn. I'm running the business from now on and that's final."
"Now you just hold on one minute!"
"Don't make me tell Mother what you pulled."
"Listen, Mike, I don't know what you're talking about. Of course I wanted the marriage! Why wouldn't I want the…"
"Oh don't even bother. I'll get the business one way or another."
"What do you mean by that?"
"I mean I know how to do books. You may fool everyone else. I *know* that the mill's in trouble! The whole nation's heading for trouble. Hell the Union Pacific just went bankrupt…"
"What?"
"You didn't know that? How can you sit here pretending to run a business when you don't even know what's going on in the world around you? Wake up! Everything's about to go bust and you're taking all of us right down to bottom with your stupidity."
          For the first time in his life Mr. Warrant felt aged:
good meals, warm bed, expensive clothes…it had been a long time

(*a generation's time*)
since destitution loomed over the senior Warrant.
        Like a masthead
(cloven * eternally asleep)
Mike Warrant Sr. plunged deep into his thoughts—his fears—his
                        self-defeat.
"Dad?"
        Silence

"Dad, are you alright?"
        Silence
Then
Mr. Warrant
stood
gave the keys
to the mill
to his son
and never walked through the doors of his office again.

When Roy read the headline, "Industrialist Found Dead," he
full-belly-laughed.
One down
***

When Tristan came into the house of Hannah Lee Watkins he was overcome with a smell of sickness and a feeling of heat.

Instinctually, he remembered advice
(from somewhere or someone longforgotten) to keep oneself, as a physician, out of situations that placed you between your fever victim and their flaming fireplace. Only Tristan's visit was not during winter; heat could not be avoided. It was the stifling of summer's onslaught; the everyday norm for a homestead built on the baked side of a mountain's toe.

Still, Tristan opened the window
(defying much medical literature cautioning against such things) believing that fresh air revitalized
(plus it helped him breathe). Then he began his examination of Hannah Lee:
"Hello Hannah," he said softly.
She whispered, "Hello Dr. Tristan."
She remembers me. That's good.

"How are you feeling today?"
She shook her head, ever so slightly, side-to-side, in a "no."
She can move her head. That's good.

"How long have you been sick?"
She shook her head, ever so slightly, side-to-side, in a "no."

Tristan looked over his shoulder to John Thompson,
"How long has she been like this?"
"I don't know really. One of her heifers got into our just-planted vegetable garden. The wife got real mad and said I had to come over here to give her a 'what-for' for not taking care of her beasts. When I got here she was like this."

Tristan felt her pulse. He'd become quite an expert with his 'touch' and could determine much of the body's overall vitality just by its
strength & rapidity.

He gently lifted her
{as if a small child} for she'd lost weight, carrying her to the one pane of windowbright. It was not enough for observation; the small home (though cozy) had very bad light.

221

He returned her to her bed.
"I need a candle."
John Thompson looked around
(like a child looking for a sock or shoe when what they really want—
if preference given—is to be barefoot) then quickly replied, "Can't
find one."

Tristan
(whose temper had become none-better by the jarring wagonride up
the mountainside riding beside Mr. Thompson—who incessantly
derided the entire medical profession as being nothing more than
snake oil charlatan hucksters) yelled, "Well find one!"

Then John Thompson looked around the room
(like a child in fear of being switched if they didn't find a shoe) and,
miraculously, found one straightaway.

Tristan observed Hannah Lee:
eyes : tongue |
temperature
skintone (poor. Like a cold, greasy eggwhite left sitting in a pan).

He didn't like how her breathing suddenly shifted rapid
(without reason) then (just as mysteriously)
reassumed its prior lethargic cadence.

"Hannah," he asked.
She shook her head, ever so slightly, side-to-side, in a "no."
She's well into fever.

"Get me some water for her to drink."
of water.
a pail
to fetch
went up the hill
John Thompson

When Tristan tried to make Hannah drink she vomited
(violently) until nothing but putrescent yellow came.
Her bile is speckled with blood.

222

"Go outside," he instructed John Thompson, "and wait."
"But I have to get…"
"DO as I say Man!"
"Yes sir."

John Thomspon sat on the front step, chewing an oatstraw
he'd picked from the field. When along came a spider and
(though it tried to hide from…) John Thompson stepped it to death
with the heel of his shoe
those fat black spiders with hourglasses are dangerous I just know it

while inside Tristan hovered the candle's light over Hannah Lee's
body trying to find some clue:
what had happened,
what he could do…

for he could plainly see…she was dying.

That's when he noticed the lump on her wrist.
A bump with two prongs filled with pus.
A cyst. That might be important

"Hannah,"
She shook her head, ever so slightly, side-to-side, in a "no."
"What's this?"

He held her wrist up to her eyes and held the candle by its
side. She flittered her eyelashes, trying to focus…
…but shook her head, ever so slightly, side-to-side, in a "no."
"Try harder, Hannah, I need to know."

She looked
again
and again
and again
back-and-forth
back-and-forth between
the light that hurt her eyes   and the man   and the palm of her hand
and then…
she remembered…
something…
somewhere…when she was…
"The well."

"The well?"
"The well."

 then she fell back to sleep.

 Tristan sighed.
 Stood.
 Went to the door that, when opened out, pushed John Thompson aside.
"Well Doc. She's going to die right?"

 He wasn't particularly offended by or angry at the man's views. It went hand-in-hand with living so close to the land.
"I hope not."
"Well. I best be going now."
"Wait!" Tristan grabbed the strong man's shoulder, "You can't leave. I need you to take us to town."
"What! I got three more fields to plow."
"Can't someone else do that?"
"Well," he rubbed the back of his straw-brown neck, "My boys are at it now but…"
"Listen, John," Tristan appealed, "you have the chance to save a life. Your boys, how old are they?"
"Eight, ten, twelve, fourteen and eighteen."
"So you have five people…"
"No six…my girl, whose sixteen, does as much work as my eldest and middlest boys put together."
"Okay six, then. I'm sure they'll be fine for just today. I really need your help. I'm going to have to try to save Mrs. Watkins while you drive the wagon. I fear if I don't work on her constantly, the ride alone will kill her."
"So why not leave her be?"
"Because leaving her would be killing her too."
"If you ask me," John Thompson said, kicking a bit of ground with the tip of his shoe, "I'd rather die at home in my own bed then in the back of some wagon…or …some physician's 'stablishment.'"
 Tristan nodded his head. It had been a long time since he'd been in the presence of Farmer Wisdom.
  But…he had to try to save her.
  Then he thought about the cyst on her wrist.
"Hannah said something about a well."

"Yep, just been up there myself for the water."

"And there is a cyst…a swelling filled with liquid that's full of bacteria and…"

"I know what a "sist" is doc. Sists and sties. We get them lots."

"Okay, well, she has one on her wrist. And there are two little marks, perhaps a bite from something…something maybe poisonous around here."

"Yes!" John Thompson nearly screamed, "I TOLD them these buggers were bad but no one would believe me. You think that's what's done the widder in?"

"First, she's not 'done in,' second, what are you talking about?

John Thompson reached down and (using a dead brown leaf) scooped up the smooshed spider. Tristan observed that huge man shudder.

Scared of spiders…now that's funny!

But there were its fangs—and a bright red hourglass neatly torn in half by the farmer's fatal heel-blow.

"I see," Tristan mused. "Have you ever been bitten?"

"Me? Oh no no no. I keep clear of 'em."

The farmer looked at Tristan, his head lowered just so that he peered through the hairs of his bushy eyebrows. Then he said

(in a great effort to deepen his voice)

"They give me the creeps, these black fatties."

"Do you know anyone who has been bitten by one?"

"Nope."

The mystery was still on. Tristan feared time was running short.

"Okay, thanks John."

"No problem Doc. You want this spider?"

The man held it up near to Tristan's nose.

"Uh…yes. Yes! Bring it. Wait. I've a better idea." he exclaimed, reaching into his doctor's bag, "I'll put it into one of my specimen jars."

Then I can look at it under my new microscope. Maybe…could it be…

"Let's get Mrs. Watkins ready to go."

While John prepared the team for the journey, Tristan prepared the woman. Before they left Tristan asked John,

"Did you happen to notice if there were these kinds of spiders anywhere near the well?"

"Well…these kinds of fat blackies…they love dark places like wells. I even find 'em tucked in my winter wood. When I put them on the fire they 'pop.' Spurt lots of guts…"

"Uh…that's good…"

"…one time one had a sticky sack and out came so many little tiny ones I thought we'd be all dead…but the fire got each one. I made sure 'a that. Darn things. Give me the creeps."

"I have one more favor to ask of you."

"Now what?"

"I need you to take one of my specimen jars up to the well…"

"But I just TOLD you how much I hate those spiders!"

"I know. I'm sorry but I have to stay with Mrs. Watkins and I HAVE to have a sample of her well water."

"Can't you do without that?"

"No. I'm sorry John."

The big man kicked dirt with the toe of his boot.

"Okay. Fine. Give me your darned jar!"

That being done, they began their descent down the mountainside.

"Now you drive as gentle as you can."

John Thompson snorted. "Yeah right. What do you think this is…Wells Fargo?"

Slowly the farmer drove his team
slowly the doctor doctored the woman who slowly
(yet incessantly)
shook her head, ever so slightly, side-to-side, in a "no." An easy "no" (like a young girl's insistence against being kissed though wanting nothing more than for it to happen) like a drowsy dream.

Tristan gave her opium, holding her head when she vomited and stroking her sweaty hair. She cried out:
"Burt…Burt…"

Tristan shushed her, never looking away from her pustuled wrist, wondering if all of what he saw could possibly be the result of spiderbite.

***

Dr. Manfred knocked on the hydrotherapy theater door. No answer. He knocked again. There came from within a scuttling noise. He flung wide the door to find Dr. Hague firmly stanced behind Mrs. Bigewol with his pants round his ankles and she in throes of ecstasy as he manually massaged her.

"Dr. Hague!"

The woman and Roy both looked:

Roy grinned.

she shook (as he continued his manual stimulating).

"Dr. Hague, stop that immediately!"

Begrudgingly, Roy withdrew (himself and his hand), collected himself, stroked back his hair and with airs said, "Dr. Manfred. I must speak with you."

Then he turned to Mrs. Bigewol and charmingly smiled, "My dear Mrs. Bigewol I do apologize for the interruption. I'll not charge you for this session but do, please..."

and he bowed, most courteously,

"...reschedule...immediately."

The woman scurried off to dress.

Inside Dr. Manfred's office raised voices could be heard clear outside the building. Dr. Manfred ranted/raved about how Dr. Hague had ruined his professional career. Then he got melancholy, envisioning his life dashed into as many fractured bits as the #

    of

          tiles

   lining his

      hydrotherapy

            floor.

"The scandal will destroy my practice!"

As certainties go, there can be ways found round their directives or (at least) maneuvers to avoid the full extent of their blows. This, circumventing, was what Roy did best.

"Dr. Manfred I've been meaning to talk to you."

"Talk! Talk! You have ruined me!"

"Now, dear Dr. Manfred. No need to be so dramatic. If you please..."

"Dramatic! Dramatic! You...you...you CHARLATAN! Get out of my practice! NEVER step foot in here again!"

Roy rose, "If that's the way you feel..."

"Feel! Feel! I'm ruined because of you!"
   Roy
waited

waited

waited for the passion to ease
(as passions do). He waited for the surrender—the moment when Dr.
Manfred slumped in his chair to mutter, softly,
"What am I to do…I'm ruined. What am I to do…"
Roy took his cue.
   Sprung (like a Jack) he boxed him into a scheme he'd been
'working on' every evening since he'd come to town…
"Haven't you ever noticed," Roy assuaged, "how often I go to
Ashland? At night, after work?"
Dr. Manfred looked up, "Now that you mention it…yes. I'd
wondered…" then returned to burying his forehead, mumbling,
"I'm ruined, ruined,"
"What if I told you…"
"ruined…"
"you could be…"
"ruined…"
"rich."
   He waited for his last word to sink into the doctor's head
(like a fisherman's sinker all weighted with lead).

"…ruined
   ruined…
     rui…rich…rich? What do you mean rich?"
Without missing a beat, Roy continued, "There's a new thing
happening around the country."
"You said rich, right?"
"Right. Rich. This new thing…"
"But how…you…YOU! You get out!"
rich …I suppose he can't do any more harm now…might as well
listen to him

"As I was saying this new thing is a spa."
"Oh dear God! Now that *is* it! Get out!"
"Just listen."

"No Dr. Hague, YOU listen. Every 'legitimate' doctor knows that spas are nothing more than lurid dens of...well...disrepute. So if you don't mind. I'm going to try to salvage what's left of the practice YOU'VE single-handedly destroyed.

Roy boasted in thought, *Not always single-handedly*

Then Roy resorted to the one-failsafe weapon he'd learned to skillfully use

(those many years ago—amidst European streets): knowledge.

Each person kept a key to his or her dreams.
Dreams were keys to undoings.
If a person wouldn't surrender their key then locks could always be picked.
The strongest shackles (clasped round those dreams) often featured the weakest locks.
It was always just a matter...of...time...before the person betrayed their one...perfect...click...

"Besides," Dr. Manfred sighed, "all those spas are in Europe."
click

"That's where you're wrong!"

Roy settled into his seat in preparation for his well-ordered (practiced) pedantic speech:
"You see spas were made great in Europe. Myself having traveled there."

Pause

"You have?"

"Oh yes. Beautiful spas. And the doctors—sooo well paid."

Pause

"Really?"
"Oh yes. And do you know WHY the spas do so well in Europe?"

Pause

"No."

"Because in Europe doctors treat their patients like clients—their clients like people—and people are just like themselves."

Pause

229

Silence
Let it soak in

Pause

Silence...
"Oh...I see...?"
"No, doctor. You don't see. You can't see because here we doctors are reduced to symptoms + signs, tonics\procedures..."

Dr. Manfred looked at Roy as if he were a raving lunatic.

"...and here...Doctors hardly make enough not to starve..."

Dr. Manfred looked at Roy as if he were a brilliant genius.

"...but there...doctors are allowed to intuit people's needs. They assist them. They heal them. *Their* clients go on to lead happy lives."
"So do ours. We help people. We heal them."
Roy mocked, "Really?"
"Yes, really." Dr. Manfred insisted (out of professional loyalty).
"Fine." Roy retorted.
"Fine." Dr. Manfred snipped.
"Fine. Then tell me the last time you cured a woman of hysteria!"

"Well,   that's   different."
"Yes,   why?"

"Well it's a terrible disease. Some diseases just don't, well...don't cure easy."
"You mean you haven't come up with a way to cure it at all!"
"The PROFESSION! Not me personally."

Roy sneered. He loved cleaving a person from their ideologies.

"Well I think you can cure it."

"Oh yes. I saw how YOU cure it."

"Exactly. I did…

　　　Pause

Silence

"…whatever it took."

　　　That was the hook

(lined lead sinker) that snagged Dr. Manfred onto Roy's designs of establishing a spa from a hotspring water source he'd discovered, himself, traversing Ashland.

"We must act now," Roy insisted. "The land may be tied up shortly in legalities. You see, the hot springs is on Isaac Inns' land and with the recent wedding of his daughter—

　　　(I'm sure the wedding was an exorbitant expense for a man of
　　　Isaac Inns' means)

—so just now he might entertain selling some acres to us in order to: recoup,

recover,

assist the new wedded couple."

Silence

Then Dr. Manfred said: "I don't know anything about running a spa!"

"Just leave it to me," Roy assured. "Now let's talk about what you saw…in the hydrotherapy room."

"Oh yes! That! I can't believe…"

"You just sit there and listen. I've revolutionary news to share with you. Mrs. Bigewol's hysteria is *nearly* cured thanks to this:"

　　　he produced A.F.A King's obstetrical observations about
　　　hysteria being linked to the physical need of preservation and
　　　perpetuation of the human species

to which, Roy continued—adding his bit—

"…what is more germane to perpetuation of the species than what you witnessed, Dr. Manfred. By the way, in conjunction with the old-fashioned hysteria treatment of manual stimulation…well, I think upon further examination even you'll find—my dear Dr. Manfred, that Mrs. Bigewol is just about, nearly almost, very *very* fine."

　　　Dr. Manfred thought. Shifted in his seat. Rubbed his scalp. "So why the spa then?"

"Because of your own very reaction! Doctors won't accept it here," Roy pointed round the office, "but in a spa. Well, we can REALLY heal people there. We can be free to be the healers we were called to be!"

Dr. Manfred nodded. Rubbed his scalp. Shifted in his seat. "The cost?"

"Well now, that's the hard part."

"Yes. I figured. Let me guess, you've already come up the figures."

"Then you're getting to know me quite well." Roy grinned. "It will only cost…around (x). Now, for my part, I can contribute what I've managed to save, but we both know: doctors don't hardly make enough for bread."

Dr. Manfred nodded. Nodded. Agreed.

If he could be sure of Roy's scheme he'd happily put every penny he'd ever earned into it. For (although it may not have seemed the case) Dr. Manfred still hoped (still dreamed) that the world could be bettered if only people bettered their health. After a few more conversations with his revolutionary (visionary) partner, it seemed to Dr. Manfred that there was absolutely nothing better

(in the wideness of the entire world)

than for him to open a hotspring spa (near Ashland) for the treatment of hysteria.

***

Chapter Fifteen

Tristan was still away at Hannah Lee Watkins' farm when Wendy Waeh rushed into Dr. Hill's office.

Dr. Hill (who'd been working less since his young, energetic partner had begun handling most of the cases) was almost glad to see someone in need of his assistance.

"Miss Waeh, how can I help you?"

"It's my father. Please! You must come quick."

He quickly grabbed his bag (knowing the Waeh's flat was near enough that he could return for additional supplies, if needed) and followed Wendy outside. While they walked he asked her for details about her father but he noticed that she seemed nervous. Shy? He couldn't quite put his finger on it. When he asked what her father's specific symptoms were or how long he'd been suffering…she seemed evasive. Guilty?

Inside the apartment the first thing Dr. Hill noticed was the stench. He put his handkerchief to his mouth % nose.

"Miss Waeh, what on earth is that smell?"

Wendy looked at the ground.

Dr. Hill didn't ask her again for he'd already answered himself: dying flesh.

In one (of two) bedrooms, Dr. Hill found Mayor Waeh lying on his side, staring out the window with wild, uncomprehending eyes.

"Mayor Waeh," Dr. Hill asked   [trying to keep his distance]
I'm so close to retirement. Wouldn't it just figure now I'd get diseased

Mayor Waeh didn't respond.

Dr. Hill felt his pulse. It was racing very, very weak.

"How long has he been like this Miss Waeh?"

"You mean, like he is now?"

"Yes child. As he is now."

"You mean staring out the window like that?"

Dr. Hill stood up, staring the girl eye-to-eye. When she tried to look away he grabbed her chin, firmly—assertively, raising her eyes back to his: "Now you listen to me, Young Lady. Your father is dying and if I don't get some straight answers from you this very minute…"

She started crying.

"Well?" Dr. Hill insisted.

"I think something went wrong."

234

"Yes. Obviously." Dr. Hill shook her chin when she tried to dart her eyes away, "Now tell me what happened to Mayor Waeh!"

She pointed to her backside.

Dr. Hill looked less shocked than puzzled. "You mean something, say, from going to the bathroom?"

He'd treated many many patients for hemorrhoids.

She nodded.

Oh dear Lord. If what she says is true and he's in this state...it can only mean...oh dear Lord

Dr. Hill rushed to the door.

"Dr. Hill?" Wendy began to protest.

"No time, Child. I must get some additional things from the office. I'll be right back. Whatever you do DON'T try to move him or do anything! Just, maybe, talk to him or...do you sing?"

"Yes, a little."

"Good. Sing then. I'll be right back."

Wendy began singing (in as quietly tender tones as she could) the one song she knew her father loved—

Sleep, Baby, sleep
Your father tends the sheep
Your mother shakes the dreamland tree
And from it falls sweet dreams for thee
Sleep, Baby, sleep.
Sleep, Baby, sleep.
Our cottage vale is deep
The little lamb is on the green
With snowy fleece so soft & clean, so
Sleep, Baby, sleep.

For it was the song he'd sung to her all the years she'd grown up

(...without a mother who'd died birthing her...)

and the tune

(that lulling croon)

always seemed to her his way of saying sorry for what he'd just done.

Dr. Hill rushed back into the apartment. As gently as he could he gave Mr. Waeh the injection. "There, that should help him be more comfortable while I examine him."

235

He looked at Wendy (whose face could not hide the fact she'd been crying). "It's to help with the pain. Now you go wait in the living room."

She obeyed.

When Dr. Hill lifted the blanket off the man, warm stink rose like haze.

The buttock skin is lacerated with infected bedsores. There is dried blood on the lower cheek. I must examine the rectum.

When he tried to separate the two mounds of flesh the man groaned in such an agonizing manner that Dr. Hill decided to belay that exploration until finishing the rest of Mayor Waeh's physical examination.

He looked at Mr. Waeh's vacant eyes.

Opened his non-resistant mouth % looking at his tongue

Dry. Yellow. Halitosis. Needs fluid

When Dr. Hill tried to give Mayor Waeh some water the water simply glided over the man's prostrate lips, dribbling onto the pillow sham. *Not good.*

After he'd done all he could, minus examining the anus, he said to Mayor Waeh, "Be brave Man. This is going to hurt. Be brave:"

he forcefully pried the cheek

Mayor Waeh screamed

(which had been seared together by dried fluids:
pus?
Blood?
?)
apart to reveal a mass of the most infected flesh he'd ever seen.

Wendy

(upon hearing her father's screams)
ran into the room to find Dr. Hill's face contorted by a stench so overwhelming that she began to wretch.

Dr. Hill
(who'd put his kerchief back to his face) waved her out of the room
without uttering a word
(trying to keep the vapors from entering his mouth).
What on Earth am I going to do? What can I do?

Dr. Hill felt himself nearing tears. Never, in all his years, had
he felt so helpless…so overwhelmed.
*Where do I even start? I can't just leave him here. I can't operate.
Dear God! What can I do?*

Dr. Hill could hear Wendy sobbing.
*That poor girl but that DAMN girl! How could she let her father go
like this! Negligence I tell you! She should have gotten help. But
that does no good. Pull yourself together, old Boy…what to do.*

For the moment Mayor Waeh had returned to silent staring.
Still, Dr. Hill administered another shot, whispering, "This will make
you more comfortable." Though Dr. Hill rose, he couldn't make
himself leave that room. Not because he didn't want to (for he
wanted nothing more in all the world) but because he had nothing to
say (nothing he could offer to ease pain) and he knew Wendy Waeh
was waiting for him to tell her what was to become of her father.
Dr. Hill stared out the window.
*Come on, Man. Think. The flesh needs to be cleaned. Definitely
septic. But…to what end? It will hurt too badly…*
Dr. Hill looked at Mayor Waeh. The man's face looked as if it
was Pain itself—
(something beyond physical or temporal, perhaps ephemeral) and yet
it seemed he'd become, relatively, comfortable with it.
*…then there's his daughter. How do I tell her it's too late…Damn
her! If only Tristan were here. He might have an idea…something
new…Dear Lord!*

Mayor Waeh's breathing grew labored, stentoric.
*That's it then. The infection is all through him. Probably peritonitis.
Maybe even full septicemia. If that's true then the best thing to do is
make him comfortable…and her too.*

So, with that understanding, Dr. Hill gathered his things, packed them into his bag and went into the living room to inform Wendy Waeh that her father had only a very short time left to live.

He asked if she could give the shots.

She nodded yes.

He wanted to believe her so he did, leaving her to tend to her father and to administer the drugs he left behind and in her care.

On his way out he looked back to see the young woman kissing her father's forehead. She'd resumed singing:

Sleep, Baby, sleep

and Dr. Hill forgave Wendy Waeh, for it really wasn't her fault. She wasn't a doctor. How could she have known? When he walked out their door he fully expected that the man would not live through the night.

***

The moment after Dr. Mereth Hague returned to his office (seating himself at his desk) there came a knock on his door.
Now what!

"Come in."
"Hello Dr. Hague." Dr. Jones smiled.
"Mereth, please. How can I help you, Dr. Jones?"
"Paul, please."
"Okay. Paul."
"It's just that I noticed, couldn't help really noticing…"
But of course
"…that you had a visit from a rather strange looking fellow."
"Is that so? Strange? Can't think of any students that strike me as strange. Can you be more specific?"
"Well," Dr. Paul Jones continued, "that's just it. I don't think that man was a student."
"You don't. Don't you?"
"No. In fact, he looked…well…perhaps nefarious would be too strong of a word."
"You think?"
"Yes, too strong. Well, just back to my original observation: strange."

Dr. Hague leaned his elbows on his desk, resting his chin on his fingertips^
(like a tripod for a great human mind)
but all he said was… "hmmmm."

Dr. Paul Jones nodded, joining in the, "hmmmm," until he added, "Oh, and he was wearing pretty shoddy clothes."

Dr. Hague pursed his lips,
leaned back,
folded his arms against his chest,
sighed,
then… "hmmmmm."

Dr. Jones scratched his head.

Dr. Hague waited for frustration to drive the nuisance-of-a-man away from his office.

Dr. Jones pointed his index finger to the ceiling,
"I've got it!"

"Say!" Dr. Hague feigned anticipation.

"He reminded me of those White Chapel blokes, well more specifically—maybe—like one of their victims. You know, in Chicago?"

"I don't know what you're talking about."

"Ah come on now. You being from City, I mean, surely you know about the White Chapel guys."

With dishonest sincerity, Dr. Hague shook his head in the negative.

"Oh yes you do! You know the ones who have 'secret' meetings with skulls,

coffins,

swords,

daggers, you know all that stuff."

"Dr. Jones," Dr. Hague piqued, "I don't have the slightest idea what you're going on about. I can't recall any student who came looking…strange or evil. I've had nothing besides a normal day and I'd appreciate if you'd leave me to the vast amount of work I have yet to accomplish before the end of it."

Dr. Paul Jones could take a hint. He knew when he wasn't wanted yet he also knew (intuitively) that there was something wyrd about the man he'd seen earlier that day. Walking back to his office he kept shouting, "I know you'll know who I'm talking about…you know…the White Chapel guys…weird, strange…he was here…earlier!"

Dr. Hague listened to the little man's voice fade away (like an expert pianissimo) until he was quite silently alone with his thoughts.

Of course I know about White Chapel. That idiot Jones. What's he playing at anyway coming in here with accusations?

Dr. Hague stared out the window, watching tree limbs waving in the afternoon's breeze

I wish I could forget. It seems just when I get away…something brings me back. I wish I'd never let myself…damned ambition! Me. A great scientist. Discovering what? Nothing but sorrow. Heartache! Even here, in this God-forsaken place…this wild of

un-civilization…worms like Jones smitten by Sherlock Holmes and
Jack the Ripper…I can't get away from my past. HOW I've tried!
Lord, how I've tried.

    There was another knock on the door
Oh God NO!
    This time it was Dr. Stanley Hahn.

"What's this I hear about some strange man coming to see you?"
"I swear I'll kill that Dr. Jones. That's who you heard it from, right?"
"No. Doris told me."
"You seeing her?"
    Dr. Stanley Hahn grinned, "Oh yes. She's a keeper. I'll tell
you. If I wasn't 20 years older than her I'd ask her to marry me
today."
"So what's stopping you?"
"She says, her dad."
"God help you then, Stanley. If I were you I'd call it off right now."
Stanley shrugged, "Ah…but love…anyway, back to the man."
Dr. Hague grew serious. "It was Big Bob."
"It can't be! How did he find us?"
"Says he went to the medical school asking for me specifically."
"Not me?"
"Didn't mention you at all."
Dr.Hahn sat down, mumbling, "Well that's good."

They both sat silent for a while.

"Do you think that other guy, the mean one. You remember?"
"Roy." Dr. Hague replied.
"Yeah. Yeah. Roy. Do you think Roy's still setting us up?"
"Could be, I suppose."

Dr. Hague walked back over to the window and stared…"Do you
think," he pondered, "one's
      time passing
           here, on Earth, amounts to much?"

Dr.Hahn retorted, "Well of course! It just depends on who you are
and what you do."
"Does it? Does it really depend on anything?"

Dr.Hahn held the door's handle before he exited, "You'd better keep it together. I like it here and, if you remember, it was YOU who'd suggested my name to Big Bob and Roy…so it was YOU who's gotten us into all this trouble in the first place."

Exactly

              …it's

                                    as if…

***

By the time Tristan and John Thompson had brought Hannah Lee Watkins down to town she'd grown worse.

She vomited black,

and her stomach was bloated and sore…very sore…to touch.

When Tristan touched her fingers she either acted as if his touch was the most painful thing she'd experienced or that she could feel nothing at all…both simultaneously, yet intermittently.

Tristan gave her laudanum and rectified whiskey.

She vomited everything

(and more).

The pustule had broken and was oozing fetid fluid (mixed with blood).

It—

soaked through the muslin Tristan had applied.
Her skin had turned cold (like marbled stone).

Tristan carried Hannah up to his apartment. When she saw the room she winced (reflexively motioning—as if her limbs remembered her broken arm) but her grasp fell, limp.

Tristan took a sample of the pus from her pustule. He was looking at it under the microscope when Genevieve came in.
"How is she?"
"Poorly."
"What's wrong?"
"I don't know."

He told her all the symptoms he could recall.
"What about typhoid?"
"Yes. I thought of that too. The symptoms are similar. Why do you suggest it?"
"Well," then Genevieve seemed anxious, "it's just that I know a little about typhoid."

Tristan smiled, half unbelievingly, "Oh really? How did you come to be an expert on typhoid bacilli?"
"I never said 'expert' I simply said I know a little about it."
"From midwifery?"
"No!"

She took offense to his belittling tone so, reactively, responded, "From one of the world's leading scientists in the study of typhoid fever!"

Taken aback by Genevieve's defensiveness, Tristan knit his brow: "Is that so!"
"Yes! And I was just wondering if you might have ruled that out or not!"

Hannah giggled.
Why? No one knew. In fact, she never even opened her eyes. Perhaps it was a dream…lover's quarrelling (or other things of a life she'd led long ago…with love).

Whatever the reason it—
stopped the argument between Tristan and Genevieve.

Tristan went back to looking at the pus/blood sample.
Genevieve stood by his shoulder.
"What do you see?" she asked.
"A lot. Would you like to look?"
"Oh yes," seeming near-excited, "I see," she said, "so what do you think it is?"
"I don't half wonder if it has something to do with this spider."

When he lifted up the specimen jar containing the black arachnid with the fat belly wearing a red hour's glass for Genevieve to better see, she shrieked! =…and bolted for the door. If there was one thing she could not bear…it was spiders…and that one (as far as she could tell) was the scariest she'd ever laid eyes on.
"It's dead," Tristan quipped.
"It doesn't matter. I hate spiders."
"Oh, you're silly!"
"Am not! Look what it might have done to poor Hannah Lee."

Then [as if bolted by lightening] Tristan remembered Hannah Lee (the person) not as specimen keeper. He sat beside his patient and gave her, yet, another examination hoping (somehow) she'd show signs of improvement. There was no such luck. Tristan looked up at Genevieve, who was still standing at the doorway, "In or out?"

Genevieve inched in…(never taking her eyes from Tristan's spidery jar).
"So," Tristan began (in his coy voice) as he sat back to at his microscope, "tell me about this scientist you worked so closely with." Tristan grabbed Genevieve around her waist, pulling her close to him, "Were you lovers?"

As if answering a questionnaire of one's work history, Genevieve stated, flatly, "Yes."

To which Tristan nodded (he knew she'd had others), "Was he
French?"
She nodded. "His name is Ernest. Ernest Duchesne."
"Did you...love him?"
Genevieve put her hands to Tristan's cheeks. Pulling his lips to hers:
"Yes."

For the first time it all became real for Tristan,
(like a needle piercing the skin—an injection of Truth: she loved him
and the others—it delivered a jolt of pain like the opposite of
morphine: opposite but the same, for he wanted more of it. He
wanted to know), "Did he love you?"

She smiled though tears came to her eyes. "I think—he loved
his work best. And he was...a military man...and was"
"Killed?"

She laughed. "No! Silly! After his work on typhoid bacilli
and penicillium glaucum was published—it was his dissertation...that
was how we met...at school. After meeting him, I'd decided I didn't
want to be a midwife any longer—just his."

Tristan could see pain seeping from the core of her in every
word she uttered. His heart ached for her...ached to ease
her..."Please, you don't have to tell me any more."

She sobbed.

He took her in his arms. Her body quaked.
"I've never been able to tell anyone. It was all a secret."
"You poor thing." He kissed her hair.
"And it hurt! It hurt so very badly...that I never wanted to be..."
"I understand. Shhhh. It's okay. You don't have to tell me..."
"Then he went away...so I went ahead with midwifery and he...he
married someone else."
"That's terrible! I'm so sorry. I'm so sorry!" Tristan grabbed
Genevieve's face in his strong hands: "I love you! I've always loved
you. I want to marry you. Say you'll have me."

Genevieve smiled (tears running into the corners of her mouth,
her nose draining over her lips' edge) "But you need to know
something."
"Yes, my love. You can tell me anything!"
"I never loved him like I love you. You don't have to marry me...we
both know my past."

Her head tried to droop but Tristan held it firm: "I WANT to
marry you."

Hannah giggled again.

Tristan and Genevieve laughed.

"If I didn't know better, Genevieve, I'd swear she knew exactly what we were talking about."
"How do you know she doesn't?"
Tristan held up (in front of Genevieve's eyes)
a bottle of laudanum
and a bottle of opium
and the bottle of whiskey.
"I see what you mean," Genevieve replied.
Still, slowly (surely) Hannah Lee Watkins began to recover.
***

From his home, Dr. Hill pondered:
I wonder why I haven't heard from Miss Waeh. I'm almost positive her father could not have made it through the night…but I've been wrong before. I hope he did die. That poor man. I hate to see suffering drawn out. Still, I'd better go check.

Dr. Hill grabbed more opium.
At the Waeh's apartment he knocked. No one answered.
That's odd. Certainly Miss Waeh wouldn't leave her father alone.
He knocked again. Harder.

Nothing

He knocked again. Harder + longer.

Nothing
That is strange indeed.

He tried the door. It was unlocked.
Certainly, it is my duty to check on my patient.
"Helllloooo. Anybody home?"

Nothing but stench replied.
He walked through the living room. It was as it had been the day before. "I say, is anybody home?" That was when he saw the most shocking thing he'd ever seen!

There…on the bed…lay Mayor Waeh
(still on his side just as Dr. Hill had last seen him) only in his arms was Miss Wendy Waeh—and she was stark naked. (Upon Dr. Hill's closer observation) she was also…quite dead. So was her father. That was when he saw the hypodermic|
Why, child why!

He brushed back Wendy's lock from her bluing cheek. For the first time in his entire career he was suddenly seized with an urgency to vomit—which he did (to his utter embarrassment) all over the floor. So he went into the living room (to recollect himself). Sitting on the sofa, he thought of what to do:
Cover the poor girl's body.

247

Get the police.
Get Tristan.
    This isn't good for us.
It was the prescription I gave her…of course not FOR her…but…
    well, I hope people understand the difference.
I mean how was I to know?
    She seemed perfectly fine, considering…well…
no use brooding.
Cover the body. Get the police.

So that is what Dr. Hill did and
    (as it is in small towns) news spread. It wasn't more than two hours after Dr. Hill's unfortunate discovery that Curt Bell learned of his one true love's death.
***

Chapter Sixteen

Emily Marie settled into married life quickly. It wasn't hard to do. Ever since the wedding Mrs. Warrant (then senior) became ardent in retaining her daughter-in-law's affection (something about gaining a daughter), which she tried to accomplish through purchasing:

expensive dresses,

expensive jewelry,

expensive hairstyling,

and displaying her new possession (her daughter-in-law) to Society as if the new Mrs. Warrant (a Mrs. Warrant, Jr.) was a priceless porcelain chinadoll.

 (The new) Mrs. Warrant (Jr.) rightly perceived that her marriage had imbued her with a certain strength, which she exercised first by convincing her mother-in-law and her new-husband to, from then on, call her Emily Marie

 (she just hated living lies—at least when it came to her name) explaining that "Julie" had been the name given her by her abandoning mother whereas Isaac Inns

 (her devoted father)

had always wanted to name his baby girl: Emily Marie. Of course, they consented. After all, Julie or Emily Marie, they were all getting used to using each other's names. There was, however, one truth Emily Marie did not share with her husband

 (or his mother): the truth of Ida May. And it—

  was the one truth

(if truths be told) that hurt Emily Marie:

every hour

of every day

in every way a mother hurts when separated from her child.

Ida May, however,

(being the resilient toddler-of-a-girl she'd grown into) was doing quite fine for the most part. Because Isaac Inns gave her every single bit of attention he had within himself to give. You see, it—

 suited him. Ever since the day Emily Marie had begun to connive/marry Mike, Isaac had pined, dreading the day that the mother would take the child:

the only child he ever known...

the child that had awakened in him a paternal spirit

(so foreign to Isaac, therefore precious)
the child he knew he'd long for when she was gone.

It was this very preciousness that tugged at his heart every
time Ida May said, "Eye-zsay"
To which Isaac would say, "Yes, my beautiful Ida May?"
And she'd say, "Dat!" to whatever it was she wanted him to get for
her.

That she grew like she did amazed Isaac Inns. Sure, he'd been
a rancher all his life (having seen life\death/death\life) but he NEVER
had seen how complex a human child could be. Her facial
expressions, alone, kept Isaac busy.
One moment:
funny face—Isaac would laugh until his sides hurt.
Next: sweet—the most beautifullest things he'd ever seen
oh, and burpface: that's when she'd cross her eyes.

(Truth) Isaac secretly wished Emily Marie would never come
back to his home. He was fine pretending to be a sucker for stage
women, if it meant he could keep Ida May. However, life isn't
always as neat as stage. That one-day (Isaac just knew) when he
heard the clopping of horse feet (Emily Marie had come to take his
precious girl away).

Needless to say, when Isaac hoisted Ida May onto his shoulder
("For a ride," he said. She squealed—peeling in laughter) he was
quite surprised to find a young man. A young man that seemed
(somehow) familiar to him. A young man that stopped his horse dead
in its tracks, staring (entranced) at the tiny girl-reflection of himself.
"Can I help you?" Isaac asked.

Jake tried to mumble something about an actress...but kept
staring at the little girl's bright-as-lazuli-eyes.

Isaac didn't like the way he stared at Ida May. "Nope, no
actress here. Best be on your way."

Stupefied, Jake remained on his horse's back (mouth agape
with words failing)—pointing his index finger (it trembled a bit) at
the little girl.
"Mister," Isaac's tone became threatening, "You'd best be getting off
my property."

Isaac (still holding Ida May on his shoulder) slowly stepped
back inside the doorway, reached down (without taking his eyes off
the stranger) and hoisted his shotgun.

That snapped Jake right back.

"Wait, Sir, I'm sorry. I mean no harm, please. Put the gun down. I must speak with you. You are Isaac Inns aren't you?"

"Who's asking?"

Isaac kept the barrel raised.

"My name is Jake Kalmar. I've come from…"

All he needed to say was the first four words. Isaac knew fullwell who Jake was. He'd heard Julie call for him some nights from inside her dreams. Isaac didn't need dreams to know that Jake was Ida May's father—it was etched in the features of each of their faces. So he lowered the barrel but kept Ida May (who'd begun blowing spit bubbles % giggling) atop his shoulders.

"You'd better come in," Isaac said to Jake.

Jake went in. The two told each other stories:

Jake—of how Emily Marie became (stagename): Lily.

Isaac of how (stagename)Lily became: Julie.

Both watched the toddling girl.

***

The first time Jake tried to see Emily Marie he found himself waiting outside a small but nice house. Jake waited for her husband, Mike (for Isaac had told him everything) to exit (presumably for a day's work). Once he had, Jake tried to approach but a man (wearing riding gear and carrying what Jake knew to be a doctor's bag) discreetly entered immediately after the husband's departure.

He wondered if Emily Marie was ill. The doctor stayed for nearly half-an-hour. When the doctor exited he caught his first glimpse of Emily Marie. He thought, she did in fact, look ill.

After the doctor rode off, Jake (once again) made his way…but (quite unexpectedly) Emily Marie's husband turned the corner and headed for his front door. Jake receded…waiting (hoping the man had simply forgotten something and would be leaving again soon. That did not prove the case). Still he waited. Unable to get the image of Emily Marie (simultaneously juxtaposing in his mind between her look of illness and her hotel-nakedness) clean out of his head so he waited. He saw shadowbodies moving on the other side of draped curtains.

He thought he heard shouting.

Was it a man's voice…or hers?

He knew firsthand she could be a handful when she wanted to be.

He thought he heard: "Ida May."
He couldn't be sure. The wind liked playing tricks.

Finally (with the sun's dip) Jake made his way back to Isaac Inn's home where the wind's whisper, on that long ride, had set his heart to a sore-missing of new-found girl.
***

News of Wendy Waeh's suicide spread like summer forest fires. The very day Dr. Hill had found the needle in her arm (and after the police came) everyone knew. There was an under-the-breath chorus brewing lips that whispered:

"that poor girl"

"how bizarre"

"I never knew Mayor Waeh was ill,"

and on and on it carried its tune.

Curt Bell's eardrums wished to burst: when he heard—he fell to the ground (lifeless as the corpse of his lover except...breathing...blinking).

Curt's mother called for Dr. Andersen. Tristan's smelling salts revived the stricken young man who then began weeping.

Tristan administered opium.

Curt's hysteria calmed.

They talked (they'd talked before though neither considered the other to be a 'close' friend, rather polite fellow practitioners with the same, general, goal: helping). Tristan always thought Curt a bit like the volcanoes he'd read about in school.

Curt thought Tristan a cucumber...coolcoolcool.

Both smiled whenever they met. This time, however (once Curt had fully recovered) Tristan warmed up.

"Curt," Tristan began, "I must beg a favor."

"Anything."

"Well first I have to ask you a, rather, personal question."

"Okay."

"Are you planning on attending Miss Wendy Waeh's funeral?"

"Good God No!"

Curt began re-fluttering.

Tristan reached for the salts; Curt waived him off (flickering his hand).

Tristan continued: "I'm sorry to be so indelicate it's just that Dr. Hill feels our whole office should be there because Dr. Hill was the attending doctor. Well, I don't have to tell you, the thing was rather a terrible result. The problem is, we have a patient convalescing in the upstairs apartment and even though she's nearly recovered, it just wouldn't feel right leaving her unattended. Especially now."

"Understandable."

"So would you?"

"Me? What exactly do you want me to do?"

"To sit with Mrs. Hannah Lee Watkins while Mm Pardieu, myself, and Dr. Hill attend the Waehs' funerals."

Tristan went into greater detail of the Waehs' deaths (hoping to convince Curt the importance of his entire office's attendance at their funeral) saying: how Dr. Hill had left the young girl in charge of administering her father's drugs because he didn't suspect the girl unstable, and how loving towards her dying father the girl had been and how…

Tristan did not notice Curt squirming with every utterance.

…since it was Dr. Hill's prescription that killed the girl, the three of them (Mm. Pardieu, himself and Dr. Hill) needed to be available to: "…answer the Community's questions surrounding our parts in the deaths."

Curt shook his head back&forth like a dog trying to shed water (or an attic chasing bats).

Tristan rose to leave, assuming Curt's actions meant no, "I'm very sorry to have bothered you Mr. Bell. I'm sure Dr. Hill will understand."

Curt looked up at Tristan. His pupils dilated when the sun splintered through the window glass.

"Fine." Curt said.

"You'll do it?"

"Yes."

Tristan grabbed Curt by the arm, hoisted him up, shook his hand vigorously and thanked him over and over so that by the time Curt watched the back of the young doctor exiting he'd quite forgotten why he'd been swooning in the first place. It did not take long for him to recall.

His mother, who'd been in the lurches—watching and listening—then stormed off to her apartment, scolding, "A grown man falling to pieces over a girl like 'that'!"

Curt shuddered, remembering his beautiful (complete) love and wept as he threw the almond oil into the wastebasket—for it had finally arrived too late.

***

"Listen, Mr. Inns," Dr. Manfred insisted, "I'm offering you a fair deal."

"I don't want to sell my land."

"You won't be selling ALL of your land, just a small part of it."

Ida May came tramping out from the bedroom all pinkyrose-cheeked and glitteryeyed. "I—zay. Want milk."

"Not now Ida May."

"WANT MILK!"

Isaac looked at Dr. Manfred. "Please excuse me, doctor. The girl knows what she wants."

Then Isaac laughed.

Dr. Manfred watched the girl slurp and coo (happy as a lark). "You were saying, Dr. Manfred."

"I didn't know you had a daughter? I was under the impression, with the recent wedding of your daughter, that you were—once again—a bachelor."

"I am...I mean well she is...uh...anyway you were saying?"

Dr. Manfred looked back and forth between the faces of the toddler (who'd climbed onto Isaac's lap) and the man's. Seeing absolutely no resemblance, he continued, "I'm suggesting you sell to me 100 acres here." Dr. Manfred pointed to the rich black ink encircled section of the map he'd brought with him.

Isaac knew that land. It was worthless. Too many canyons, creeks, even a cave (it wasn't even any good for livestock). Still, he wondered why someone would be willing to pay good money for something so worthless.

"What do you want it for," Isaac asked.

"We want to build a health spa."

"What on earth for?"

Dr. Manfred acted indignant.

"To help people."

"That land's no good. What are you going to have them do? Climb up^^down canyon walls?"

"What WE will have them 'do' Mr. Inns is of little concern to you, I'm sure. What IS of concern to you (I would think) is our arrangement."

"We?"

"Yes."

"I only see one of you?"

"My partner and I."

"Oh, I see."

"Yes. We are willing to offer you (x)."

"That's a good price."

"I think you'll find it better than anyone else would offer you for the same parcel."

Ida May finished her milk.

"Now go play." Isaac told her, putting her feet, gently, to the ground.

"O-tay I-zay."

The little girl toddled off. Isaac leaned back in his chair. He folded his arms. He looked at the tips of his wornout boots. He thought of Ida May and…agreed.

The land was deeded.

Cash exchanged.

That very night Isaac waited for Jake (who'd returned quite late) before he saddled up his horse and left (with the cash) into the dark hours.

He thought:

"It's best I leave them alone together. Get to know each other. Besides, I like the hotel in town. Boy, won't she squeal when I bring her home some pretty clothes, some new shoes and maybe a real nice fancy doll!"

He rode into the dark only mountain nights can proffer as enthusiastic as a six-week old puppy.

***

"Please listen," Emily Marie pleaded.

"We can't." Mike replied.

Emily Marie sulked:

huffing

<|>folding her arms so forcefully their angles seemed to pout out her lower lip}.

Mike (not numb to her charms) knelt beside the chair she'd flung herself onto. "My dear," he cooed.

"Don't call me that!"

"Emily you just don't understand."

She sat forward pressing her forehead to his. "Then help me understand."

Mike didn't have the heart to tell her that they were nearly bankrupt. "It's complicated."

"So you think I'm stupid! That I can't understand complicated things?"

"No. No! That's not it. It's just that the mill is..."

Emily Marie knew that look (the look that crossed his face). She'd seen it all her life—it was the tight look. The look that meant there'd be less to eat—less of everything.

"How bad?" She asked.

She thought she saw tears in his eyes but couldn't be sure.

"Not...so bad."

She knew he was lying.

"It's just you ask so much money,"

If he only knew why

"and the mill isn't...hasn't...for a long time now—been doing. I'm boring you!"

"No. Please. Continue."

So he sat down with his new wife and told her everything: how his father had been irresponsible during the economic crisis...

"Crisis," he animated to Emily Marie, "I might add, that shook the world round."

...and how, against tradition, his father had...

"For some bizarre reason." Mike pondered. "Maybe he was losing his mind. He was a suicide after all. Anyhow..."

258

...given Isaac Inns a significant amount of money just for him to be able to marry her (which had actually been borrowed against the mill)...

"Very bad. Very bad." He shook his head.
　　A reprimand of the dead.

　　...and that after they'd married then his mother...

"Poor woman. It's understandable. In her grief," he excused.

　　...had begun spending too much.
　　Emily looked at the new shoes her mother-in-law had purchased only the day before.
"And you, my love,"
　　he kissed her cheek then noticed that her eyes had gone grave.
"Oh never mind. Never mind it all my beautiful Emily Marie. It will all be okay."
　　Emily Marie kissed his cheek. "Will it?" she asked.

"Oh yes. These things happen in business. Just the nature of the beast I suppose. Only I wish Father hadn't...it's no use. What's done is done. Let the dead rest. Can you see, now, why we can't take on the financial responsibility of your little sister?"
"No."

"Then damn you! You haven't heard a word I've said!"
"I've heard. But she's just a baby."
"Exactly! Babies are expensive!"
"What if I were pregnant?"
　　His eyes goggled. "You're not are you?"
"No but"
"I have to go. I can't sit around here listening to 'what ifs.' And I mean it about Ida May. She absolutely can NOT stay with us. We can't afford it. Besides,"
　　Mike's anger-mask assumed rationalism,
"your father should know better than to keep getting into trouble. If he can't learn that...then he should at least take responsibility for what he's done."
Emily Marie burst into tears. "You're cruel!"

Mike put his hat on. "Yes. I'm cruel. But I have one duty. OUR family."

And with that the young man strode out the door.
Jake was waiting across the street.

Maybe this time I will get to speak with Emily Marie

But as before, when the husband had gone the doctor came. Time passed. The same glances exchanged between the physician and Emily Marie upon his exit.

This is my chance

Jake crossed the street.
Knocked.
Waited.

Nothing—silence.
He knocked again.
He could hear her behind the door.
"Emily! Emily Marie! It's me, Jake."

From behind the wood a broken voice
(one that sounded as if it came from strained tealeaves or from below a deepcarnality):
"Is that really you?" she asked.
"Yes. Now let me in."

Silence.

"I can't."
"Why not?"
"I just can't."

Her voice chilled him.

"Are…you alright?"
"Yes."
"I saw the doctor."
"Oh please don't! Don't mention that."
"Open the door!"
"No. I can't. I can't."

There it was again…in her voice…

The hairs on the back of his neck stood up.

Danger

"If you don't open the door this minute I'll break it down!"

"You wouldn't dare!"

He will. He will because he has to save me. He's always had to save me

She unlatched the door.

When Jake's eyes re-focused (within the dark curtained room) his heart sank to his stomach—before him stood a woman who'd (quite obviously) been abused.

"My God! What happened?"

"It's a long story," she said, collapsing to the floor wearing nothing except a torn chemise.

Jake took her into his arms.

My love! My beautiful love. What have you gotten yourself into

She felt limp (like damp).

"Oh Jake," she cried, burying her face into his vest. "It's so terrible!"

"Tell me, my love."

Emily Marie looked up at his face. The face she'd been recreating in her mind's eye ever since she'd said goodbye to him that night…that fateful night…at the Greenspring's Inn. That night she'd refused to marry him. That night she rode away with Isaac. And then there was Ida May.

"Oh Jake! I've made such a mess of it all!"

Her tiny hands grasped {clung like mouse claws}.

"It's okay. It's okay," he murmured into her silken hair.

"No…no…no…" she wept.

He held her convulsing body, wiping tears until she eased. That was when he whispered, "I've met Ida May."

When Emily Marie saw his eyes (eyes of wild doe…eyes like her own dad's every time he'd looked at her) she realized how wonderful it was for them to have met.

Sensing this Jake said, "She's beautiful." He brushed a strand from Emily Marie's forehead, "Just like her mother."

It was the first time Emily Marie could remember smiling about anything to do with her daughter.

"And," Jake continued, "I know she's mine."

Emily Marie's eyes glazed.

His voice.

His cream-rich voice.

How she'd dreamed of hearing his voice in her ears…but…things had all gone so wrong.

"Jake," she said, "You must leave here at once."

"Why?"

"Because. I'm married."

"I know."

"And if my husband comes home…it will ruin everything!"

A man (in love) can only take so much (when it comes to their intended's concern for other's feelings, well-being, or state of any affair). For those kinds of loyalty binds cut scalpel-deep (and quick) with—typically—only one calming salve|one balm: anger.

"Fine!" Jake yelled, storming out the door, "What would your precious husband think of your Doctor's visit!"

Oh dear God! It's all coming unraveled

    With Jake gone,

    with Dr. Hague gone,

    with Mike gone: Emily Marie sat.

Rocking herself

    back ~ forth,

        back ~ forth,

I have to keep paying Dr. Hague or he'll tell Mike that Ida May's my child. But he takes SO much. I can't bear his touch on my body. Doctor Hague! I wish I could rip out his eyes! And Mike I know he doesn't love me…really…I think anyway it doesn't matter…I don't love him…I love Jake. I've always loved Jake and now he knows about Ida May…Oh God! The way he says her name…he loves being a father…what am I going to do…

    The scenes corded inside her head

(looped round % round)

        <until the ends came tapping>

    slapping her back to the inside

[of her home]   for the light had changed.

It was getting near evening. Mike would be home wanting supper. She hadn't even cleaned herself up from the doctor (his semen ran from her rectum along the backs of her legs).

She rose.

Cleaned.

Cooked.

Smiled and played her greatest part.

***

The funeral was macabre. It—
could be nothing else.
A daughter's suicide: naked in the arms of her naked father.
Of course. There was talk.
But people try not to lend voice to speculations
(when it comes to the dead).
They whisper instead.

***

Chapter Seventeen

After Tristan left Curt Bell's Apothecary he returned to the office to check on Hannah Lee Watkins. Her situation had much improved. Which puzzled him. After Genevieve's revelation about her expertise in typhoid bacillus, he'd analyzed Hannah Lee's well water only to find that it had, in fact, contained bacteria.

Tristan then began wondering if Genevieve's suggestion of Typhus had been the case (which would have meant that the poor widowed woman would simply have died).

Yet there she was…living.

Recovering.

Growing stronger day-by-day.

On the third day after coming to the office she passed blackness from every orifice, looking Death its very self. Then she drank a little…ate a little…even got up on her feet a little. The only thing that worried Tristan was that she still seemed to have

phantom nerve pain

    in one of her fingertips

(and, for no rhyme or reason,
        would
suddenly
        lose her
        balance…
or burst out crying
in terrible fits of melancholy—

though all of the abovesaid symptoms rectified themselves, quickly).

Tristan wondered if…perhaps…the widow (as it would be natural for a woman of her situation) might not be suffering…from hysteria.
***

In Ashland, Big Bob stuck out like a Jacksonville gold nugget.

He didn't look the part of:

millworker,

miner,

farmer…he just looked eerily big and leery. *That* look made the Ashland folks offput. Big Bob didn't (or couldn't) be bothered with such things. He simply roamed the streets looking at each and every person's face that passed. Waiting, patiently (his predator-self) for that instantaneous recognition. Waiting to spring the moment he saw those eyes (Roy's eyes) in order to lock his pupils to those pupils.

Like a recurring dream, Big Bob re-envisioned killing him. But he'd seen nothing of Roy in that town.

***

Returning to Isaac's house, Jake pulled Ida May to his lap, curled his fingers through her fine, fine baby's hair, and kissed her chubcheeks every time she apexed the upswing of her 'hoe-sey' ride atop his knee.

Isaac was nearly bursting from excitement. "Wait here," Isaac beamed to Jake and Ida May.

Jake kissed Ida May's earlobe. "Wonder what Uncle Isaac's up to?"

Ida May looked.

Isaac returned with three boxes.

He gave Ida May one at a time:
the first was a lacy, frilly little dress,
the second, a pair of dainty girly shoes
and the third a doll with a porcelain face.

Jake knew how dear these things were. "No Isaac, we can't take these."

"Now you just hush, Jake. It's from Un-kull I-zay."

Jake grinned. "Thanks Isaac. You shouldn't have."

"Why not?"

Jake didn't have an answer.

Ida May kissed the doll's cold, hard cheeks and fingered its hair before she laid it backward (watching the real eyelashes close/open) and then she cried. "Mommy. Mommy."

The two men (as strong and capable as they were) were as helpless as she was. They could not be what she needed (though not for lack of trying). The three had to finally accept (after hours of failing) that the only peace little Ida May would find was when she'd worn herself completely out with crying…and slept (clutching her doll to her babychest).

The two men went out on the porch and sat. Looking out over Isaac's valley view.

Jake asked, "What is going on with Emily Marie."

This time Isaac told him…everything:
about the night she came to his house,
about the letters she'd received,
about the strange man he saw (always off in the distance) riding across his land.

"Did he look like a doctor?"

"Too far off to tell. I'll tell you though, every time I saw him...I can't really explain it...my hackles got up."

"I bet I know who that was."

"Oh yeah?"

"Yeah. That doctor."

"What doctor?"

"I don't know his name. What are the names of the doctors here?"

"There are only two in town...and an apothecary."

"Maybe he could be an apothecary. What's his name?"

"Curt...Curt Bell."

"What does he look like?"

"Tall, blonde..."

"Nope. Not him. What about the others? The doctors?"

"There's Doc Hill. He's old."

"No that's not him. The other one?"

"Doc Andersen, he's new. Young. Tall."

"Blonde?"

"Yeah! Quite handsome some say."

Jake paused for a moment. "His given name wouldn't happen to be Tristan would it?"

"I wouldn't know. I never go to doctors."

"Well that's not him. The man I saw was darker-haired. If he was blonde then he was as dark a blonde as I've seen."

"Saw where?"

"Coming out of Emily Marie's house."

"A doctor? Is she ill?"

"I thought the same thing but this man (if he is a doctor) is treating Emily Marie badly."

"Badly? What do you mean?"

"I mean, after he'd visited her." Jake looked up and down his body (moving a certain way).

"No!"

"Yes! I don't wonder if this 'doctor' isn't the same man you saw on your land. Perhaps the same man who'd written Emily Marie. Maybe some secret affair of hers."

"No! I wouldn't think it of her."

"I don't like to, believe me. But what else could it be?"

They looked out over the horizon.

Clouds brewed.

Both contemplated whether or not "their" girl could, in fact, be acting a whore. Jake interrupted their silence: "You wouldn't happen to have one of those letters would you? Maybe the guy signed them?"

Isaac led Jake into the house and they searched as quietly as two grown men can (when searching for something a woman has hid). "She kept some in here," Isaac said, reaching into the flour bin (whose mesh had been chewed through by rats so—although useless for the makings of bread—served a perfect hiding place).

Nothing.

Then Isaac lifted the kindling box lid. "I found one in here one day," he pushed handfuls of slivery wood to the side, pointing to the bottom.

Nothing.

Then both rose up (standing from their crouchings) to come eye-level with the Good Book resting on the fireplace mantle. "There?" Jake asked.

"No. Well. I really wouldn't know. I haven't picked up that book in a long time."

Jake lifted it.

The book left no dust silhouette. He opened it. Out fell three letters.

Only none were signed except by "Your Admirer."

They were back to nil.

Jake stopped (thinking). Perhaps Ida May was the key. "Isaac, let's wake Ida May and tell her she's going to see Mommy." Isaac frowned. "You think that's wise?"

"I think," Jake paused, "it's necessary."

Isaac stood for a moment. "Okay."

The three made their way down their side of the mountain while the little girl squeaked (peeling with laughter) gibberish and all the excitement a baby leaks when getting to be with its too-long-absent mother.

***

Newspapers can be (like specters) eyelids for lives that might otherwise remain unseen. Big Bob loved newspapers:

> they kept him warm
> and he liked the pictures.

It just so happened that that day Big Bob saw (on the front page) a picture that made him really warm: Roy.
That grin! I'll cut that grin right off his face!

Roy was standing beside another man and both were in front of a grand opening of something. What? Big Bob couldn't quite tell (for he could only read a VERY little and newspapers used such big words).   So he asked strangers to read it to him. Unfortunately, the townsfolk of Ashland avoided him

> (a transient—a plaguey pestilence that they just knew was
> spreading)

minus one—a girl

> (not more than ten years old and whose mother was inside a
> store).

She proved quite kind (reading to Big Bob every line and stumbling over a mere word here and there). Big Bob kept poking his finger deep (and hard) into the paper's news as if he were poking the image's (Roy's) eyes and kept repeating: "Him. Him there. What about him?"
The little girl replied, "He's at a health spa."
"Where?"
"South of here."

> She pointed south.

"How far?"

> She shrugged her shoulders.
> Her mother came out of the store (glaring at Big Bob as she

whisked her daughter away).

> Big Bob waved. "Thank you little girl."
> The little girl looked over her arm (an arm bruising beneath

her mother's pinching fingers) and waved, smiling back at him.
I liked her.　　　　　　　*South.*

> Big Bob walked and walked.
> Clear into the night's dark until he found a clump of tall grass.

Pulling Roy's photo over himself he fell into fitful—wonderful

> —dreams of

how—

when

he'd meet Roy again.

     His legs twitched
(like a sleeping dog's) when his mind split Roy's skull in two. With
his eyes flickering behind shut lids he chewed, murmuring:
"In one blow…one…one blow…two"
***

The newspaper's specter had a beastly reach (it liked to touch and touched many); the spa's grand opening page (with Roy's photo) made its way into the hands of Jake and Isaac (who'd been secretly waiting outside Emily Marie's house), which made them simultaneously, exclaim: "That's him!"

They both read: "Dr. Mereth Hague's Health Spa."

Meanwhile, Mike kissed Emily Marie goodbye.

That's when Ida May cried: "Mommy!"

Isaac covered her mouth, "Shush, child! Shush!"

Mike had heard the child's scream and changed his course (from the sidewalk leading to work) to Isaac's wagon.

"Say Isaac. What brings you here?" Mike Warrant asked.

Isaac held Ida May close. "We just came to see Emily Marie." Ida May cried out, "Mommy!"

Mike looked at the child. Then at Isaac. "Why's she saying that?"

Jake piped, "It's natural. With no mother. A child calls any woman mommy."

Mike looked at Jake. Then back at Isaac. "Who is this?"

Isaac (failing bit by bit to hold against Ida May's squiggling wriggling) said: "This is Jake. He's my friend."

"Oh," Mike said, holding out his hand, "Nice to meet you."

Jake tipped his hat.

"Sorry gents. Duty calls." With that, Mike Warrant disappeared back down the way he'd originally set out upon.

When Isaac and Jake saw the back of Mike they both looked to Emily Marie (who'd been standing in her doorway, mouth agape and tears running down her cheeks). Jake carried Ida May to her mother's outstretched arms.

"Mommy!" the girl cried.

"My Sweet Girl!"

The mother cried.

Both held each other in vices.

Jake pulled Isaac aside.

"Isaac. I need the wagon. Can you stay here in town with Ida May?"

"What are you up to?"

"I have to find that man. That Dr. Hague."

"I don't like this. I should come with you."

"No. You'll have to take Ida May home with you before Mike returns."

"I'm sure she can stay with Emily Marie, even after Mike gets home—for a little bit—until we get back."

"No! You didn't hear how Mike argued with her over Ida May. I don't want you to leave her here. Not around him, okay? I know she'll be safe…" Jake patted Isaac's shoulder (from that very first day Jake knew exactly how much Isaac cared for his daughter) "…with you."

Isaac's beam-smile quickly fled. "What if something happens to you?"

"Then…you take care of her."

Isaac nodded.

The two men shook hands.

Jake rode down the road to find Dr. Mereth Hague.

Unfortunately…he did.

***

Love buds in strange ways and mysterious places.

"Love!" Curt Bell cursed as he climbed the stairs to Tristan Andersen's apartment (to look in on the widow, Mrs. Hannah Lee Watkins).

"Love!" Curt Bell grit his teeth, driving (—with pieces of broken heart—) resolution into his clomping feet.

"Love," he thought, knocking on the door (with enthusiasm as fluid as sticky cold honey).

When the softness and succulence of a woman's voice called, "Come in"

Curt Bell's heart made a skip: "Love?"

Curt Bell sat beside her (listening how she'd been at her well) watching sunlight glitter the red of her redbrownyellow hair. And when Hannah Lee told him about the awkwardness she'd felt (finding herself waking at the doctor's apartment—knowing how a spider had bit her) Curt loved how her greenhazel eyes dartingly danced whenever she smiled.

"Love."

***

Tristan and Genevieve went straight from the funeral to the office (in order to check up on Hannah Lee) only to discover (quietly ascending the stairs—in order not to disturb her) sounds
of laughter,
of giggling,
of scraping about.

But when Tristan looked as if he meant to burst into the room, Genevieve grabbed his arm, put her finger to her lips and: "Shhh."

There came an ever-so-slight rhythmic squeaking (one that Tristan and Genevieve knew—themselves—very well).

Tristan looked at Genevieve, whispering, "I can't believe it!"
Genevieve grinned, "What?"
"They're making love."
"Yes."

Genevieve clutched his elbow more emphatically.
"Is there something wrong with that?"
"Well," Tristan teased, "I guess 'widder' Watkins is feeling better."
Genevieve giggled. "I guess so."
So they left the new lovers to their love making…only they forgot about Dr. Hill. The Dr. Hill who was terrified that it—
had been his fault.
It—
made Dr. Hill want to make darned sure that Mrs. Watkins (the only currently living patient in his care) recovered (well).

"Can't have anything happen to her," he thought.
He unlocked the front door.
(Lost in his thoughts) he climbed the stairs.
(Thinking about how Society was fickle: "one minute they love you for saving someone's life, the next they want to string you up as a criminal because somebody died") Dr. Hill did not hesitate to
fling wide
finding Curt atop Hannah Lee (the widow, whose legs tented the sheet in a big white 'V').
"Dear God! What's going on in here!" Dr. Hill exclaimed.
Curt dashed his naked self into the corner, dressing.
Hannah Lee Watkins pulled the sheet over her nakedness and—
to Dr. Hill's utter astonishment
—started laughing.

Dr. Hill (as if the whole situation were a personal affront) "Mrs. Watkins! I'm shocked!"

Hannah Lee adjusted herself (sitting with her back straight) "Dear Dr. Hill. I'm shocked...you're shocked."

Dr. Hill (though he couldn't seem to take his eyes off the lovely woman's naked shoulders) "To think," he scolded, "here! In my medical office."

Hannah Lee softened (such that Dr. Hill could hardly stand her softening so) and spoke her Siren-voice, "I'm terribly sorry. It won't happen again. You see. I'm just so happy."

She held out her hand to Curt who clutched it—
as if it were life itself and,

in unison, they chimed: "We're in love!"

One could have blown Dr. Hill over with a single puff of pipe smoke.
Now...I've seen it all

Dr. Hill shut the door   behind him.   Walked

downstairs,   grabbed a note   and scribbled:

"Tristan,

I retire. The practice is yours.

P.S.   remember our business agreement: 15% for 15 years.

Sincerely, Dr. Frank Hill."

Still, (perhaps out of habit—or nostalgia) he loaded his medical sachet the same way he'd done every day (for all those years) yet went—directly—home.

***

Ida May would not allow her mother to let go of her, literally. Emily Marie carried her on her hip as she made herself and Isaac a pot of tea. Isaac watched out the window. Hoping Jake would return soon (he didn't like him going to find that man all alone).

Emily Marie steered the conversation.
"Isaac,"

Ida May imitated her mother,
"I-zay-kuh"

"Good, Ida May," Emily beamed at Ida May, then at Isaac, "You've done a great job taking care of her, Isaac. Thank you."
"And you?" Isaac asked, "How are you?"

Emily looked at the wallpaper (at nothing). Her dress was fine, her hair fine; she was polished and shined. She could not answer that question so she began to cry.
"No cry mommy,"

Ida May wiped away every tear that even attempted a fall from her mother's eyes.
"It's okay, sweet girl. Mommy's okay."
"O-tay."
"That's right, my beautiful Ida May. O-Tay!"

The little girl squealed to hear her mommy sound just like her.

Isaac watched mother and child. He'd never...never seen a more beautiful thing in his life. Then (suddenly) he found Ida May (unexpectedly) jumping into his lap: "No cry, I-say-kuh. No cry!"

He thought it funny how (with him) she was so firm. He stopped right away.
"Show Mommy your doll," Isaac said. Hoping to keep Ida May's attention away from grownup tears.
"Look:" Ida May:
pointed
touched
kissed her new doll (all while Emily Marie's eyes pleaded with Isaac's to understand that which he never could).
"Why did you do it," Isaac finally asked.
"Money."
"Please don't say that."
"It's true, Isaac. And you knew that. You DID. I know you did!"

He wagged his head sideways, in a numbing rhythm, for she was right. He knew her marriage to Mike had been for the money.

She'd told him that much (he always believed there was more) then he remembered.

"There was more!" he cried.

Emily Marie hung her head.

"I knew it. What?"

She looked at him through her eyelashes:

"I fell…"

"In love?"

"Oh dear no! I mean, perhaps I thought, but no. The only person I've ever loved was Jake."

"I don't understand. What about those letters?"

A clock bonged.

Emily Marie started, then counted.

They had only a little time left (before Mike returned).

"Dr. Hague. I didn't know that was his name. I didn't know what kind of man he was. I was young and foolish. Arrogant…and it was…"

"Tempting?"

"…my undoing."

Isaac knelt beside her.

"Are you in trouble Emily Marie?"

She threw her arms around Isaac's neck. "Yes! Yes! I'm in terrible trouble!"

"Tell me. Just tell me what I can do!"

"There's nothing. Nothing! If I tell Mike about Ida May he'll divorce me. Then no one will ever want me, especially Jake."

Isaac pulled away from her (so as to make sure she could see his eyes), "Now you just listen here. That boy LOVES you. He wouldn't care less what Mike does. He's wanted you ever since I've known you and…he wants you now. If I'm sure of anything it's that!"

Emily breathed deep, "You really think so?"

"Absolutely!"

"There's something else," Emily Marie's tone shifted to caution, "Dr. Hague told me that if I ever double-crossed him, he'd kill Ida May."

"I'd like to see him try! I'll kill him myself before I let him touch a hair on my girl's…I mean Ida May's head!"

Suddenly Emily Marie grew very distant. Her eyes glazed. Her voice came strange and slow, "He's an evil man. Pure evil, Isaac. You just don't know. I'm afraid of him."

Isaac knelt back beside her and drew her hand in his. "Now don't you fret yourself about THAT man. Between me and Jake we'll take care of you and Ida May. Now you go pack your things. You're coming with me and Ida May and Jake."

Just then Mike walked through the door.

"What's this?"

Isaac stood tall and firm. "Emily Marie is coming home."

Mike ran to his wife (who was still far far away). "What are you talking about Inns! She's not going anywhere. She's MY wife and I'll not have you...and your BASTARD upsetting her!"

That was it. (A man's adrenalin can be dammed only so long before it bursts—and Isaac's had been raging since the moment Emily Marie had told him the truth about Doctor Hague.) The punch landed square. Mike fell hard.

Ida May screamed horror only innocent children can scream.

Emily Marie swooped her child up, shielding her eyes from the blood that gushed from a gash just above Mike's lip.

"Don't you EVER say that again, about that child!" Isaac yelled.

"Get out of my house," Mike snarled (still on the ground) "and don't you EVER come back. You hear me? Never!"

Isaac looked at Emily Marie. Emily Marie (brushing her little girl's hair with her fingers) looked between Mike and Isaac. Isaac mouthed, "Believe me." Emily Marie (carrying Ida May) followed Isaac Inns out of the Warrants' house.

Mike (suddenly struck quite dumb) simply lay back on the floor, bled, and wondered: *Why God? What's all this for?*

Isaac was too late.

Emily Marie was too late.

It was late when they got to the hotel where they waited...
        and waited...for Jake to come.

Only he never did.
***

At Genevieve's apartment there came a knock. It was the police: "Is Doctor Andersen here?"
"Yes."

Tristan tucked in his shirt as he walked (barefoot) to the door. "Please come with us, Dr. Andersen. There's been a murder."

At the newly-opened Health Spa, Dr. Manfred paced. For when his feet stopped his mind started. All he could think was: *I'm ruined ruined ruined. I'm ruined ruined ruined*

The body of a young man (a stranger to Dr. Manfred) had been found in one of the hysteria treatment rooms.

A young hysteric (who'd been told by Dr. Mereth Hague to enter and wait inside for him to perform treatment) had the misfortune of finding the body (which did NOT improve her condition one bit). The investigating police officer asked, "Where is Dr. Hague?"
Dr. Manfred shrugged, "I can't seem to find him anywhere."
The police officer looked at his partner, "That might be important."

Tristan followed the police to the room. When the door was opened for him, Tristan felt himself loose consciousness. Never (in all his life) had he seen so much blood. But the blood wasn't it... wasn't what made his mind need to leave its senses...it
was that plunging pain in his heart
(as if God himself had struck lightning into its nerve endings)
because there (before him and lying dead)
was his best friend—Jake Kalmar.
***

Chapter Eighteen

Isaac (with Emily Marie clinging to his arm) walked through the front door of Dr. Hill's office.

"How do you do. Mr. Inns? Mrs. Warrant?" greeted Genevieve.

Isaac answered, "Not well, Miss. Not well. Is the doctor in?"

"No. The police took him."

"What!" Isaac exclaimed.

Genevieve chuckled, then quickly corrected her indiscretion, "No no. Nothing like that. There's been a murder and…"

Emily Marie cried out, "What!"

Suddenly Genevieve realized she was making everything worse. "I'm sorry Mrs. Warrant. I should have been more delicate."

"Who was murdered!" Emily Marie verged fainting.

"I really can't say."

"WHO!" Emily Marie screamed.

Genevieve looked at Isaac Inns. "What's wrong with her Mr. Inns?"

"It's a long story Miss. I came here because I was wondering if you might give her a little 'something' to help calm her down."

Genevieve looked at the young woman, who'd begun swooning, "It's him. I just know…it's him."

"Who is she talking about?" Genevieve asked.

"She thinks a bad end has come for someone she loves."

"Mr. Warrant?"

Isaac lowered his eyes. It was all he had to say.

Genevieve left the room, briefly, returning with a needle. "This won't hurt very much."

Emily Marie was so far off she didn't even feel it penetrate her. She felt something else…something unexplainable, as if her very guts…her intuition…her soul itself were being ripped apart.

Withdrawing the point Genevieve said to Isaac, "That should do."

"Thank you Miss."

"Now, perhaps we can talk. A little more calmly? What is this all about?"

"You see," Isaac began…

Emily Marie looked out the window,

                                                    watching

every wagon, praying t
                          he next four wheels would

carry her

                    lover—her life—safely back.
***

Meanwhile, Tristan allowed himself a whiff of ether before reattempting entrance to the room where Jake's body lay.

He wasn't the only one. He ended up administering whiffs to the police officers too. For none of the officers there had ever seen anything so...

(mind, they'd seen plenty of murder—gold does that to people—
plenty of bodies:
hacked/slashed,
shot,
hung,
beaten to death)

.....perversely foul.

On the floor (beside a vibratory table) Jake Kalmar lay on a crimson rug gone rust with blood. He'd been slit from his throat to his pubis. His head had been nearly cut from the spine (the initial slash having to have been savage to accomplish this). His nose had been cut off. His penis % testicles had been cut off.

The three (nose|> penis % testicles) were placed neatly (bloodily) upon the table beside the vibrating apparatus.

His internal organs had been removed and placed in a pile between his feet.

And his left hand (with its virginal weddingring-less finger) had been stuffed into his empty thoracic cavity.

Tristan explained it all clinically to the police:
"This is a surgeon's work I can tell you that!
Whoever did this knows his anatomy...and,"
        he pointed to the clean cut lines,
"uses his knife better than any butcher could. Besides,"
        he knelt next to the body

- the ether had helped to remember how to detach
        |life[from]death|—|bodies[from]friends|

"look how he's specifically detached the intestine at the sphincters. Only a medically trained man could do such a thing. I'm sure of it!"

The police looked between each other, scribbling (like mad) on their individual pads. A young officer came in. He'd not seen the scene yet and puked on the floor. He kept saying, "Sorry. Sorry," as an older officer escorted him out the door.

The older officer came back to tell Tristan: "There's no sign of Dr. Mereth Hague." Tristan knelt beside his friend. The ether was wearing off. He saw that Jake's eyes had been wide open—
He looks scared, God. Why? Why him!

Then Tristan heard a woman's cry (a frantic high-pitched screaming) and the scratching of materials:
a dress,
a uniform,
a door—clawing (like a phantom).
For you see, the screeching had come from Emily Marie
(who'd been brought to the scene by Isaac and Genevieve
because they believed
that when she saw the murder scene
and saw that the body, was in fact, not *his*, then she'd calm).
However *that* plan went TERRIBLY wrong!

Even a policeman, holding her arms,
(saying she could not go nearer)
did not prove strong enough to keep her from *him*
and she found herself able to pass (that policeman)
by becoming wriggly, squiggly…(like Ida May)
and so found herself falling to the floor
beside the body of Jake
kissing him hard, fast,
rubbing his cheeks as if…to wake him…"No! No! No!" she cried.

Tristan looked at the strange woman and sat back on his haunches—still feeling the end effects of the ether:
Is that my little sister?

"Emily?"
He grabbed her/| she clawed his face.
"Ouch! Dammit!" he recoiled.
She heard his voice.
Could it be? It's impossible!

"Emily Marie, is that you?"
"Tristan?"

      Tristan put his hands on her shoulders. "Come with me."

      She looked up at her big brother with glassy drugged strangewild eyes: "Tris? Is that really you? "

      They held each other
(both sobbing) there

      where Jake's blood ceased to mean death and did what blood does best…
coagulatingly congeals—
***

Meanwhile, Dr. Manfred told the police (over & over again) how he'd met Dr. Mereth Hague.
What his credentials said.
What his physical characteristics were.
They asked if he'd found the man strange.
He told them everything

> except *that* one thing—*that* one thing he'd rationalized didn't mean anything so why tell *it*—
> (that Dr. Hague had visited him…bloodyhanded, saying: "If you breathe a word of what I'm about to tell you I swear I'll find you and do what I did to him |>to you. "
> The deal was half the spa's profits
> {from that day forth, indefinitely} sent to:
> The White Chapel Club
> In Care Of: The President
> Chicago, Illinois).

Dr. Manfred fantasized that The White Chapel Club was a group of:
suffragettes?
missionaries?
Zionists?
Methodists?
"Helpers, I bet. Besides. It can't be all bad. It has a president."
***

Meanwhile, the police notified police
who notified police
who notified police
until a great manhunt brewed. Everyone:
layman,
policeman,
(maybe even cats and dogs)
feared every stranger they saw.
Every stranger was *the* brutal murderer.
Who was it?
You?
You!

Police stations buzzed buzzy buzzes of|from all kinds of busy bodies.

Only it was too late.
You see.
Big Bob had been at the scene where Jake's body had been
discovered. He knew Roy's tricks. So Big Bob waited outside the
thick crowds (in the fringe of tall grass, near the road out of town).
(Sure enough) while everyone was in commotion Roy
slithered out,
calm as milk in a kitten's bowl,
carrying an expensive bag and dressed in a real nice suit.
"One whack," Big Bob thought, but then, "No…wait. Wait. It'll be
better if I wait."
So he followed him.
In Middleford Roy bought a train ticket.
Big Bob went to the counter,
"Where's he going?"
"San Francisco."
"I'll go there too."
Big Bob gave the last of his money to the man.
Roy sat (pretending to read a newspaper though he never
turned a page).
"I bet he's thinking about what he done," Big Bob thought. "He likes
murderin'."
The train came in.
The train went out.
Big Bob (always distant) never let Roy out of his sight.

After they'd arrived, Roy went to *that* side of town where he could make his next mark…a young lady with cheap feathers and thick painted lips.

"He'll kill her," Big Bob thought, "His lips twitchin' like a huntin' dog whose onto strong scent means he's thinkin' about killin'."

Big Bob followed Roy (who was following the prostitute). Eventually both men ended at the docks. It—
made Big Bob angry enough to bite off the tip of his tongue and spit when he saw Roy spewing the 'friend schtick'
(the same he'd used on him that day by the sea)
on a big guy
—a dockman—
who even looked like Big Bob
(big and dumb).
"That's all I was. A sucker!"

Still. He waited.

He'd know the moment.

The perfect moment.

Then inspiration came…there (on the docks) in the dark (with the bay's black water sloshing) with Roy standing snugly alone (waiting for his big dockworking friend to return).
"Big Dummy's probably getting him that whore," Big Bob thought, "he likes to fuck after killing."

Sure enough, along came the big dockman with the painted woman beside him. Big Bob followed them to her room.

He listened at the door of the whore.

He heard the grunting. Next came the woman's muffled screams (Roy liked it rough after murdering). Then that moment came…that window of time when everything went quiet inside. "This is it!"

Big Bob effortlessly flung the door wide (nimbly shutting it behind him).

Roy (still quivering inside the whore—quite naked and quite far from his clothes where his scalpel tucked in) tried to manipulate Big Bob with his eyes (being a mesmerist). But when Roy realized Big Bob's eyes would not cow down, he tremulously pulled himself out of the woman. "You'd better go," Big Bob said. She didn't need to hear anything more. In a flash (like a cockroach) she was gone.

Without taking his eyes off Roy, Big Bob shoved the dresser in front of the door. Roy sneered. He didn't once look at his clothes. They both knew what they held. "You're a dead man," Roy sibilated. Big Bob stood (as if his legs were Redwood trunks and his fists—boulders) not saying a word.

He didn't move an inch.

He just waited.

Waited for the one perfect moment…

it was coming…he knew it.

That one perfect moment when Roy would kill himself.

Roy leapt.

Big Bob lunged.

Roy's throat, cleanshaven, felt—to Big Bob—almost womanlike.

Roy's feet dangled.

His breath tried to pass through the closing way.

Roy kicked and hit, but to Big Bob it felt like mosquitoes.

Roy hissed.

"What?" Big Bob asked.

Roy hissed.

"What?"

(After as long as it took Big Bob to eat an egg) Roy's leg kicks got weaker and weaker until only his toenails tried to claw free. *That's just about…right…he's just about…done*

So Big Bob set Roy free.

On the ground, Roy lay still.

Big Bob kicked his ribs. "Now I know you're not dead so don't go play it."

Big Bob knelt down beside Roy, whispering, "T'wont do you no good."

Roy's throat crushed—no more voice—only air rushed past.

"Now," Big Bob said in a sleepy way, "You like the cutting. I hate blood. That's how it all went right?"

Roy watched Big Bob pull his scalpel out.

"And…if there's one thing I know you like, Roy," Big Bob knelt beside the man (pulling Roy's head up by his hair, resting his skull in his lap…like The Madonna) "is your face…so that has to go."

Big Bob cut round the edges of Roy's jawbones, earlobes, forehead…and pulled!

POP!   off it came.
"Now that 'twernt too hard,"
          Big Bob said (using Roy's own clothes
                    to wipe off Roy's own blood).
          Roy lay limp (alive, barely).

"There was one other thing you love…now, what…was it?"

          Big Bob acted as if he'd forgotten (then remembered). He
          was enjoying it too much to give away what he'd envisioned
          ever since the day Roy had set him up to take a murder rap.

"Oh yeah! Your cock!"
          Big Bob spread the man's legs and…
CHOP!
          Roy still clung to life.
God, only, knew why.

          Big Bob stood up, opened Roy's bag to find plenty of nice
nice clothes. He held them up to himself. "Too small," he said to
Roy, throwing them onto Roy's bleeding body.
          Big Bob grabbed two bundles of money. "I bet if I asked you
where this came from," he said, waving the money in front of Roy's
blood-filled eyes, "you'd say a nice little girl in Ashland gave it to
you…only you wouldn't say you'd been blackmailing her and raping
her. You SON-OF-A-BITCH!"
          That is when all the reserve Big Bob had (with great effort)
used to hold back burst, flooding the spillway of his infantile restraint:
he kicked
and kicked
and kicked
          the beast from the man called Roy
          until nothing remained but a mass of meat.

Big Bob took a deep breath.
          Collected himself.
          Washed (as best he could with the half-filled pitcher of water)
leaving behind one money%bundle on the whore's bed.
          If anyone had noticed him leaving, no one said a word.
***

Meanwhile, police had arrested the infamous Dr. Mereth Hague in Portland, Oregon.

Dr. Hague opted for a bench trial.

At the train station in San Francisco, Big Bob's phantom (the newspaper) pricked his eyes when he saw the picture of his favorite doctor,

"The Lollies,"

on the front cover.

For Big Bob, a kind man read:

"A Jack-the-Ripper murderer…"

Big Bob said to the ticket agent, "Portland, please."

***

Chapter Nineteen

Meanwhile, (Jake's murder aside) Tristan could see that Emily Marie was not well:
her color,
her tone,
perhaps what some might say aura.

Tristan had seen it—
that was not good.

Throughout Emily Marie's crisis, Genevieve had proven a rock. In fact, the two women bonded such that it was Genevieve's arms (not Tristan's, Isaac's, or even Ida May's) that Emily Marie clung to whenever she envisioned Jake Kalmar's body (which was too often for her own good).

Although Hannah Lee was still occupying Tristan's room when Jake's murder had occurred, the moment the widow laid eyes upon the young girl (Emily Marie) she instinctively offered up her (rather Tristan's) bed claiming to be fully "healed."

When Tristan asked where she would stay that night, she replied that she had her own ideas, adding: "Don't you worry about me."

Some rumored that Hannah Lee and Curt Bell had secretly eloped that night (though the truth was: no preacher or rings had been involved). And (after time) people accepted Curt and Hannah Lee as husband|wife. They worked (all the rest of their lives) on Hannah Lee's farm and Curt found that he liked wrangling cattle, tilling soil, fathering (and delivering) his own children much more than his past of peddling pills.

In fact (and it was a fact) that no one in the Watkins|Bell family ever took a single thing that they hadn't culled from the earth (all living well into their twilights).

And old Mrs. Bell, well she was left (all alone) to run her husband's|son's apothecary (and rumor had it—
she ran it very well).

Tristan felt it his duty to inform Mike Warrant, Emily Marie's husband, of his wife's health condition. He was surprised when Isaac said, "Don't bother with that man. He'll not have anything to do with her."

And Isaac was right (that night Emily Marie left Mike prostrate on the floor he went directly to his mother who went directly to her lawyer who directly annulled it all).

After the laudanum Emily Marie was calm. Genevieve stayed by her side (they slept together like sisters). Ida May curled up on her mother's belly (as if trying to be reborn). Tristan scoured his journals and books for "that" look of his sister.

He did not like what he found:
Uveitis
Optic neuritis
Conjunctivitis
Retinitis
Dacryocystitis
Scleritis

He palpated her lymph nodes:
Swollen pelvic

She stirred.
He injected her.

He turned her hands palm-up in the palm of his hand:
Just as I thought

He lifted Ida May (who'd fallen down into the deep sleep gifted by God) and gently settled her on the floor.
He pulled back the bedcovers from Emily Marie's feet but before he examined her soles he prayed:
Dear God...please!

He made notes.
Then there was only one thing left to do.
He lifted Emily Marie's dressing gown,

pressed her knees in opposition so they fell apart.
There…before his denying eyes…his worst fear realized:
Chancres

Emily Marie had contracted syphilis.

Without covering her (or shifting her) he woke Genevieve.
"What? What is it?"

Tristan held his finger to his lips (miming her to come
whisper-close). When Genevieve looked at her lover's face she knew
it—

something terrible, something shattering. She felt her own nerves
surging but had learned (over her years with hysterics) to fight nature
with artificial calm.

She whispered: "What's wrong?"

Tristan pointed to Emily Marie's sprawled legs. Genevieve
drew close to girl's body. She knew what she saw. "Dear God! what
are we going to do?" They both knew that there was nothing
Medicine could do for it…

…Time. And Passing (It)…

        …and lives…

…like fishing line—

       simply   floating

    atop {within} amongst

       forces.

So when Tristan kissed Genevieve (leaving her to care for his
little sister and his littler niece) Genevieve knew:

It interested…

        …the Crux of It…

   …All…

       Divergently.

Dr. Hill was shocked to hear knocking at his door. Though (if
truth be told) it pleased him—excessively—to hear it because during
his brief hours of retirement

(after he'd broken his decision to his wife, and had spent:

afternoon, evening, and twilight

doing nothing but keeping her company)

Dr. Hill had begun to wonder if he hadn't (in a fit of passion) perhaps,
made a terrible mistake. So, when Tristan (explaining his and his

sister's situations) said that they needed to leave for their home in Iowa, immediately, a look of near-joy flooded Dr. Hill's face. "Certainly, my Boy. Take care of your family. Don't give the practice another thought! I'll come right back to work."

Mrs. Hill
        (who'd been pressing her ear to the kitchen's door—secretly
        shared her husband's joy;
                for after:
                an afternoon,
                evening
                and twilight
                of nothing but keeping her husband
                company she'd become quite sure
                that she absolutely opposed the idea
                of her husband *ever* retiring)
smiled ear-to-ear.

Tristan was all apologies.
Dr. Hill, who at first was all graciousness, quickly reverted to business. A bargain was struck.

        It
        [Dr. Hill's buying out of Tristan's part of the business]
was enough for Tristan and Genevieve to make their new start.
***

Meanwhile, Dr. Hague's trial took place. Dr. Mereth Hague was:

examined,
cross-examined,
scrutinized,
stared at with horror-eyes,
hissed at,
spat on,
manhandled by guards whose own fear of Humanity's capabilities bred iron fists.

There, in the gallery, Big Bob sat.

Dr. Mereth Hague never said a word. In fact, when asked about his guilt, he simply nodded his head (like a man bobbing for apples...or drowning). It was struck into the court document: affirmation.

When asked if he had anything to say in his own defense:
mute

It did not take long for the judge, upon hearing of the mutilation|torture nature of the Ashland murder in conjunction with a "guilt" plea
(combined with the fact that the police always wanted swift justice,
["open|shut" cases]
because rapidity bred public favor, in general, which improved their too-often precarious 'public relations')
to declare Dr. Hague guilty.

Big Bob sat, listening to every morsel (as if a jackal) feeding his own sense of glorification because he'd rid the world of (Roy) a person who could do the things that he was hearing his good friend (the Lolly Doctor) had done.
"Why," he wondered. "Why did Doc do that? Was *he* like Roy? But he had kindness...didn't he?"
Then Big Bob shrugged his shoulders. "Never can tell who's a murderer."

Still…

he decided

(even murderers could be kind. The doc had been kind to him)

so he'd go see Dr. Mereth Hague

(if he could).

He deserves at least one friend in the world

At the jail the guard looked Big Bob up/|\down & up/|\down.
The guard ran his hands round every inch of Big Bob's body.
"How d'ya know the pris'ner?"
"I'm a friend."

The guard looked Big Bob, again, up^down & up^down. See,
rumors had been twirling round that the murder might have been done
by two men (instead of one). But they were just rumors (nothing
substantiated) so the guard let Big Bob in because even in the
wildness of Oregon—there was etiquette: a man, sentenced to death
by hanging, was entitled to a visitor…a meal…and a priest.

Big Bob sat on the cot beside Dr. Hague.

His weight made the rather-flimsy wooden frame cry out.
When he tried to settle himself in (to get comfortable, if he could) it
creaked and screeched as if it would break.

The guard yelled, "Settle it down in there."

Big Bob got rigid. And sat still.

Dr. Hague stared at the stone's wall.

Masonry. Now that's a skill

"Why'd ya do it?" Big Bob interrupted the quiet.

Dr. Hague remained silent.

They shared looking at the wall.

"I mean I never picked you the murdrin' type." Big Bob went on (his
face flat cold like the wall's).

Dr. Hague said nothing at all.
"See, I've known murdrin' types all my life."

Big Bob shifted.

The cot scritched.
Nothing.

It was as if the two held steerage on a fareless ship…a vessel of forgotten title—

Big Bob turned to face Dr. Hague.

"See Doc. I don' care wha'cha done. You was kind to me and that's all that counts."

Still, Big Bob stared at the man's statue-face…it seemed to him as if…it began to crack…right uptop…right at the scalp…

because that was when Dr. Mereth Hague finally spoke:

"You see, Big Bob, there is a very common application to everything…

    …and nothing else more so

                  —the crux of what It is—is

Passing."

Big Bob scrunched his face.

"Wha'cha say?"

Dr. Mereth Hague laughed. A good hearty belly-rolling laugh!

"Yes!" the doctor cried.

The guard told Big Bob it was time to go.

The public wasn't officially allowed to watch the (evil) doctor's hanging

    (though men, women and children climbed atop roofs to get a

    glimpse of the Sheriff's rope).

Big Bob relied on his oracle-demon to bring him the news. The photo showed a man's head (covered with a sack)…

resting?

    …a body.

A kind man read the title to Big Bob:

"Murderer Hung in Portland…" the article went on to say what Dr. Mereth Hague had eaten for breakfast, how he'd refused to pray and how the minister asked God to be merciful on his soul…

***

~~~~~~~~~~~~~~~Finale~~~~~~~~~~~~~

The train ride across the country proved hard on Emily Marie. She did not hold up well and had it not been for her brother's medical care (and Genevieve's) both were sure....it

would have killed her.

Ida May had become obsessed with the doll Isaac had given her and cried inconsolably whenever it was not either in her direct sight or pressed to her tiny body.

Isaac (who'd driven the four of them to the train's station) tried his best to keep strong but could not—would not—hold up when Ida May cried:

"I-zay...I-zay...no go!"

He thought he was going to die when the train lurched, the wheels turned, the rails rocked...

he clutched his chest praying:

Dear God! Take me! I can't bear this!

Rusty (who was also waiting at the station) began to whine and whimper. Isaac patted his head...and neither died (for very long times).

***

Elaine and George: Jan and Greet—all four waited at the train station in Council Bluffs. Each taking their turns reading the telegraph Tristan had sent (which simply said): "We're all coming home. There's been tragedy but also great news. Stop."

The telegraph operator had asked Tristan if there was more he wanted to say.
"I...can't. How much?"

When the train pulled in the parents clambered like children (each trying to be the first to spot their own kin). First, came Tristan (he carried the luggage). Then came Emily Marie (with a strange lady beside her—holding her arm—helping her along...as if she'd grown quite old). Then came a little girl that neither set of parents knew.
Like lions in a pride, Elaine and Greet lunged (tearing at the little child) both lifting, looking, (seeming-to-almost-be-smelling) the little girl (who proceeded to scream at the top of her lungs). Tristan grabbed his mother's shoulders, wrenching the child from her grip. Greet would not be so easily pried from (that which she instantly knew was) her son's living flesh (Jan had to pinch his wife's fingers from the child's frame).
"What on earth!" the two husbands yelled, in chorus, "Has gotten into you two!" They were men—they could never know.
Then Ida May discovered that (in the scuttle) her Beloved Doll's face (the porcelain white face) had shattered: the little girl wailed at the decimation.
Tristan knelt beside her. Rubbed her tiny back. Tried to console her. All the while scornfully looking at his mother (whose hair, he then noticed, had turned gray). "Sh," Tristan cooed. But Ida May would not be consoled.
Emily Marie listened to her daughter's voice and watched her daughter move, thinking, "She'll be a great performer."
Tristan deftly made use of his trade (a few drops of ether) and Ida May made like warm clay in his arms. He carried her small frame to his father's wagon and they all began...their journeys.

Meanwhile Jan and Greet claimed the [casket]body of their son.
***

It wasn't until years later…

after:
Emily Marie had passed away (just a single year before
Dr. Paul Ehrlich's Magic Bullet that would have saved
her)
and…
Ida May had grown into a young woman…
and…
Genevieve and Tristan had married (adopting Ida May
as their own)…

…that there came a certified letter from an attorney in Oregon.

It read:
"The last will & testament of Mr. Isaac Inns…"

He'd bequeathed all his lands to Ida May.
The country was turning its head to the World's grand staging:
war.
George and Elaine had retired from farming:
Tristan (with Genevieve) had finally taken his rightful place
on the farm.

Sometimes (when the setting sun's breeze let the day's humidity cool)
Genevieve and Tristan would sit on the porch of the Andersen
family's home and talk.

Genevieve would speak of economics: "It's Capitalism that's made
people worth nothing more than their skin."
Tristan would laugh: "It's treated us alright."
She'd huff.
He'd grin.
He'd talk about the Bible: "Much has changed, it
seems…yet…all has stayed the same."
She'd laugh: "I remember when things were different."
He'd grin: "You do? "
She'd teasingly fondle him, "Like when you and I made lots
of money…"
That's when Tristan would grow dark.

305

He didn't like to think of those days. Those days when he'd believed that he was helping, treating…maybe even curing those poor women. Those days before the newsreels (and other types of film not suitable to mention in polite company) turned all he'd worked for into something…disgusting…and dirty.

"You see," Genevieve would say (rocking back in her rocking chair, triumphantly), "There is only one truth…"
To which Tristan would reply, "Amen."

> Truths happened to be what shrouded Emily Marie's deathbed like when she told Tristan how she'd longed to sing (like Lotta Crabtree and Marie Duret) on the riverboats in Oregon. Just before she died she asked him why he'd never been a preacher.

> Tristan looked at his little sister, "Because."
> " 'Cause why?"

> He thought he saw the faintest sparkle (like the ones that streaked from her eyes the night he'd taken her to her first burlesque…so he answered) "Because when I studied with men who said they were preachers I couldn't tell."
> "Tell what?"
> "The difference."
> "I don't understand."
> "I couldn't…separate…what was Godly from what was them."
> Emily Marie looked, then, very wise: "Like magicians. You believe what you want…and you see what you can."

> She died holding the thumb of her big brother's hand.

On their porch, Genevieve parroted: "Amen…(adding) so the truth is that there is no truth."
Tristan would shake his head, "No Genevieve, there is truth…we're just too busy watching the act."
   He knew she didn't believe what she said (that she embraced her contrarianism simply to be interesting) because at night (when she thought no one would find her) she'd sneak into the pages of her

Good Book and she'd bow her head, praying (aloud): "God...if you can hear me I'm sorry for what I said. Thanks for:
　　　Tristan
　　　Ida May
　　　It..."

　　　And Tristan would tiptoe back to their bed where he'd wait for his beautiful wife to slide in beside him, nestle her head to where his chest met his arm and fall...
　　　Slowly, surely
　　　into dreams
　　　softly snoring, softly...passing time.

fin